UNBRIDLED

UNBRIDLED

BETH WILLIAMSON

Lori, Enjoy the ride! Beth Williamson

HEAT BOOKS
New York

THE BERKLEY PUBLISHING GROUP
Published by the Penguin Group
Penguin Group (USA) Inc.
375 Hudson Street, New York, New York 10014, USA
Penguin Group (Canada), 90 Eglinton Avenue East, Suite 700, Toronto, Ontario M4P 2Y3, Canada
(a division of Pearson Penguin Canada Inc.)
Penguin Books Ltd., 80 Strand, London WC2R 0RL, England
Penguin Group Ireland, 25 St. Stephen's Green, Dublin 2, Ireland (a division of Penguin Books Ltd.)
Penguin Group (Australia), 250 Camberwell Road, Camberwell, Victoria 3124, Australia
(a division of Pearson Australia Group Pty. Ltd.)
Penguin Books India Pvt. Ltd., 11 Community Centre, Panchsheel Park, New Delhi—110 017, India
Penguin Group (NZ), 67 Apollo Drive, Rosedale, North Shore 0632, New Zealand
(a division of Pearson New Zealand Ltd.)
Penguin Books (South Africa) (Pty.) Ltd., 24 Sturdee Avenue, Rosebank, Johannesburg 2196,
South Africa

Penguin Books Ltd., Registered Offices: 80 Strand, London WC2R 0RL, England

This book is an original publication of The Berkley Publishing Group.

Cover illustration by Phil Heffernan.
Cover design by George Long.

PRINTING HISTORY
Heat trade paperback edition / July 2010

Library of Congress Cataloging-in-Publication Data

Williamson, Beth, [date]–
Unbridled / Beth Williamson. — Heat trade pbk. ed.
p. cm.
ISBN 978-0-425-23614-7 (trade pbk.)
1. Ranch life—Fiction. 2. Cowboys—Fiction. 3. Wyoming—Fiction. I. Title.
PS3623.I5668U63 2010
813'.6—dc22

2010006713

PRINTED IN THE UNITED STATES OF AMERICA

10 9 8 7 6 5 4 3 2 1

To my dad,
the real-life hero who has always inspired me,
supported me, and loved me

CHAPTER ONE

Alex looked out at the beautiful backyard, the pool sparkling in the late-afternoon sunlight, the patio furniture arranged just so. Everything appeared perfect, as beautiful as any Southern California yard. It seemed the world should be weeping instead of continuing on as if David hadn't died, as if her life hadn't come to a screeching halt.

She'd been granted a day to leave the house, to vacate the only home she'd had for the last ten years. David's family hated her, likely assumed she'd been the cause of the sixty-year-old's death. She wasn't, of course; she had loved David more than she thought possible.

And now he was gone.

Alex managed to swallow the enormous lump in her throat, then turned without looking back. It wouldn't do her any good to regret her choices—she couldn't change them. There was no do-over button to frantically press.

Her footsteps echoed on the marble foyer floor; the clack of her heels sounded so damn lonely. As she passed the hall table, she stopped and picked up the African violet. She'd purchased it when she moved into the house, promising David to leave when it died.

It never had.

With the constantly blooming purple-flowered plant in her arm, she left David's house for good. The warm breeze caressed her face, drying any leftover tears she'd missed. She slipped on her sunglasses and walked to the car, back straight, spine as stiff as a steel rod.

It was time to emerge into the real world, out of the protective cocoon David had kept her in, to face the ghosts who constantly rode beside her. He'd known she didn't want to return to Wyoming, but it seemed the universe had a twisted sense of humor.

She had no place else to go, and she could almost hear his melodic voice telling her to follow her heart. Alex had learned to listen to him, to trust his judgment. This time would be no exception. He'd left her one thing; his family had seized the rest upon his death. And of course it was the one thing she needed to go back to Wyoming.

A 1967 Camaro.

It got shitty gas mileage, but ate up the road like it was an all-you-can-eat buffet. Alex had loved that car from the moment she saw it. David's family promised to allow her to keep it provided she disappear, and quickly. Her presence in his house had caused them no end of embarrassment. A wealthy man who died living with a woman half his age was like inviting the tabloids to rip them to pieces.

The rich green color of the car contrasted sweetly with the white stripes up the center. It was in cherry condition and it was hers. The pink slip was firmly in her purse, and it would take an act of God to pry it from her.

Alex slid behind the wheel, the seat warm from the afternoon heat. After setting the plant in a box on the floor of the front seat, she turned the key and it roared to life. The thrum of the engine vibrated through her, giving her just a hint of what it could do if she opened it up.

As she drove down the horseshoe-shaped driveway, she mentally said good-bye to the man who had been nothing short of a substitute father, mentor and friend. She managed to lock away the grief, but just barely. David would have been proud of her.

The steady bass thumped from the dance club, calling any and all into its depths. Alex needed this, needed to have a night to release her emotions, to feel as a twenty-six-year-old woman should, to recover from David's death.

It had been a shock to everyone. He'd been so healthy, so full of life and verve, until Fate had sunk her deadly talons into him and yanked him away. Alex had been more than just his beard, the woman by his side night and day to keep the wolves at bay—she was his best friend.

Deep in the night, they would talk of everything, anything. She told him about her past in Wyoming, how she'd run from the death of her mother, the abandonment of her father. He held her close as she'd sobbed just as she held him as he cried about losing his only love at twenty-one. The young man had simply vanished after appearing at David's side at a family function.

David had suspected his family, a bunch of vampiric money-sucking bastards, of either paying the young man a disgusting amount of money to disappear or perhaps even killing him. There was too much money at stake with David's legacy from his industrialist grandfather. They couldn't have a gay man at the helm.

Alex suspected she wasn't the first beard David had had by his side, a constant female companion to share his life, his bed, but never his heart or his body. Oh, she knew he loved her, but it was the love of two human beings who lived together and cared for each other as friends.

In return for her role, he provided everything she needed. When Alex first came to him, she expected to be his whore, and she was desperate enough to accept the offer. He was so gentle, sweet and funny—a balm to her wounded soul.

Yet all he'd wanted was for her to be his companion, and eventually his friend.

After ten years, they were as close as a man and a woman could be without being romantically involved. No one knew of their real relationship except for his friends, a bisexual couple named Kent and Don.

She'd flirted with them and they with her. Kent had even gone so far as to make out with her once when they'd gotten drunk on Christmas. And he'd been an amazing kisser. David had never limited her sexual partners, but he insisted on her being completely discreet. Now he was gone and she was full of pain—she needed to escape it if only for a little while.

As she stepped into the club, she was surrounded by the music; the steady thrum of the beat echoed through her body, through her flesh and bones. She reveled in the feeling, the sensation as foreign to her as being alone in the world again.

Alex walked in, watching others as they drank, danced, laughed, lived. It was as if she were an outsider looking through glass, unable for anyone to hear or see her. She scanned the crowd for Kent and Don. They had cried together at the funeral the day before. When she'd told them of her plans to leave L.A., they invited her to the club for a last hurrah. Kent had kissed her and held her close, whispering in her ear that they could comfort each other. She wondered if it was an invitation to finally fulfill the flirtation, the attraction, that had lain between them for years.

Truthfully, she was just a bit nervous about being with Kent and Don finally, about what might happen. They had enjoyed a sexual flirtation for so long, she never expected it to go beyond that. Yet Kent, the blond-haired charming one, had told her on more than one occasion they'd always wondered what she might be like in bed. Don, the dark-haired quiet one, had simply watched them with a sizzling gaze. Now she needed that closeness with them, a connection to another human being, or two. Her grief was pressing down so hard on her, she had to escape it for at least a little while.

Alex found herself vibrating to the music, swaying with the crowd as mindless as the notes around her. She realized what she was doing and glanced around to see if anyone else had noticed. No one was paying attention to her, of course. She knew she shouldn't be embarrassed, but she was never one to make a spectacle of herself in public.

She wandered to the bar and managed to shout loud enough for the curly-haired bartender to hear her. She paid him twice as much as she needed to for the bourbon before she downed it in two gulps. He raised his brows, either at the tip or at her slamming back the booze.

Alex held up her finger to request one more. That was all she would indulge herself with. If she allowed the buzz to sneak into her body, she'd lose control completely. That was the last thing she needed. Alex was a sloppy drunk, and seeing as how she'd just buried her best friend the day before, it wasn't the time to show everyone else just how sloppy she could get.

She sipped the second bourbon as her eyes scanned the crowd. If she didn't find them before the drink was gone, she was leaving. There was no need to prolong the discomfort any longer than necessary. The idea of letting go, of feeling everything life could throw at her, was intimidating to say the least. Alex might appear hard as brass on the outside, but inside she sometimes felt like the scared sixteen-year-old who had arrived in L.A. ten years earlier.

"Hey, gorgeous." Kent appeared on her right, a tight white shirt gracing his nicely muscled body. Damn, the man took care of himself. His blond mane was perfectly arranged with nary a hair out of place. He smiled over her head. "Told you she'd be here."

Alex turned to find Don on her left side. His dark brown eyes were expressive, telling her without words that he understood her loss. Before she could say anything, he gathered her up in his arms and pressed her to his own firm chest. She was nearly overwhelmed.

Then Kent embraced her from the other side and she was an Alex sandwich.

Suddenly the comfort Don had initially given her turned into something else altogether. Heat poured through one man, through her, and into the other. She had no idea touching two human beings at once, being enveloped by them, was so intense.

Kent leaned down and kissed her ear. "I'm glad you're here, Alex." He pressed his cock into the crevice of her ass and she felt every inch of it through the thin material of her pants. The man was well endowed and Alex felt the stirrings of arousal low in her belly.

Then Don leaned back and kissed her. His lips were soft and plump, tasting slightly of rum and Coke, sweet and intoxicating. She kissed him back, surprising both of them. His sweet kiss turned into an openmouthed dueling of tongues and hot, wet heat. Kent brushed the undersides of her breasts, and the nipples popped like pink diamonds.

"Wanna dance?" Kent leaned past her to insert his mouth between them, to lap at their tongues like a kitty reaching for a treat.

Alex could hardly catch her breath. The idea that these two hot men would want to share their bed with her, which was patently obvious now, made butterflies explode in her stomach. She'd come to the club expecting this—it was no time to be a pussy about it. She chased away the lingering apprehension and smiled.

"Yes, let's dance."

The dance floor was crowded with gyrating bodies, pulsing with heat and arousal. Alex was already warm from Don and Kent, and the mixture of their sexual titillation made her temperature rise even more.

As the beat thrummed through her, Kent stayed behind her while Don took up position in front of her. She expected them to be good dancers, and they didn't disappoint her. Kent put his hands on her hips and swayed behind her, his cock just brushing against her ass.

Don's dark gaze held hers as he approached her from the front. His chest came close to hers, close to the aching nipples clearly visible through her white blouse. It was a tantalizing dance, a tease to keep her wanting and needing more.

Her breath came and went in pants; she could hardly get enough air in. She wished she'd tossed back the rest of the bourbon; her body burned for something, anything. As she swung her hips around and moved as one with her dance partners, her pussy began to throb with the music.

Don slid down the front of her, his tongue leaving a path from her throat to her breasts. He nipped at her, leaving her almost dizzy with arousal. Kent pulled her toward him, putting her ass in the saddle of his obviously hard cock.

She closed her eyes and Don pressed her front once more. The music thrummed through her as she twisted and turned with them. Hands and bodies rubbing, touching, inciting. Alex was on fire, had never been so aroused in her life.

She grabbed Don and yanked him until his lips slammed against hers. Tongues tangled, rasping against each other as Kent reached around to tweak her already aching nipples. She came up for air, meeting Don's dark gaze. He smiled and she knew she was ready to do more than dance.

Kent whispered in her ear, his voice husky with need. "I want to fuck you, Alex. I want to taste your pretty pussy and feel your mouth on my cock."

Alex looked into Don's gaze as his partner had sex with her in words. He licked his lips, as if tasting her, and she did the same. With a smile, she turned to Kent. His brows went up as she backed into Don, reveling in the feeling of his hardness against her.

Kent's nipples were hard beneath his white shirt. She longed to taste them, bite them and make him hiss. Her sexual proclivities had always leaned toward the experimental, although this would be her first ménage, and with two bisexual men to boot.

She could hardly wait.

Alex took Kent's hand and brought it to her throbbing pussy. "I need you."

Instead of looking shocked, he smiled and met Don's gaze over her shoulder.

"Let's go."

The ride to their house was excruciating. They'd put her in the backseat alone. She almost tore her clothes off and masturbated during the fifteen-minute ride just for some relief. As it was, she kept touching her nipples, tugging at them through her blouse.

"Are we there yet?"

Kent chuckled. "Anxious, *ma petite*?"

It was David's nickname for her, and the sound of it made her heart clench. She was there to escape the pain of his death, to give and receive comfort. Kent's reminder put an instant kibosh on her arousal.

"I'm sorry, Alex."

She shook her head. "Don't be sorry. I want to be here more than anyplace else in the world."

Kent turned to put his hand on her knee. "Same here, doll. Now, let's see just how much fucking we can get done tonight."

She laughed, reveling in his honesty, his ability to put her at ease. Don was a lucky man. If Kent had been entirely straight, she might have to fall in love with him.

They pulled up to the beautiful adobe-style house and Alex was calm, yet there was still a steady beat of need within her. Kent helped her out of the car as Don opened the front door. By the time she entered the house, he'd lit a series of candles leading them to the bedroom.

Her stomach jumped in anticipation, wondering exactly what she'd gotten herself into. It was enough to make her just a tiny bit nervous, but it wasn't fear; rather, it was the unknown. A ménage had always interested her, but it had never gone past the fantasy stage.

When they entered the bedroom, an enormous king-size bed dominated the room. Don stood by the bed, lighting one more candle, throwing a light blue glow in the room. She heard the snick of the door closing behind her and she closed her eyes.

As if it were their standard position, Kent stood behind her, his warm hands sliding down her arms. Don cupped her chin and kissed her, his fingers unbuttoning her blouse. Their hard bodies surrounded her, bringing back her arousal as if they'd found the magic switch deep within her.

"I can smell you, Alex." Kent nibbled at her ear. "I told you I want to taste that pretty pussy of yours." He cupped her throbbing mound. "And judging by the heat I feel, you're ready for it."

"God, yes." It came out in a rush of air.

Kent's breath puffed against her skin as he chuckled. "Let's get the rest of these clothes off, then."

She stood and watched as they undressed her. Wet, hot kisses accompanied each inch of skin they revealed. Alex was almost beyond the point of no return, and was afraid one touch of any appendage to her clit would make her come instantly.

By the time she was naked, somehow both of them had removed their clothes too. Dark and light, they were images of muscle and sinew, and fucking sexy as all hell. She drank in the sight of the six-pack abs, the well-hung cocks, and the idea they were to spend the night in bed with her made her giddy.

Alex lay back on the bed, never taking her eyes off the men. They crawled up on the bed after her, like big cats stalking their prey. A shiver raced through her at the thought.

Kent grinned as his hands slid up her thighs even as his erection pressed against her hip. He was hard as an oak tree, smooth and silk wrapped.

Don seemed to be the kisser because Kent focused on her pussy, while Don used his formidable kissing skills on her mouth. Kent's lips and tongue teased her inner thighs as Don's teased her lips.

It was an onslaught of sensation. Alex closed her eyes and reveled in the feel of two hard bodies pleasuring her. It was a dream, a celebration of life, a fitting end to the worst week of her life. She needed them maybe as much as they wanted her.

Kent's tongue swiped her slit from one end to the other. She sucked in a breath and held it as Don licked her neck, traveling down to her aching nipples.

Kent lapped at her, alternately nibbling and kissing her throbbing center. It took only moments, really, when Don bit one nipple and Alex exploded with the most powerful orgasm of her life. She screamed and bucked against Kent. He absorbed her twists and turns, his mouth locked on her clit, sucking every last drop of orgasm from her.

Tears slid from her eyes as she came down from the high. They laid down on either side of her, petting her, gentling their touches until she had calmed down.

"Okay, doll?" Kent turned her head until she looked at him.

She smiled at him. "Yeah, I'm okay, just a little overwhelmed."

"Then stay there and we'll give you something to watch." He waggled his eyebrows; then his gaze locked on Don's. They reached across her body, kissing hard, the sounds of their rasping tongues and heavy breathing loud in the quiet room.

Alex watched with fascination as Kent climbed over her to reach his man. She scooted over and turned on her side to get a better view. She'd watched her share of porn, of course, but seeing the real thing, two men pleasuring each other, was far beyond anything she'd experienced.

It was clear Kent was the bottom and Don the top. They grabbed each other's cocks, tugging and sliding their hands up and down, even as they continued with the punishing kisses. Soon Kent was on his knees sucking Don with a tremendous amount of skill. He lapped, sucked, nibbled and laved at his partner's erection.

The wet sounds of his mouth, the small moans he made as he pleasured Don, made every hair on her body stand up. Kent's erection bobbed between his legs, forgotten as he gave Don a blow job.

Alex couldn't let that happen, not after the tonguing he'd just given her. She slid closer until she could take him in her mouth. He was salty and delicious on her tongue. One thing she could do well was suck a man off. Kent groaned, and when she looked up to meet Don's gaze, he nodded his approval.

It was a cock-sucking fest and she couldn't have been happier. She fondled his balls, her finger sliding back to his puckered hole. He groaned and jerked against her. No doubt if he didn't have a dick in his mouth, he'd tell her to keep going.

Alex tasted a bit of cum on her tongue and she swallowed his essence. Kent let Don's cock loose and looked down at her.

"Let's get busy, doll."

She didn't know what to do, so she simply moved out of the way and watched as Kent got on his knees. It was the most erotic moment of her life. Her heart beat a steady rhythm as Don put lube on his lover's ass, sliding a finger in the hole, then two. Kent closed his eyes, his entire body shuddering.

"Get under him, Alex. We'll do this together or not do it at all." Don's quiet voice was strained with arousal.

She smiled as Don handed her a condom. After sliding it down Kent, Alex waited until Don was positioned to enter him; then she slid back under Kent. Kent's face was tight with pleasure as Don fucked him.

"Now."

Kent obeyed his partner and slid into her waiting pussy as if she were coated with the same lube. She was so wet from watching, from sucking Kent off, and from his tonguing. It was the slickest she'd ever remembered being and, damn, it felt better than she could imagine.

Soon they began to move in unison. Don slid into Kent as Kent slid into Alex. It was a symphony of fucking and of life. She pinched her nipples, sending jolts of pleasure through her body even as Kent's pace quickened within her.

The moans, the stuttering breaths, the wet sounds of her pussy, of their cocks. The entire room turned into an inferno of pleasure and Alex felt her orgasm building somewhere near her toes. It traveled up her body until it landed in the walls of her center. She tightened so hard, Kent groaned.

"Alex, Jesus Christ. Ah, shit, Don, I'm fucking coming."

Don seemed to catch the same rhythm and together they groaned and thrust.

Yes, yes, yes. That was it.

Right there.

The wave of her orgasm washed over her, stealing her breath, nearly stopping her heart. She arched against Kent, even as Don arched into him. They came with a cacophony of primal, animalistic growls. Alex could barely catch her breath, and her heart beat so hard, she swore it would burst from her chest. She smiled up at Kent, then up at Don. When they smiled back at her, she knew she'd be all right.

Alex woke as the pink light of the dawn painted the horizon. She stepped into the shower, intrigued by the mixture of masculine and feminine touches in the bathroom. Both Kent and Don were amazingly neat.

There was a guest towel with tiny shampoo and soap, a little tented table card on top with her name on it in masculine handwriting. She smiled as she stepped into the hot spray and took a quick shower. The two of them had been sweet, sexy, solicitous and wonderful friends. She couldn't have asked for a better catharsis to begin the next section of her life.

As she toweled off, she tried to think of an appropriate way to say thank-you and good-bye to them. It would be difficult to keep her emotions in check; that was for sure. Alex had felt like a foolish woman all week, weeping and moping. It was time to find her backbone and stop whining.

She dressed quickly and brushed her teeth, hoping to leave before both of them were out of bed. Alex wasn't a coward; she was just ready to leave, to finally say good-bye to her life in L.A.

After calling a cab, she gathered up all her things and stuffed them in the small bag she'd brought in last night. Then it was time to wake them up, but much as she wanted to leave, she also wanted to crawl back into the bed between them and stay. They were safe, whereas the unknown of Wyoming loomed in front of her.

Alex knew there was no permanent place for her in their

relationship. Kent and Don were together for life, a perfect couple who indulged with a woman only when it suited their moods. Alex understood all that, but still, a little part of her wished they'd invite her to stay. It would give her an excuse not to face her past.

The bedroom was awash in the gray light of early morning. As she stepped in, her shoes made barely a whisper of a sound, yet Kent sat up when she walked in. His blond hair was tousled from sleep, among other things, and he smiled at her.

"Ready to go, then, love?"

She sat down on the edge of the bed and embraced him, drawing in his scent, his life force. "I'm as ready as I'll ever be."

"You know you always have a place to stay." Kent took her hands and kissed the backs of her fingers. "You're wonderful, sexy and fucking amazing."

"Best we've ever had." Don, usually the quiet one, spoke up from the other side of the bed.

Alex reached out to take Don's hand too. Her throat closed up as she leaned forward and kissed Kent, then Don.

"You take care of yourself, doll." Kent squeezed her hand. "If you need us, call and we'll come to you. They do have airports, right?"

Grateful his teasing broke the tension, Alex managed to smile. "Yep, they finally closed the pony express office and stopped the stagecoach runs." She rose from the bed and picked up her bag. "Thank you for everything. I feel as if I can say good-bye now."

They both knew she wasn't talking about saying good-bye to them. Alex backed out of the room, the two gorgeous men in the bed watching her as she closed the door. She took a moment to stop shaking before heading out of the house.

It was time for Alex to return to her past and begin her future.

CHAPTER TWO

As she turned onto Interstate 15, Alex had a moment where she could have turned back. Perhaps even would have if there hadn't been a long line of cars behind her turning right up the exit ramp. She was one car among hundreds headed somewhere.

The sun bathed the concrete in a golden pink glow while the warmth of the morning breeze caressed her face through the open window. It was a beautiful day, again, and she was like a butterfly emerging from a ten-year chrysalis, spreading her wings and flying off alone.

In reality, she should have left David's protection long ago, but hadn't. His death put her in an awkward situation with no place to live, no income other than the accounting work she did for him, and no friends other than his own. She had hidden from the world, licking her wounds and burying her head in the sand.

It was past time she began a life of her own, rather than live as David's shadow. She'd become too comfortable with it, lulled into complacency by his need to protect her, by her need to be protected.

There was nothing for her in California, and too much in Wyoming. The thousand-mile journey would be bittersweet, a review of all of the choices she'd made in the ten years since she left. Then, she had been a scared kid full of grief and righteous fury.

Now she was a scared adult, full of grief and regrets. Neither one of them was a palatable choice, but sometimes in life, there simply was no choice. Alex knew she was textbook screwed up. Her father had abandoned her and her mother; then her mother had died.

She finally allowed the door to her memories to open, and they washed over her like a musty blanket. Life had been perfect as she grew up on a beautiful ranch at the base of the Big Horn Mountains. Her parents had loved each other and managed to keep a ranch afloat when many others were folding under the pressure. At one point, when money was tight, her father had suggested renting out rooms for people as guests. Her mother had refused, finding a second job teaching riding to girls. Katie Finley had more pride than to turn her husband's legacy into a dude ranch.

Alex remembered the day her parents had told her about the cancer. About how it was stage four and there was nothing they could do but comfort her mother. At first, Alex was so angry, she ran off, got drunk and lost her virginity to some cowboy in a bar. It was a stupid thing to do, and she had regretted the impulse as soon as he'd taken her innocence.

She finally came to terms with her mother's impending death, and then her father began to pull away. It was subtle at first; he would stay away all day, supposedly taking care of ranch business. Then it bled into the evening hours too. Days would go by when Alex didn't see him, and she began to understand he could not handle his wife dying, so he hid from her.

Alex had been angry with him, but tried to talk to him. Unfortunately her temper got the better of her and she said some things that were way over the line. With the emotional pressure of her mother's sickness, Alex's mouth pushed him too far. It was the first and only time her father had struck her. She swore she could still feel the sting of the slap. He'd never apologized, and basically stopped providing any care for his wife as she lay dying in their bed.

Thank God for hospice nurses and the help of friends, or sixteen-year-old Alex might have lost it. She struggled daily with the knowledge that the woman who had given her life would soon die. Yet Alex got through it, knowing her father would eventually have to face his wife's death.

Then the unthinkable happened.

Alex had been asleep in her bed when she woke to the murmur of voices in the hallway. She recognized her father's voice and the night nurse, so she'd gone back to sleep.

The next morning she discovered her father had left, simply packed a suitcase and abandoned them. The pain from that particular moment in time still sliced through her ten years later, enough to make her gasp.

The worst, however, was yet to come. When her father returned a month later, after her mother's death, he brought a woman with him. One to replace his dead wife before her body was even in the ground. He walked around the ranch he'd left behind as if nothing had changed, king of the castle, and he had the balls to tell her to calm down.

His betrayal was complete and brutal. When she'd left Wyoming, she told him in no uncertain terms she would never return, that he was dead to her. And she would not grieve for him.

Yet here she was, ten years later, finally willing to face him, to come to terms with the horrendous mess she'd run from. Alex didn't want to, but she needed to. She knew there was no way to move forward with her life until she put the past where it belonged.

If she drove straight through to her family's ranch, it would take her eighteen hours or so. Since she had only the car, and a thousand dollars for gas and food, she opted out of stopping at a hotel. The truck stops were not happening either—she'd tried it once on her westward journey. After being scared nearly to death by a big trucker with more tattoos on his skin than hair, she'd vowed never to sleep at one again.

She'd stopped at the all-night store and stocked up on Diet Coke, chips and other staples to get her through the next day. The cold can in her hand felt comforting as she kept her eyes on the road. It was a long and boring journey in some areas, while there was breathtaking beauty in others.

The déjà vu was almost frightening. She didn't want to remember the girl she had been ten years earlier. Not yet anyway. Once she arrived at the ranch, there would be time enough to confront her father and exorcise all the ghosts in her closet.

Wyoming offered her the opportunity to start again, or at least she hoped it did. She had no idea what awaited her, but since she really had no place else to go, she had to return home.

The desert of Southern California gave way to the forests of Utah. The Camaro performed like a dream, climbing the hills with its teeth bared and engine revving. She remembered the drive out to L.A. and how she'd wondered if her mother's Buick Regal would make it that far. It was a beater, with a great deal of dents and scratches, not to mention bald tires, but it had heart. It got her to her destination and even served as her home for a year.

The uncomfortable memory of those miserable twelve months made her shudder. There was nothing glamorous about being homeless, about selling her mother's things in order to eat. Without David's assistance, Alex was certain she would have died years ago. At least she could say she hadn't gotten to the point where she needed to sell her body; thank God for that.

If there was one thing she had an excess of, it was pride. Pride was what drove her to L.A., and kept her safe at the tender age of sixteen from the big bad wolves of the world. It was also pride that kept her from returning to Wyoming, to confronting her father and coming to terms with his abandonment.

Of course, she'd turned around and abandoned him and the only home she'd ever known. Alex was almost tempted to liken her own flight to his, but not quite. She'd stayed until her mother had died, had seen it through to the end, cried buckets of tears, and survived. He'd run like a coward, leaving his daughter to take care of his cancer-stricken wife. There was no excuse for that.

Alex had never forgiven him.

She was an adult now, and if she was honest with herself, she should have gone back to Wyoming long before now. David had always encouraged her to, even offered to buy her a plane ticket to fly into Billings, the closest big city to the ranch.

Yet she'd refused and eventually come to realize it was a matter of her pride getting in the way again. Now that she finally had the courage to face him, she wouldn't be foolish enough to think everything would be resolved and she'd be welcomed into the house with open arms. The thought of standing on the stoop made her feel as if she'd break out in hives.

Her father had always been her hero, a larger-than-life man with a booming voice who had a gift for riding horses and raising cattle. When he left them, Alex's entire world crumbled, and she survived by focusing on taking care of her mother, on managing one day, one hour, one moment at a time.

The drive back to Wyoming gave her the opportunity to replay the agonizing month over in her head. The entire trip through Utah was spent with a box of tissues and a headache as she wept alone. Alex always wept alone.

By the time she'd crossed the Wyoming border, her ass had grown bedsores and her leg was permanently crooked from holding the gas pedal down. As she pulled into a gas station and exited the car, the fresh air hit her and she sucked in a lungful. She'd forgotten how crisp and clean everything was in Wyoming, or rather, how dirty and rank it was in L.A.

As she worked out the kinks in her short frame, she pumped gas into the Camaro. A dozen pickups were parked in various spots around the station, some pumping gas, others putting air in tires or chatting with a neighbor. It was as if she'd stepped into another time, another planet, where neighbors knew one another's names and helped out whenever they could.

Alex remembered how all their neighbors had relied on one another, using CB radio to communicate over the miles between ranches. It was the days before there were cell phones in everyone's pockets, before instant communication replaced good old-fashioned, face-to-face conversation.

She grabbed her purse, locked the car and walked into the gas station to pay. The tiny little store barely fit three people, and that was only if they didn't mind getting cozy. She stayed outside until the two rather large cowboys left, each of them tipping his hat to her and saying, "Ma'am," as he passed.

Alex couldn't help the bemused smile on her face. It was possible coming back to Wyoming would remind her of the good in people. She doubted it, since she was going to see her father, but possible and probable didn't always meet in the middle.

As she paid for the gas, the cigarette display was directly in front of her, rows and rows of Marlboros, Winstons and Camels. No fancy shit here, and no Virginia Slims or clove cigarettes for these country folk. She licked her lips and reminded herself it had been two years since she'd quit smoking. It wouldn't do her any good to start again—she'd worked her ass off to kick the habit the first time.

But her nerves got the better of her, and when Alex left the little gas station, she had a pack of Marlboro Lights in her hand, and a guilty conscience.

A man with a nicely shaped ass in a pair of Wranglers was staring at her car, hands on his lean hips, and a big black ten-gallon hat on his head. He turned to smile at her as she walked up.

"Evening, ma'am. This your car?"

"Yep, and it's not for sale." She unlocked the door and was about to slide in the seat when he put his hand on her arm.

Alex's instincts kicked into high gear and she leveled an unblinking stare at him. "And neither am I, so hands off."

"Whoa there, little filly, just wondering if you were looking for some company tonight." He smiled, a blindingly white example of teeth. He tried to move in closer, crowding her against the car. She told herself to keep calm.

"That would be a no. Listen, Donny Osmond, you heard what I said. If you don't back off in the next half a second, I'm going to break something off." She'd learned to protect herself; David had insisted on it. Given her small stature—barely more than five feet—and her large breasts, men assumed she would be an easy target. Her martial arts training gave her an advantage they couldn't see, especially when they were staring at her tits. This guy went further than that though—he was leaning toward her more with each second.

"Oh, now, why do you have to be so mean to me? I just—" He reached for her, pressing her into the side of the car.

Alex twisted his thumb, then his arm, up and behind him until the bastard was on his knees on the oil-stained blacktop. "If a woman says no, it means no, bucko. Now, get the hell out of here before I break off an appendage you want to keep."

The furious gleam in the fool's eyes should have made her nervous, but she held her ground and kept her face as hard as granite. He finally nodded and she let him up. As he meandered away with a sullen expression, she hopped in the Camaro, locked the doors and got her ass out of there. She still had four hours to go, and the sun was going down quickly.

Never mind that she pulled out a cigarette and took a deep drag to calm her nerves, then coughed so hard she nearly peed herself. Alex threw the smokes out the window, put the cowboy out of her mind and focused on the spectacular scenery that passed her. The brilliant, vibrant colors of the sunset—purples, pinks, oranges and yellows—came together in a symphony of beauty, as if brushed on there by God's own paintbrush. She'd never seen anything more beautiful in L.A.; hadn't really since she'd left Wyoming.

As full darkness settled over the prairie, the long, dark highway stretched in front of her. The familiar road up State Road 751 led her to the foot of the Wind Mountains. They rose majestically in the distance, reminding her of just how small humans were, how tiny life was for those struggling to exist. Their big brothers, the Big Horn Mountains, awaited her on the final stretch of her journey.

Melancholy and introspective, Alex finally reached the city limits of Lobos, and as her car crossed the line, her entire body clenched. She didn't know if it was fear, hesitation, frustration or exhaustion. The only thing she could think of was that she'd made it back home.

The town had changed, though not a considerable amount, since small Western towns never really did. There was the cineplex, still showing a mere two movies; Albertson's Furniture store; the Methodist church—the only stone church within a hundred miles—and the town park. Aside from all that, there was a Holiday Inn with a bar, a shiny, well-lit gas station and even a brand-new town hall.

It was nearly eleven o'clock; she'd made terrific time flying across Interstate 15, and the lack of cops made it easy to do ninety in her muscle car. The deep purr of the engine echoed across the parking lot as she pulled into the Holiday Inn.

She was grateful for the bar since she highly doubted there was anyplace open to buy liquor. Alex needed a drink in the worst way. The hotel would give her an excuse to wait until morning to go to the ranch, the bar an excuse to forget why.

After checking in and ignoring the pimply faced desk clerk's stare, she left her traveling bag in the room and headed back downstairs. The squeaky-clean lobby gave way to a small bar in the back of the hotel. The twang of country music greeted her as she stepped in and made a beeline for the booze.

It had been a long damn day, as if she'd spent the last twenty-four hours in Ebenezer Scrooge land—facing the ghosts of the past, present and future. She ordered a double bourbon and downed it a lot more quickly than she should have, but hell, she didn't have to drive anywhere. What did it matter if she got a little tanked?

The second double slid down even more smoothly than the first, warming her from throat to stomach with the burn from the not-so-fancy hooch. Her head buzzed as the bourbon began to work on her, loosening her up more than she expected. Yep, this was exactly what she needed.

She tried to get up off the stool with her third drink, and slipped, spilling the booze on her hand. As she licked at her fingers, she realized someone was watching her. She looked up to find a cowboy, this one in his early thirties with green eyes and chocolate brown hair hidden beneath—what else—a Stetson. He had what was likely gin and tonic in his hand and was gazing at her in what could only be amusement.

Alex couldn't muster up enough energy to get pissed at him. Instead she shrugged and continued licking the bourbon from her hand. His gaze changed from amused to heated as her tongue caught his attention.

There was no way Alex should be looking at him as a one-night stand. She'd just spent the night with Kent and Don, an unusual and highly emotional experience. She sure as hell didn't need to pick up a stranger in a bar, even if he did look like a really good fuck.

"Something you find funny, cowboy?" She was amazed to realize she slurred. Two doubles and she was already hammered? It had been quite a while since she'd spent time slinging back drinks in a bar.

"No, not funny." His voice was deep enough to be a DJ, a late-night one who would give his female listeners the hots. "Just wondered if you were okay."

She managed not to fall off the stool when she nodded. "Just ducky. I needed a drink."

"I can see that." He sipped at his own, while his gaze kept returning to her lips. Obviously he was entertaining fantasies about her that involved her mouth and tongue. That was intriguing.

"Don't judge me, cowboy. I'm tired and don't have the energy to deal with anyone else's opinion right now." She took another healthy dose of bourbon and the world tilted to the right. "Oh shit."

He caught her by the elbow before she landed on her ass. His hand was warm and strong on her skin. Alex smiled at him.

"Aren't you the dashing knight? Rescuing me and all that." She laughed like a hyena, snorting and guffawing. What the hell was wrong with her? Alex never lost control, and yet here she was, drunk in fifteen minutes or less at the Holiday Inn in East Bumfuck, Wyoming. If it wasn't true enough to be pitiful, she might have cried.

"Do you have a room here, ma'am?"

" 'Ma'am'? Don't call me that. Jesus Christ, I'm twenty-six, not eighty-six." She leaned toward him, intrigued by the clean scent and the musky cologne he wore. "You smell good."

He looked at the bartender. "Do you know where she belongs?"

The blonde behind the bar shook her head. "Never seen her before. Likely someone driving through town."

"Oh, no, no, no." Alex leaned into the man, pleased by the feel of his muscled chest and firm body. He was definitely in shape. "I belong here, I swear." She laughed like a hyena again, recognizing the fact she really didn't belong there. Not anymore.

Alex didn't remember leaving the bar, but suddenly she was in the elevator. The stranger was carrying her, and she wondered if she was going to get lucky.

"Hey, I'm not that kind of girl, dude. I don't fuck on the first date." She giggled at her own joke. "I mean, not that we're on a date, but, ah, hell, I don't want to catch some kind of disease or anything like that."

"Shut up, already. I'm not going to, ah, take advantage of you, ma'am. I'm just making sure you make it to your room all right." He set her on her feet and pulled her key card from his pocket.

That was when she noticed he wore the same tight, faded Wranglers as every other cowboy, but damn, they fit him like a glove, outlining the nice package between his thighs. She could do worse than hopping into bed with a stranger with a cock like that.

Alex felt the world tilt beneath her feet, and then his strong arms were around her again. Her stomach lurched and it was all she could do not to puke all over him.

He pushed the door open and dragged her inside. Alex should be frightened by her stupid behavior, by ending up in her hotel room with a perfect stranger. She could get raped, beaten or worse. Yet all she could think about was that he smelled fucking awesome.

“Here you go, ma’am.” He led her to the bed and set her down on the edge, then got down on one knee to take off her shoes.

She pulled off his hat and ran her fingers through his hair. Soft as silk and full of dark curls. “Mmmm, that’s just the best hair I’ve ever felt on a man. What kind of product do you use on it?”

He ignored her and snatched his hat back, which he promptly slammed on his head. “I’m being a gentleman here, so please keep your hands to yourself.”

Alex snorted and fisted his shirt in her hands. “Kiss me, Galahad.”

Connor Matthews didn’t know what to make of the little spitfire. She tossed back the bourbon as if it were water, then almost passed out in the bar. If he hadn’t found the little cardboard sleeve with her room number on it, he might have had to leave her there. No doubt one of the randy assholes who frequented the bar might have taken advantage of her.

She had a haunted look in her blue eyes, one he sure as hell didn’t want to explore. The woman was walking trouble, and he wanted no part of it. But the gentleman in him had to make sure she was safe and sound in her room.

Then she kissed him, and he forgot exactly what it was he wasn’t going to do. Her lips were soft and firm at the same time, moving over his with ease. He tried to pull away even though his entire body reacted to the kiss, yet she held firm, surprisingly so, considering how drunk she was.

She opened her legs and lay back on the bed, pulling him on top of her. Damn, she was all curves and softness, except for her nipples, which were currently hard enough to cut glass. They rubbed at his chest, taunting him, even as she kissed him with surprising skill.

The woman was plastered, yet she still kissed like nobody's business. Her sweet, wet tongue curled around his, sucking it into her mouth. Lips moved across lips as he forgot why he shouldn't be kissing her and joined in fully.

Connor's dick hardened until he thought he'd lose consciousness as all the blood rushed to the pulsing stick between his legs. Her legs were open in an inviting vee, and he nestled in there nice and snug.

Oh, but he shouldn't be doing anything with this stranger he'd literally picked up in the bar. Yet she was perfect beneath him, the right combination of sexy and soft. She wiggled her hips, pushing her pussy against him as he groaned into her mouth.

With a giggle, she scratched at his ass. "Mmm, I like my cowboys hard and, damn, you are hard as steel."

Connor didn't want to be hard, but he couldn't seem to help himself. The woman was wrapped around him like a vine, squeezing him, pulling him closer and closer. He sure as hell wasn't a helpless victim, since his body didn't seem to want to be let go. Obviously he outweighed her and could easily leave her there on the bed.

But he didn't.

In fact, his hand crept up to her right breast, weighing the delicious roundness in his palm. Oh, but she was perfectly formed. Large enough to fill his hand, but not too big. He tweaked the nipple and she let out a kittenish moan.

"Oh, that's good. Do it again." She nipped at his earlobe, laving at the outside of his ear until shivers raced down his back.

Connor needed to stop, he had to stop, or he'd end up fucking a nameless woman at the Holiday Inn. But no matter what he told himself, he didn't stop, and his dick roared to be let out, to find the wet pussy it scented.

He took a deep breath and told himself to get up. She was too damn drunk and he was still a gentleman. Connor pushed himself up to get off her when he realized she wasn't squirming against him any longer. She'd passed out, for better or for worse. He hopped up and walked around the room for a few minutes, trying to remind himself why it was a blessing she'd actually lost consciousness.

None of it worked, of course. He had a hard-on that wasn't going anywhere no matter how much he told it to. With a string of curses, he went into the bathroom, leaving it in darkness. Connor was embarrassed to admit he needed to jack off, desperately. The woman had whipped him into a sexual frenzy and he needed a release.

The night-light in the bathroom provided him enough illumination to find the toilet. As he pushed his jeans down, his dick sprang free and he breathed a sigh of relief. The fabric had been cutting off the circulation.

He closed his eyes as he sat down and grabbed his dick in a punishing grip. Imagining it was her hand, her stroking him, Connor pleasured himself in the bathroom of a stranger's hotel room. He imagined her mouth, her tongue, her nimble fingers all over him, pulling him closer and closer. Her pillowy breasts would be against his chest, the nipples on his tongue. He came quickly, the orgasm sweeping through him with the power of a hammer strike.

Connor leaned his head against the wall and caught his breath, even as his dick grew soft in his hand. He cleaned up quickly and dressed, more in control, although he was mortified by what he'd just done.

He peeked into the room to find her still passed out on the bed. Thank God. He repositioned her boneless form until she was on the pillows. Connor contemplated making her more comfortable by stripping off her clothes. Not the best idea, considering how he'd already lost control of himself. In the end, he took off her fancy boots and pulled the blanket up over her. She snuggled into it, rolled over and started snoring.

She'd said she was twenty-six, and had the look of someone who'd had a few hard years in her life. He knew the look well—saw it in the mirror every day, as a matter of fact.

His civic duty done, he put the key on the dresser and left the room. If he was honest with himself, she wasn't his type, but something about her made him react more strongly than he had with any other woman. He pushed the memory of arousal away with difficulty as he made his way back downstairs. When her lips had touched his, it had felt as though a lightning bolt had slammed into him.

Connor shook off the memory—he'd never see her again, so what difference did it make? In the morning, she'd be gone from Lobos and just a memory he could tuck away in the dusty corners. With luck, she'd never find out what he'd done in her bathroom.

After he made it back downstairs, he started to head back to the bar, then thought better of it. No need to have another drink; the mystery woman had given him a prime example of why he shouldn't imbibe too much.

The night air had cooled enough that he could almost see his breath. As he walked to his truck, the image of the woman on the bed flitted through his memory. He didn't know what it was about the brunette that stayed with him—perhaps it was her blue eyes. They were as haunted as his own.

CHAPTER THREE

Alex woke up slowly. Her mouth tasted like old sweat socks and her head pounded as if some little creature were banging on her temple with a hammer. She was in a bed, fully clothed, thank God, and she smelled like bourbon.

She opened one eye and looked around. It was a hotel room, a generic one like many others. Her traveling bag was on the floor near the dresser, which meant this was her room. She lay there and listened to the sounds of the hotel around her. Fortunately, there was no one in her room with her.

Alex sat up like an old woman, groaning with the rush of blood to her head. She remembered getting to the hotel, had a vague recollection of checking in, then a much better recollection of the bar.

Oh shit. She'd started on bourbon; doubles if she wasn't mistaken. There was a gorgeous green-eyed cowboy she'd flirted with, and then, nothing. She finally made it to the edge of the bed, where she held her head in her hands and tried not to run to the bathroom and vomit.

Her shoes were side by side on the floor.

Alex stared at the ankle boots and tried like hell to remember taking them off. She didn't even remember getting into bed, much less taking off her shoes. That meant only one thing—someone had brought her back to her room and taken them off.

Her heart pounded at the realization she'd put herself in danger. All because she'd come back to Lobos and lost control of her emotions. Too much booze and self-pity was not a good combination.

She was still dressed, which hopefully meant whatever cowboy brought her back to her room had been a gentleman. Or she'd done something really stupid and then re-dressed herself. Unlikely, considering she didn't feel as though she'd had sex, but still a possibility.

Alex didn't drink often and this was exactly why. She usually ended up doing something out of character, but this was beyond that. It had put her in danger and she hadn't even been aware of it.

After making it to the shower, she stepped in and let the hot spray wake her up. The hangover wasn't too bad; she was more tired than anything. Coffee would be the first priority after she got dressed.

As she dropped off the key, the desk clerk looked at her as if the young man knew what she'd done the night before. Alex again wondered exactly what had happened. It was frustrating to not remember.

"There a Starbucks anywhere in town?"

He looked at her blankly. "You mean that coffee place?"

Alex held on to her patience. "Yes, the coffee place."

"No, we ain't got Starbunkers. The café down the street serves breakfast, and their coffee is good."

"Thanks." With a smile she didn't even remotely feel, Alex left the hotel.

The morning air was crisp, making her still-wet hair supercold against her face. It didn't matter; she needed to keep herself up after the night of drinking and a day of nonstop driving. As she walked toward the Camaro, the Big Horn Mountains were suddenly there.

She stopped, struck by the beauty she had almost completely forgotten about. They were majestic—a corny word to use, but the one that fit. The peaks were already covered by snow and it was only the beginning of September.

Alex took a deep breath, realizing she was smelling nothing but air. No pollutants or car emissions, just plain old air. She sucked in another lungful before climbing in the car to head to the café.

If she was right, it was Talulah's Café, a woman who had been a friend of her mother's. Alex's heart thumped at the memory of having Saturday lunch there with her mother every week. It wouldn't be easy to walk back in, but seeing as how it was apparently the only place in town to get coffee, she didn't have a choice.

Alex pulled into the parking lot and sat there for a few minutes, staring at the sign. No longer Talulah's; the sign read LOBOS CAFÉ and had a multicolored wolf, similar to a Mexican Huichol, on it The outside had been a bright blue; now it was a desert brown with green trim.

Knowing Talulah wasn't there actually made it easier to get out of the car. This would be the first place she entered that she'd been in before, albeit under a different owner. Her stomach clenched as she walked in the door and the bell tinkled merrily above her.

She was feeling far from merry that morning.

An older woman with blond hair liberally laced with gray smiled at her. "Table for one?"

"Large coffee with cream. To go." Alex wasn't ready to spend any amount of time in town yet, least of all in a place with so many memories of her mother. The table by the window had been their spot, and she couldn't even bear to look at it, even if the tablecloths were different—hell, even the tables and chairs were different. Instead, she didn't take her eyes off the waitress.

"A good breakfast goes a long way. Are you sure you just want coffee?" The waitress eyed her as if Alex were a friend of her daughter's she needed to take care of.

"My stomach couldn't handle anything but coffee right now, but thanks." Her smile was shaky but she managed one anyway.

"Okay, wait right here and I'll get it for you." The waitress went behind the counter and began pouring the coffee.

Alex told herself not to take her gaze off the woman. She didn't need another challenge that morning; going to the ranch would be hard enough. But it was as if there were a train wreck to her left and she could barely keep from turning her head.

"Here you go, honey. That'll be a dollar sixty-five."

Alex started at the sound of the other woman's voice, unaware the waitress had returned. "Oh, yeah, wait just a sec." She fumbled with her purse, pulling out a crumpled five-dollar bill from the pocket inside. "Keep the change."

Although she could hardly afford to give away a dime much less three dollars, Alex needed to get out of there. Immediately.

"I can't take a three-dollar tip for coffee." The waitress was still protesting as Alex took the cup from her and smiled.

"No worries. I'm sure it's good coffee." She got out of the

restaurant, and its memories, as fast as she could without spilling hot brew down her arm. Jesus, she didn't imagine it would be so hard to actually be there, but the café was something she'd forgotten. Until she'd walked in the door and a flood of memories assaulted her.

It proved too much for Alex, running on no coffee and a slight hangover. She left the restaurant shaking and feeling as though she'd just survived an Iron Man challenge. What the hell was up with that? Honestly, she hadn't expected such a strong reaction, but the café had been the place she and her mother had gone alone. The special place they had gone each Saturday for as long as Alex could remember.

If only there were a Starbucks in town. Alex knew she would have to get used to the slower pace of life, the lack of amenities and instant gratification of L.A. Maybe if she hadn't gotten drunk and passed out the night before, it wouldn't have hit her so hard.

She leaned against the side of the Camaro and took deep breaths, trying to calm her racing heart and actually get her composure back. No need for the world to see her falling apart, because she knew sure as a bear shit in the woods that some polite neighborly patron would stop to help her. That was how it was in the country, in small-town America. She could almost hear someone approaching and straightened up.

And, of course, spilled hot coffee down her arm.

"Fuck me." She switched the coffee to her other hand and shook off the burning-hot liquid. After wiping her arm on her pants and vowing to put something on the burn later, she got into the car.

It felt safe in there; the leather seats were familiar and welcoming. Even the violet appeared to welcome her presence. Perhaps because the car had experienced David's touch, his care applied to it for so long. He'd told her it was the first car he'd purchased, at age eighteen, and he'd vowed never to sell it. Alex would keep that vow alive for him and hang on to it for her natural life as well.

After a moment, she was able to take a sip of the coffee without risk of more grievous injury. The hot liquid splashed down her throat like the nectar of the gods. It was damn good coffee too—enough to rival the big chains with its flavor. She decided it would be a good idea to sit tight until it was gone.

The windows in the car began to fog up either from her heavy breathing or the hot coffee. She grumbled as she rolled the window down, recognizing that electric windows were something to be treasured if she ever had a car with them. The cold breeze hit her wet hair again and she shivered as if a hand had reached out and caressed her.

She wanted to believe it was her mother, that Katie Finley had been waiting for her daughter to return. To make peace with all she'd left behind ten years earlier. Alex closed her eyes and wished like hell it were true. She could use her mother's support and help right about then.

Of course, it was just the wind. Regardless, she left the windows up as she gulped the last of the coffee. But it felt comforting even to pretend it was her mother's hand stroking her hair.

Alex spotted a trash can in front of the diner and hopped out to throw away the cup, as well as the rest of the trash that had accumulated in the passenger seat of the car.

"Wow, that's a pretty ride you've got there, miss." The man's voice didn't startle her, but it sincerely pissed her off. How many men would hit on her because of the goddamn car?

She turned to tell whoever it was to fuck off and found an older man with snow-white hair and a cane. "Oh, uh, well, thanks."

The man never took his eyes off the Camaro. "Had one myself back in the day. Loved that damn car so much my wife made me sell it." He chuckled to himself. "She thought maybe I loved it more than her."

"Did you?" Alex couldn't help but ask. Sometimes she thought David had that kind of relationship with the damn thing too.

The man finally turned to look at her. She saw longing and loneliness in his watery blue gaze. "No, but the love I gave her was never enough no matter what car I had. She left me back in 'seventy-four and I ain't found a good car since."

With that strange remark he shuffled toward the diner. Alex wanted to ask him what that meant, but decided she didn't need any more bizarre conversations that morning.

She hopped into the car and started it. The roar of the engine made the old man stop and cock his head to listen. Alex gunned it and she swore he smiled. She felt good about making at least one person happy that day. God knew she wasn't going to experience that emotion for quite some time.

With more than a small amount of trepidation, she pulled out of the parking lot and headed north. Toward the confrontation with her father. Toward the final obstacle in her quest for happiness. Toward home.

The road was so familiar, she felt the ache in her throat grow tighter the closer she got. When she saw a huge black mailbox that read FINLEY'S RANCH, her stomach flipped upside down, throwing some bitter coffee back up. The bile burned her throat but she swallowed it back down and turned down the long driveway.

It was more than a mile until she got to the house, so she had time to try to regain control of her runaway emotions. She had known it would be difficult when she finally got there, but this was excruciatingly hard. Ten years ago, she'd been a scared, angry kid when she'd left. Now she was a woman and had to remember to act like an adult and do what she needed to.

Easier said than done, of course.

When she saw a sign that read REGISTRATION, at first she thought it had been a mistake. Then she saw a second one that read GUEST PARKING.

What the hell?

By the time she crested the long, sloping hill, the sight that greeted her knocked the breath from her lungs. No longer comprised of a simple ranch house and a barn, there were at least fifteen cabins now situated behind the house and a second, much larger barn.

A paved parking lot was on the left with nicely divided spaces. Like a robot, she pulled into one and cut the engine. Her heart pounded so hard, her ears hurt from the sound of the blood rushing past them.

Her family's home had been turned into a dude ranch, a goddamn *dude* ranch. Holy ever-loving shit. There were at least a couple dozen dude ranches in Wyoming, some as old as a hundred years. She never expected her father to do the same. Their property was only about five thousand acres total, but it was apparently large enough to build a bunch of cabins and suck some city folk into riding horses and fishing.

Her mother had worked so hard to keep from renting rooms, and her father had done something else completely unthinkable. Another betrayal to Katie Finley's memory and her wish to maintain the ranch as a home, not a hotel.

Jesus Christ.

She closed her eyes and leaned her forehead against the steering wheel until she felt more in control of her reaction. It shouldn't really matter if her childhood home was a dude ranch, or *guest ranch*, the more PC term. She had come to talk to her father and address the issues that had been weighing her down, preventing her from living life fully. Until she did that, she wasn't going to be happy.

She told herself she wouldn't even ask her father about the damn guest ranch. It wasn't her business anymore and it didn't even matter. What mattered was just talking to him.

It took every smidge of courage she could drag from the depths of her soul to get out of the car and walk down to the sign that read MAIN OFFICE. Or, as she remembered it, the front door to the house.

A few people smiled and said hello as she walked past them. Her heart thundered with each step she took and her mouth dried out until she forgot what spit tasted like. Her hand shook as she pulled the huge mahogany door open and walked in.

Connor tried to focus on the reservations on the computer screen, but his mind kept wandering to the woman from the bar. She'd had such sadness in her eyes, something he could relate to. However, it was the anger he remembered more—she had a deep fury within her that had its talons dug deep. That was where he could completely relate. Once upon a time he'd spent a good deal of time being angry at the world. It was tough to shake.

Of course, he also kept thinking about her lips and those damn eyes. She was like sin incarnate for him, all curves and no sharp angles. He liked women who weren't emaciated and whose ribs didn't threaten to poke an eye out. This woman, she had it all going on with breasts the size of cantaloupes ripe for picking, curvy hips he could trace with his tongue, and an ass that still made his dick twitch.

Oh yeah, she was definitely a lot of woman and exactly his type. Too bad she got drunk in hotel bars and passed out while trying to seduce strangers. It was a good thing Connor had a conscience and knew wrong from right, or she'd have woken up with more than a hangover.

Then again, it was a shame she had gotten so drunk that she had passed out. His own body reacted, yet again, to the memory of the mystery woman, and it was all he could do to tell his semierect Johnson to cool it.

A knock at the door was the last thing he needed.

"Yes?" he called out, annoyed with himself more than with whoever was knocking at his office door.

The door opened and Jennifer poked her head in. She was the daughter of Henry Avila, the head of landscaping, and a good kid. When not in school, she worked at the front desk to make money for her college tuition. This time her normally bright smile was gone. She frowned and her gaze was full of trepidation.

"What's the matter?"

"There's a woman out here asking for Grant."

The mention of his business partner, friend, and mentor still made his heart clench. It had been two years since Grant's death. Connor had finally moved past the pain of losing the man who had helped shape him into the person he was. The memory of the day they buried Grant would be with him for a very long time. He hoped whoever the woman was, she hadn't been close to Grant.

Connor didn't like being the bearer of bad news—he sure as hell didn't know how to be sympathetic to a stranger's grief.

"Okay, no problem. I'll be right there." Fortunately or not, the interruption had actually cured his semiarousal. He needed to stay focused on work and not on the drunken fish that got away.

He left his hat on the desk and walked out of the office. As he stepped down the hallway, he smiled at the pictures lining the walls. They'd build the guest ranch as a family; each cabin that had gone up was proudly displayed with a group photo of the staff. Grant had done his best to make sure the Finley Ranch was a place filled with love, no matter whose blood ran through your veins.

As Connor entered the great room that served as the lobby, he nearly went back into his office. There stood the woman from the bar with her back to him. He glanced around but there was no one else there. Jennifer pointed at her, then left the room. Jesus, the woman had followed him somehow and thought he was Grant. That was a sticky situation.

"Good morning."

She jumped at the sound of his voice and turned to look at him. This morning she wore a pair of nicely fitted jeans, a deep purple blouse and her hair up in some kind of knot on the top of her head. He was again struck by the depth of her blue eyes, deep and fathomless. This time instead of anger, he saw a deep sadness and confusion.

"I know you."

He went over and leaned against the check-in desk. "We met at the hotel last night."

Her cheeks colored slightly. "Ah, yeah, that's why you seem familiar. I, um, don't normally even drink, much less get toasted on two drinks in a hotel bar." She glanced at her feet, which he noted were encased in the same pair of fancy ankle boots that wouldn't last two seconds outside. "Was it you who brought me to my room?"

Nice to know he was memorable. "Yes, it was me. I was glad to help. Is there something I can help you with today?" Connor sensed she was genuinely distressed about something and wanted to be anyplace but right there. He'd never actually had a stalker before, if that was what she was. Of course the memory of her lips, of those fantastic tits pressed against his chest, made him a bit distracted.

"I'm looking for Grant F-Finley." She threw back her shoulders as if girding herself for battle, but her voice shook.

Ah, yes, she was looking for Grant. The name snapped him back to reality. "And you are?"

"Oh, sorry; I feel like such a dunce. I'm Alex Finley, Grant's daughter." The word *daughter* got stuck in her throat and sounded more like a croak than a word.

It was a word, however, that hit Connor square between the eyes.

Holy fucking shit.

This was Grant's daughter? The one the attorney couldn't find? The one Connor hadn't known existed until after his best friend's death? The earth shifted just a bit under his feet as he scrambled to figure out what to say to her. After knowing Grant almost eight years, Connor was still shocked he hadn't known about the existence of the other man's daughter. Where the hell had she been?

"Is there a problem?" Her brows drew together. "Is he not here?"

"Ma'am, why don't we sit over here?" He gestured to the sofa and two wing chairs in front of the fireplace. The homey scene did nothing to relieve his shock or stress. What the hell was he supposed to say? Any way he got it out, it was going to sound bad.

She didn't look too happy about it, but she sat stiffly on the edge of the left-hand chair. Connor sat on the sofa and put his elbows on his knees.

"Let me start by telling you who I am."

"That'd be helpful." Her soft murmur told him she had a sarcastic streak he didn't expect.

"My name is Connor Matthews and I run Finley's Ranch. Grant Finley was my boss and friend. We built the guest ranch together." He cleared his throat and tried to think of a way not to look at her, but her gaze was like a damn magnet. "Grant, ah, unfortunately was killed in a car accident two years ago."

Every smidge of color drained from her face, leaving Alex looking as if someone had thrown flour on her cheeks. "Excuse me?"

"They tried to find you after the attorney read the will but couldn't. Didn't know where to start, really."

"I didn't want to be found. I lived off the grid as a renter. There was nothing for me here." She narrowed her gaze. "Wait a minute, did you say after he read the will? I'm sorry; I don't understand what's going on here." Her voice was wavering on hysterical. "My father dies and you wait until the fucking will is read to try to find me? It would have been nice to know he'd actually died." She wrapped her arms around her waist. "Jesus Christ."

Grant had obviously screwed up the situation already with his usual grace. "I'm sorry I don't have the particulars of what happened. We really should speak to his attorney—"

"No, I don't want to wait for the attorney. Tell me what you know. Please." Her voice had become almost gritty.

"Look, Miss Finley, I didn't know Grant had a daughter. He hadn't mentioned you, but he was kind of private. No one looked for you because we didn't know you existed, and then when the will was read we didn't know where to start looking for you. This is awkward as hell since Grant was my friend and I didn't even know he had a daughter. I mean, maybe Claire knew but—"

"Who the hell is Claire?" Her voice cut through his like a knife.

"Grant's wife. I guess she'd be your stepmoth—"

Alex stood up and he could see in her eyes that she was going to puke. He pointed at the restroom down the hall and she ran with her hand clamped across her mouth.

Ah, hell.

Alex knelt in front of the toilet shaking and crying. The coffee sure as hell burned coming back up no matter how good it had been going down. She grabbed a handful of toilet paper and wiped her eyes and mouth.

Dead. Her father was *dead*.

She couldn't fathom it. Not even for a second had she expected this, much less a stepmother. God, she could hardly stomach the thought of facing this woman, whoever she was.

Alex had to focus on the fact that there would never be a chance to make peace with her father, to lay to rest the cackling demons she'd had riding her back for ten years.

Her father was dead.

She had no idea how long she sat there trying to absorb the unbelievable news, but it wasn't getting any easier to accept.

"Miss Finley?" The cowboy's voice came through the door.

How ironic was it that the man she'd met in a bar turned out to be her father's partner? Likely the man who'd been the son she could never be. The universe damn sure had a twisted sense of humor.

"Yes, I'm here." She leaned against the wall, pulling up her knees to rest her head on.

"I brought you a cool washcloth."

Alex didn't want to like this guy, seriously wanted to hate him, but he was obviously a gentleman, judging by the fact he'd left her intact the night before, and was now trying to be nice to her. He was damn clumsy with his words, though.

"Fine. Come in."

The door opened only a few inches and a hairy arm poked through with a dark blue washcloth dangling from the hands.

"I'm not naked, Mr. Matthews. I said come in."

She could almost hear the reluctance in the door as it slowly swung open. The cowboy was obviously uncomfortable with emotions, but she couldn't deal with his issues right then. She took the cloth from his outstretched hand.

"Thanks." Alex pressed the cool cloth to her face, surprised by just how cold it was. One thing she missed about Wyoming—just how cool the water got out of the tap. In L.A., it was practically the same room temperature year-round, no matter how long she ran the cold water.

"Look, I know this is a shock."

Alex managed a strangled snort. "Obviously an understatement."

"I know you and your dad must have had issues." Connor leaned against the doorframe, his imposing bulk blocking the view of any passersby.

"You have no idea how hard it was to come here, to work up

the courage to face him." She stopped the sob before it escaped, pushing it back down her throat until she could swallow again. "I never expected him not to be here."

"He's here in spirit, in every board in every cabin, in every guest we have stay here." The man must've realized just how little she wanted to hear about her father's good works. The fact he'd turned her home into a hotel still pissed her off. "Look, Alex—can I call you that?" At her nod, he continued. "Grant didn't talk much about his past so we had no idea he even had a daughter."

Alex barely made it to the toilet before bile coated her throat again. She heaved up nothing since there was nothing left inside her. The door shut and she wondered if puke always made the cowboy run; then the washcloth was pressed against the back of her neck. The man had surprised her again.

"I'm sorry, Alex. I seem to find just the right thing to say to make you hurl."

She half cried, half laughed at him. "You are doing a damn good job at it."

Connor squatted beside her. "Take your time in here. I'll wait for you in the office. Turn left and it's down at the end by the side door."

Tears slid from her eyes as she realized her mother's sitting room, where they'd sat and read a thousand books, was Connor's office. Alex had really never expected any of this, and it was damn hard to accept. She wanted to curl up in a ball and cry until she had no more tears, and yet she wanted to rail at the heavens, at her father, for not being here.

For Alex there would be no closure, no good-bye, no way to shut the door on her past. It was permanently stuck open, allowing all the bad shit to constantly hit her in the backs of the knees. Her father had abandoned her again.

After a few more minutes, she managed to get herself together, or at least so she wasn't in pieces on the bathroom floor any longer. She walked on shaking legs down the hallway, avoiding the photos on the walls as she went. At that moment, she couldn't have looked without tearing something into bits.

She told herself not to be angry, not to take it out on the cowboy. Connor hadn't known who she was, apparently. Her father had failed to mention to anyone she existed. He'd probably just forgotten.

Her throat got so tight, she could barely breathe. Jesus, this was so fucking hard. As she got to the open office door, Alex took hold of herself. It was time to put on her big-girl panties and face Connor.

Connor almost jumped out of his skin when Alex came into the room. She hadn't made a sound, like a sexy cat in socks. Her face was tight with anger and her eyes swollen and red. She didn't even look around the room, but rather focused on him with that intense stare.

"Please sit." He gestured to the chairs in front of the desk.

She looked at them for an excruciatingly long moment before she sat. The angle put her gorgeous tits right in his line of sight, and the middle button of her shirt had popped open. He could see a lacy black bra, and his imagination went completely apeshit. Of course, he wanted to slap himself—the woman just found out about her father's death and he was thinking about fucking her tits.

Alex sat there silently watching him and he tried like hell not to look at her shirt, but his gaze dropped. She glanced down and realized what he was gawking at and buttoned it in a hurry. This time when she looked at him, her gaze had narrowed and the look was sharp enough to cause injury.

Connor had the uncomfortable thought this woman might not be who she said she was. After all, he'd never seen a picture of her, and even if she did have Grant's cleft chin, that wasn't proof of her identity.

"Before we go any further, I'm going to have to ask you to show me your identification."

Her eyebrows went up. "Identification?"

"You could just be a woman from the bar last night or you could be Alex Finley. I don't know and I sure as hell wouldn't risk me or anyone on this ranch because I assume you're telling me the truth." He didn't want to sound harsh but he had to make sure he wasn't being taken for a ride.

"Hm, yeah, I can see that. I could be some crazed bitch who wanted more than whatever it was I got last night." She opened the cavernous purse on her shoulder and rummaged around, pulling out an enormously fat wallet.

She opened it and fiddled around, looking in various pockets and crevices before she apparently found what she wanted. With a bit of effort, she yanked it out and handed it to him.

Connor looked at the California driver's license and recognized her picture, although her hair was much shorter in the tiny image. Her name read ALEX KATHERINE FINLEY, and that was definitely the name Grant had put in the will. Temporarily satisfied she wasn't an imposter, he handed it back to her.

"How did he die?"

Connor blocked out the image of the mangled truck that popped into his mind. "Car accident. There was a bad late-summer storm and he lost control. I was told he died instantly so he didn't feel anything."

She snorted and mumbled under her breath as she put the license back in her overstuffed wallet. "Well, that's a blessing, isn't it?" Her smile was positively feral. "Now, what about the property?"

Connor was flummoxed by the change in topics. "The property?"

"The dude ranch. This piece of land we're currently occupying." She made a twirling motion with her finger. "Doesn't this property belong to me now?"

"It's a guest ranch, not a dude ranch. And it doesn't entirely belong to any one person. You see, there are other people involved and—"

"What other people? There was me, my mother and my father. She's buried up on the hill underneath that huge Bigtooth maple tree. I don't know where the hell he's buried."

Connor told himself to stay calm. He didn't need to get angry with her too. He told himself she was experiencing normal emotions after finding out her father had died.

"I think we need to spend some time with Michael Bailey—he was your father's attorney. He's out of town for a few days but he'll be back later this week."

"I don't want to talk to an attorney right now anyway. Just tell me who the hell owns part of this ranch." Alex's voice grew harder and colder with each syllable. "I deserve to know that much."

Connor wondered how much fury Alex Finley had inside. Judging by the way she reacted to the ranch not being hers, it was as much as he suspected, perhaps more. He had wanted to own a part of Finley's for years, and after Grant died, the legal tangle had prevented him from fulfilling that desire. Maybe if he handled this situation right, he might be able to buy Alex's half and then they'd both come out winners. She would have cash and he'd get half of Finley's.

Connor had always dreamed of owning his own land. A poor kid from a bad neighborhood had no hope of actually owning anything but the lint in his pocket. Land had been out of his reach most of his life, until Grant Finley had yanked him from the road to jail and given him something to work toward. He coveted Finley's Ranch, could almost taste the opportunity to own a substantial chunk of it.

He opened his mouth to speak when Daniel catapulted into the room with every smidge of an eight-year-old's energy, screeching to a halt with his sneakers squeaking on the hardwood floor.

"Connor, wait until you see this! Buttons decided he was going to—" He caught sight of the visitor in the chair and his eyes widened. Connor noted they were every bit as blue as Alex's.

"Daniel, what did I tell you about running in here?" Claire's harried voice came from the hallway, and before Connor could say a word, she came into the office as well. When she spotted Alex, she smiled and turned to Connor. "Introduce us to your friend." He thought he saw amusement in her gaze; little did she know there was nothing to smile about.

"Claire and Daniel Finley, meet Alex Finley."

He let the words drop like a boulder into a quiet lake. The splash could likely be heard in the next county. Claire's eyes widened and her mouth fell open. Daniel just looked confused as he stared at Alex.

Alex's cheeks grew pink and he could see the muscles jumping in her jaw. "Finley?" Her voice was sharper than the knife in his desk.

"Alex Finley? Really? This is Grant's daughter?" Claire held out a shaking hand after Connor nodded.

Alex didn't move. "Finley?" she repeated.

"Yes, Finley. This is your stepmother and your half brother, Daniel." Connor sat back and waited. He didn't have to wait long.

"I have a sister?"

"I have a brother?" Alex looked at Daniel and shook her head. "No, I refuse to accept that. My parents had one child and that's me."

Claire looked as if she was going to fall over. "I can't believe this is Alex Finley. We looked for you for so long." She looked at Connor. "Did you tell her about the will?"

"No, I haven't had a chance to."

"I have a sister?" Daniel gazed around the adults with wonder on his face. "And she's old too."

"What about the will?" Alex's voice grew louder the more Daniel hopped around the room. "Can you please ask the child to wait outside?"

"The child is half owner in this property and his name is Daniel Grant Finley." Claire sounded shaky but firm. "This ranch is the only home he's ever known, so I'll ask you to treat him with respect."

"Right now I don't really want to talk to you. I just want to find out what's going on." Alex seemed to be at her breaking point as her hands dug into the plush arms on the chair. "What about the will?" She enunciated each word and her stare nearly burned a hole in Connor's face.

"Daniel, please go outside now." Connor didn't want the kid exposed to too much of his sister's anger, justified or not.

"Aw, but Connor . . ."

"It's getting time for the guests to pick their saddles. I'm sure Julio can use your help." It was the right thing to say. With a whoop of delight, Daniel scrambled out the door, leaving the tension in the room behind him.

"No more bullshit, Mr. Matthews. I think I've been more than patient here." Alex completely ignored Claire, who was standing beside the desk. "Or tell me where this attorney is and I'll find out on my own."

Connor didn't want the first meeting between the women to be such a mess, but it was too late to stop it. He found himself wanting to throw Alex over his knees and spank her until she stopped behaving as if the world owed her something. She'd been through a hell of a lot that morning, but still, he prided himself on his iron control and she couldn't be testing it more.

"I told you he's out of town until later this week. I can set up a meeting when he returns, but for now I can fill you in on the gist of it. Michael can give you the particulars. The will has split the ranch and its property in equal proportions for his two children, you and Daniel. Claire gets a monthly stipend for the rest of her life. I am head of operations and receive a salary just like anyone else at the ranch, but I have control over the business." Connor heard the steel in his own tone.

Alex watched his face carefully, her blue eyes like chips of ice. "I think you need to contact that attorney so I can see this will. Not that I don't believe you, but understand that I have never even seen you before and I've learned to trust no one." Her gaze moved to Claire's. "You, however—I remember very well when you showed up here hanging on my father's arm before my mother's body was even cold. I hope you enjoyed her funeral."

Claire's cheeks flushed and Connor realized angry Alex was telling the truth. He'd had no idea Grant would have brought his new wife to his first wife's funeral. It seemed out of character for the man he'd looked up to.

"I, uh, didn't know your mother had passed away. I tried to offer my condolences but—"

Alex cut her off with a wave of her hand. "It was ten years ago and your apologies don't really mean much now. I was a scared, grieving sixteen-year-old girl and you appeared with my runaway father. Forgive me for not accepting you at your word. As I just said, I don't trust anyone, least of all you."

Connor imagined Alex as a teenager, angry and full of sadness over her mother's death. He wondered why Grant had left them and if her anger was misplaced. Perhaps Grant had had a very good reason, or perhaps his timing was just a coincidence.

"Now, if you don't mind, I'd like to review the books as soon as possible. I have a laptop, so if I can get access to the network, I'll use it to open whatever program you use for accounting purposes. Also I'd like the name of the attorney and his number so I can verify he's out of town." Alex rose and Connor couldn't have been more surprised to see her entire body trembling. She was iron on the outside, but obviously not on the inside. He wanted to comfort her, even if she'd been a bitch to Claire and Daniel.

"Where are you staying? I can get all the information to you."

Alex's smile didn't even come close to her eyes. "I'm staying here, so you either find me a room or I'll pick one. When you have the information I need, find me."

With that, Alex left the room, leaving disaster in her wake as if she'd been a tiny brown-haired hurricane. Connor met Claire's worried gaze. Grant had left quite a mess and it would take a lot of patience to sort it out. God help him if Alex proved to be as difficult as she'd already been, because then he really would have to spank her.

CHAPTER FOUR

Alex didn't even remember walking out of the house, but she found herself at the pasture, watching the horses graze. She had adored riding, and everything that went with it. The smell of the grass, the horses, even the not-so-sweet odor of the horse shit reminded her of just how much.

She swallowed with difficulty and focused on controlling her breathing. The shallow breaths she'd managed in Connor's office had done nothing but make her light-headed. That in addition to all the shocks God saw fit to throw at her helped to make her feel as if she was having an out-of-body experience.

Not only was her father dead, but the ranch was ten times its original size and a fucking hotel for pretend cowboys. She had a *brother*, for pity's sake. Her father finally had gotten the son he always wanted. No wonder he'd never mentioned Alex—there was no need since he was finally pleased with his family.

She knew it wasn't the boy's fault and didn't blame the little booger. His mother, however, definitely had a guilty conscience, and she damn well should. The memory of seeing her at Katie Finley's funeral, of the expression on her face, still made Alex bubble with anger.

No matter what her father's motives were, as soon as Claire realized what was going on, she should have left immediately. Everyone was in black; there was a hearse and a coffin. It wasn't rocket science, and unless she was masquerading as human, Claire had known it was a funeral but she'd stayed there on Grant's arm as if she belonged there.

Alex walked around the ranch in a daze. There were groups of people learning to rope a sawhorse with horns, others who were oiling tack, and some standing around watching a young woman teach them how to saddle a horse.

The morning had given way to a beautiful warm day, with plenty of sunshine and blue skies. It seemed almost sacrilegious to be so gorgeous outside when she felt so horrible inside. Nobody spoke to her, although she saw some curious stares from the people working. They all wore light blue shirts and jeans with a happy name tag that read FINLEY'S STAFF.

Alex counted at least twenty cabins nestled on the property, some with people sitting in rocking chairs outside on their small porches. Many of them nodded or said hello as she meandered past. There were signs everywhere leading people to the corral, the barn, the mess hall and a fishing hole.

There were signs leading to six different trails of apparently varying levels of expertise on a horse. Small water troughs were everywhere—one side was for a horse; the other had a spigot for human watering purposes.

It was a perfect, idyllic setting and Alex wanted to hate every inch of it. It had been her home, where she grew up, kissed a boy, learned to ride, where she'd felt loved by her mother. Now it was a stranger's dude ranch and there was nothing left of her home except the name.

She wandered back to the corrals where dozens of horses milled around. Obviously the riders hadn't gone out yet, although given that it was likely near ten o'clock, she expected the riding would begin soon in order to be back for lunch. She couldn't even contemplate eating now.

Alex pressed her forehead against the corral fence and blocked out the sight of Claire's young face from ten years earlier. Done was done, and Alex needed to focus on the now, on the ranch that was now half hers.

There was no way in hell she'd simply accept everything Connor told her. Alex had worked as an accountant for the last eight years, and the books had better be in perfect condition. If he gave her shit about looking at them, she would do what she could to make him hand over the information. Anger was good—it helped her forget just how devastated she was.

A heated gust and a wuffle caressed her face. She looked up into the brown eyes of a large bay horse. Her tight throat loosened as she stepped back enough to get a good look at him. The white blaze in the shape of a comma near his ear made her breath catch.

"It couldn't be." She rubbed him behind the ear and the horse shook his head. "Oh my God. Rusty?" With a laugh she hugged his great neck and realized there was one living creature on the ranch she knew, one who recognized her.

Rusty had been her father's favorite bay, an even-tempered gelding with an easy gait. She'd ridden him the very day her father brought him home when she was ten. It was amazing the horse was still there after so many years.

"You're still here, boy. I'm so glad to see you." He seemed to understand her joy because he allowed her to pet and glom all over him. Rusty was an anchor in the sea of confusion in which she swam. Horses had always had a calming influence on her. They seemed to have a way of listening whenever she had a problem or just needed to vent. "At least someone is glad to see me."

He wuffled again and stuck his nose in the crook of her neck.

"Old friend?"

Alex's joy at finding Rusty went south at the sound of Connor's voice. "Yes, actually, he is."

He stepped up beside her, and Rusty immediately leaned toward Connor, eager for whatever the man had to offer. Traitor.

"He's a good horse. One of the best we have. I reserve him only for the VIPs." He whispered in the horse's ear and a carrot magically appeared in his outstretched palm. So now he was bribing the equines. Rusty delicately took the proffered orange treat and it disappeared into his great mouth.

"What do you want?" Alex kept her voice steady even as she wanted to get some distance between her and the man who confused her. She didn't want to like him, but it seemed the universe had other ideas. Even standing there upset and reeling, she was still aware of him as a man, the tight jeans, the well-worn boots, and those hands. She loved a man with wide palms and calluses.

Connor Matthews was her type exactly. Damn. She had a rather vague but intense memory of kissing him too. Bourbon was not her friend.

He scratched Rusty behind his right ear, and Alex wanted to

smack his hand away. "Just wanted to make sure you were okay. You took a lot of hits in there."

Alex had taken more than a lot of hits. She'd just found out her father was dead; she had a brother and half ownership in a dude ranch. She felt like she had two black eyes and had taken half a dozen body blows.

"That's an understatement. I was hoping to be alone for a while." She couldn't make it more obvious than that. The man confused her even more than she was already.

Connor's hand stopped in midmotion. "You disappeared an hour ago and I was, well, worried."

That was interesting. She wondered if he was worried because she had the ability to find out exactly what he'd been doing as the man responsible for running the ranch. "I'm a big girl; no need to worry about me."

A semitruth. She was definitely a big girl, but she was far from okay and needed someone to worry about her. It should be someone who knew her, who actually cared about her. But there was no one left who did.

That thought made her heart pinch so hard, she gasped. It was true she knew plenty of people, but Alex was completely alone in the world. Again.

"I've arranged for you to have the VIP cabin. It's a quiet, two-thousand-square-foot cabin on the west side of the property. There's a lot of privacy and a gate with a combination lock. No one will bother you." He pushed his black hat firmly down on his head. "You can find it down the path past the blue water trough. Gate combination is zero, five, zero, one, eighty-four."

Alex didn't watch him walk away. She didn't want to nor could she bring herself to. He'd given her exactly what she wanted, after all: a nice quiet, private place. She'd definitely be alone, very much so. A tear slipped down her cheek as she headed toward her car to get her bag.

Her father might not have mentioned her to Connor, may have kept her as his secret from everyone around her. But he obviously hadn't forgotten her.

The combination to the VIP cabin gate was her birthday.

As the morning wore on, Connor made his rounds but he didn't really pay attention to what he was seeing. Before he headed back to his office, more than one employee asked him if he was all right. The look on Alex's face when she'd been hugging the horse gave him a glimpse at the woman beneath the anger. She looked so damn young and full of joy as Rusty had done his best to snuffle her.

He had felt sorry for Alex when he first found out who she was, but he hadn't liked her. Not until he saw how much she loved that horse. No one who loved horses that much could be a bad person, and that was something Connor firmly believed.

What Connor had to focus on was getting his money together to buy Alex's share of the ranch. He had offered to buy Daniel's share, but Claire refused outright. Daniel deserved to be a part of his father's legacy, and Connor appreciated that fact.

He'd almost adopted the role of partner when they couldn't find Alex. In case they never found her, he wanted to have enough funds to purchase her part of the ranch. He never imagined she'd come strolling up in the middle of a September morning and set their world on end.

Connor had to remember she'd just found out her father was dead, that she was confused and hurt, that she likely had a hangover from the bourbon she drank. Yet the one thing running through his head was the feel of her body pressed against his, the softness of her lips.

And how much trouble he was in.

He picked up the phone from the desk and started dialing. Time to call Michael Bailey on his cell and figure out how to untangle the fucking mess Grant had left behind before Connor ruined everything by obsessing about Alex Finley.

Alex found the cabin easily enough, pleased by the secluded spot so she wouldn't have to see just what her father had done to their home. Connor had given her the best cabin on the ranch; of that she was certain. As she entered the combination on the six-foot gate that surrounded it, her fingers shook, forcing her to do it twice.

Her breath caught when she finally got a good look at the building. Huge picture windows decorated the front of the sturdy log cabin. The rocking chairs on the porch were well tended and a beautiful oak color. There was even a table between them with a checkers set in a plastic box along with a deck of cards.

The cabin faced southwest, which would give the front of the cabin a clear view of the sunset. She decided that was where she would be at the end of the day. It had been years since she had really watched a sunset. Perhaps returning to Wyoming would finally force her to sit still long enough to enjoy one.

As she walked up the three front steps holding her pot containing the violet, her boots echoed on the wood, her heels impractical for every part of the ranch. Her feet actually hurt after wandering around for an hour in them. Perhaps there was a place in town where she could get a new pair.

Or perhaps she should leave before she had the chance to get comfortable with new boots. The only trouble with that idea was that she had no place to go and her money would run out in a month.

She explored everything, pleased by the simple luxuriousness of the cabin. The only problem she discovered was that cell phones apparently didn't work in the middle of nowhere. Not that it was a bad thing, but it was another reason to dislike Wyoming. She was cut off and isolated from the familiar and thrust back into the past.

The message SIGNAL LOST was never more appropriate.

Hunger drove her from the cabin two hours later. There was only so much bottled water and lemon slices that would satisfy her growling stomach. She changed her shoes, rummaging through her things until she found her ratty white sneakers. They were at least comfortable and it didn't matter if she got horse shit on them.

The warm breeze caressed her face as she walked down the path. She followed the signs to the mess hall and realized it was the long building beside the house. Once upon a time, they'd used it for training the horses in the winter, but obviously that wasn't necessary with all the barns and outbuildings that had been constructed.

She walked into the building, pleasantly surprised by the delicious scents emanating from inside. There were long tables, bunk style, with cushioned benches. A few smaller tables were situated along the perimeter, likely for those who didn't want to sit on a bench like a real cowboy.

She didn't want to eat with anyone. Alex could only hope she didn't run into Connor or Claire. There were a number of people occupying the long tables, so she walked around those until she found an empty two-seat table in the corner. She was about to sit down when she realized the people in the mess hall were serving themselves from the buffet.

Alex set her jacket on the chair to reserve the table and headed for the vittles. She walked the line to see what was available, then turned to go back to the beginning, and ran head-on into someone else. With a rather inglorious thump, she landed on her ass, clacking her teeth together so hard, her nose actually hurt.

When she looked up, she saw an older woman with an impressive bosom, a smirk on her face and a red flannel shirt over a denim skirt. Her thick black hair was in a braid, then wrapped in a circle at the back of her head. Alex's mouth dropped open when she recognized the woman.

"Bernice?"

"Hell, look what the cat dragged in. If it ain't Alex Finley."

Bernice had been her mother's choice, a woman who served as housekeeper, cook and conscience to everyone who lived at the ranch. She didn't sugarcoat anything and was known for speaking her mind.

She and Alex hadn't always seen eye to eye on things, but Bernice had a good heart and always did what she felt was right. Even if it meant tattling on a thirteen-year-old girl who snuck out to ride under the moonlight with a boy.

"Bernice, I can't believe you're still here." Alex managed to get to her feet, even with a throbbing jaw and a sore ass.

"A' course I'm still here. Where else would I be?" Bernice pushed at Alex's shoulder. "Look at you, all grown up. You're the spitting image of your mama."

Alex nodded, knowing each and every day she looked in the

mirror that she favored Katie Finley in every way except her eyes and her chin. Those she'd inherited from her father, like it or not.

"What are you doing here after all this time?" Bernice eyed her with excruciating honesty. "And why do you look like shit?"

"If you don't mind, I'd rather eat before we talk. I haven't had anything today and I'm hungry enough to eat my own cooking, which is saying something." It would also give her time to gather her thoughts before Bernice yanked every smidgen of information out of her.

"Hell's bells, then you'd best eat then before you keel over. Plates are over yonder; trays are next to them. Help yourself and find a seat. I'll be there in a jiffy." Bernice walked toward the kitchen, leaving Alex with her thoughts.

She filled her plate with turkey and mashed potatoes, a biscuit and green beans with almonds. It looked and smelled so good, her mouth actually watered. She didn't remember the last time she'd had real food, not nouveau cuisine or fast food or whatever David's chef had made with mushrooms. Alex hated mushrooms and ended up eating a lot more junk than she should have simply because she couldn't eat anything other than rice at home.

The truth was, she could have cooked for herself, but Alex had never learned how. Bernice hadn't had the patience to teach her and Alex's mother didn't like to cook. It didn't matter now, though, because she was back at home, eating Bernice's good cooking. Not everything would be as satisfying as this delicious food.

She sat down and realized she'd forgotten to get a drink. Before she could get up, a glass of iced tea was set in front of her, the lemon nicely positioned on the rim. She looked up into Bernice's smiling face.

"Thanks." When Alex took a sip, she groaned aloud at the

cold concoction in her mouth. "God, I forgot what good tea tasted like."

Bernice sat down, her large callused hands in front of her on the table. "Dig in."

Alex didn't need to be told twice. She took a huge bite of turkey, and the flavor exploded on her tongue. The gravy was creamy and salty, the turkey juicy and just right. She took a second bite, this one with a smattering of mashed potatoes included. It was almost a sexual experience.

"I'm glad you're enjoying the food, but I'm curious as to where you've been the last ten years." Bernice sipped at the large mug of coffee in front of her.

"L.A.," Alex managed to say around the mashed potatoes.

Bernice's dark eyebrows went up. "That so? Long way from home, and I don't mean miles."

Alex shrugged, then took a gulp of iced tea. "I needed that distance."

"I can see that. And what brings you back now, if you don't mind my asking?" Bernice did the asking whether or not anyone minded.

Alex finished the bite in her mouth before she answered. "I've got nowhere else to go." The raw and pitiful truth, to be sure.

Bernice nodded. "I'm glad you came here, then. I know things were a bit rough when your mama died. I didn't get a chance to talk to you before you hightailed it outta here." She sipped at her coffee, allowing Alex a bit more time to stuff her face.

And stuff her face she did. The turkey disappeared from the plate, along with the potatoes. As she sopped up the gravy with a biscuit, Alex realized she'd eaten far too much. She was overfull and damn, but it felt good.

Bernice's gaze found hers again. "Now, tell me why you ran and never looked back. Why you thought it a good plan to disappear."

"I had to leave, and you know why. He brought another woman to her funeral, Bernice." Alex tried to block out the memory again, unsuccessfully.

"Your daddy, well, he made mistakes, but marrying Claire wasn't one of them." Bernice held up her hand, obviously seeing something in Alex's gaze. "I ain't saying he went about it the right way. Hell, he fucked it up right good, but Claire is a good woman and her boy isn't such a bad kid either."

Alex set the biscuit down slowly. The turkey now sat in her stomach like a lead weight, her pleasure at the delicious food forgotten. Bernice had no right to defend her father's actions, or that woman who'd taken her mother's place.

"I'm not ready to forgive him, or accept the strangers in my house. Jesus Christ, Bernice, it's a goddamn *dude* ranch! After a hundred and fifty years as my family's house, a Finley heritage, it's no longer a home." Alex glanced around to make sure no one was around. She didn't want to offend people, but she'd been offended by what her father had done. "A bunch of damn city folks playing cowboy. What the hell?"

Bernice shrugged. "The ranch wasn't making any money on cattle, girl. The bigger ranches were putting Finley's under. Your daddy had the idea to keep the ranch going. It weren't easy, but it worked. Each year we made more and built more cabins."

Alex absorbed that information, knowing Bernice was probably right about losing money, but hell, most ranches did. It was a constant struggle to survive. However, turning a home into a dude ranch was still unacceptable. Her father had taken something special, something that had been in his family for a hundred and fifty years, and made it into something awful.

"I think it's going to take me a while to understand it, much less accept it." Alex was proud of the fact that her voice didn't shake. "I don't like that man who runs the place either. He's probably robbing it blind."

"That Connor is a good man, even if he started off as a pain in the ass like you." Bernice wagged her finger at Alex. "It took me a while but I like the boy, so you'd best be nice to him."

Alex frowned. "I don't want to be nice to him. He's coveting the ranch that's mine by right."

Bernice snorted. "You come back in here after ten years and strut like a peacock, but let me tell you, girl, your feathers ain't shiny around these parts. Folks have worked hard to make this ranch into something special, something to be proud of, and you ain't gonna ruin it because you want to have a temper tantrum."

Alex's cheeks heated at the chastisement. Bernice could always reduce her to a little girl facing the principal, make her feel as though her transgressions were monumental. She almost wanted to stick her tongue out, but that would just prove Bernice's point.

"I'm not having a temper tantrum, Bernice. I want what's rightfully mine, what my parents held in trust for me." Alex stood. "I have no place else to go, and no money to leave. If you want to make it difficult for me, then so be it, but I'm here to stay no matter who runs the place."

Bernice stopped her with a hand on her arm. "I ain't saying you're not welcome, girl, and I'm mighty glad to see you. I can't tell you how much. I just don't want your pride or your anger at your papa to ruin a good thing. 'Cause let me tell you, this is a good thing. It can be for you too."

"I'll make my own judgment about that. Thanks for the food. It was the best I've had in ten years."

Alex stood, took the glass of iced tea and walked away. She felt Bernice's gaze and disapproval with each step she took. There was never a time in her life that she felt smaller than when she was judged by the people she respected. Bernice reminded her of that with powerful clarity.

She wanted to dismiss her anger and hurt, and start anew, but it wasn't going to be that easy. Alex had some issues to work through, and come hell or high water, she'd do it. The first was finding out exactly what Connor Matthews was doing to Finley's Ranch.

After retrieving her laptop from the trunk of the car, Alex entered the house again and set the empty iced tea glass at the check-in desk, then made a beeline for his office. She almost hoped he wasn't there so she could snoop around.

There was no shame in snooping. Sometimes she could find out a lot of things simply by looking when no one was around to keep information from her. The hallway and the office were empty, and Alex smiled grimly as she set up her laptop on his desk. It didn't matter if he ran the place; if she was half owner, he could find another place to perch.

The laptop found a secured wireless network but she couldn't find the password anywhere on his desk, although she did look through all the drawers just to be sure. There was a bottle of mouthwash, a toothbrush and toothpaste with floss in the bottom drawer. Obviously Connor had good oral hygiene, which was a plus in Alex's book.

She found notebooks, pens, a thumb drive and a neat stack of invoices for feed, hay and veterinary services. The thumb drive intrigued her, so she plugged it into her laptop and took a look-see at the contents.

"Find anything interesting?"

She didn't look up at the voice because she knew it was Connor at the door. "Not yet but give me a few more minutes."

"That drive contains the guest records for the last six months. No trade secrets or incriminating evidence."

Out of the corner of her eye she saw him standing in the doorway as she paged through the spreadsheets on the drive. He was telling her the truth, and that pissed her off, for whatever reason. She wanted him to get caught in a lie. It would make it easier to dislike him.

"Okay, now I want access to the real books. Not just guest records, fascinating as they might be." She tapped her laptop. "Give me the network key and I'll find what I need."

His gaze narrowed. "I don't work for you, and I sure as hell don't take orders from you."

Ah, she'd finally riled the calm Connor Matthews. Good, she'd rather have him rattled than annoyingly calm.

"I beg to differ. If I own half this ranch, then you do work for me."

"There's a clause in the will giving me the position of chief operating officer for the ranch. That means I work for the estate, not you." He stepped into the room, closing the door behind him, looking more like a stalking panther than a man. She shivered at the predatory gleam in his eye.

Perhaps she shouldn't have stepped on his paw.

"Six of one, a half dozen of another. You are responsible for giving me information when I want it." She stood as he loomed over her. No need for intimidation tactics. Her pulse thrummed fast and heavy as she caught wind of his scent. Why did he have to be so damn attractive?

"I don't have to give you anything you demand. Didn't anyone tell you that you catch more flies with honey than vinegar?" He leaned in so close, she could see the flecks of dark green mixed with the lighter green of his eyes.

"Who says I want to catch flies?" Why was her voice so breathy?

"You're bossy."

"You're annoying."

She didn't want to kiss him, but damn if she didn't find herself wrapped around him with her lips locked against his. After an initial moment of surprise, he pulled her close and she felt every inch of his hardened body against hers. My, oh my, he was definitely in shape. If she had been sober the night before, she wouldn't have woken up alone; that was for sure.

Her nipples tightened fast and she ground them against his hard chest, eager for more. His hands cupped her ass, pulling her against an erection she really wanted to see up close and personal. Connor was well endowed and she couldn't have been happier about that.

Their tongues rasped against each other, sweet wet heat she wanted repeated between her legs. Their clothes were annoying and preventing her from actually feeling skin on skin. She managed to get herself up on the desk, then spread her legs wide and pulled him into the vee of her pulsing core.

Something poked into her left hip, but she didn't care. All she wanted was Connor. She yanked at his shirt until it came free from his jeans and suddenly she had open access to his chest. Crisp dark hair tickled her hands as she got to know his nicely muscled front.

He somehow managed to get her blouse unbuttoned. She felt rather than heard the groan when he popped her bra open and her breasts spilled into his hands. They were double Ds and the one part of her anatomy she was proud of. The light pink nipples were already harder than she imagined they could ever be. Then he flicked them with his thumbs.

Her lower half clenched and she could hardly wait to get her pants off. First, though, his dark head dipped and he sucked her nipple into his mouth. Oh God, his tongue and teeth were dexterous and marvelously gifted. He somehow managed to suck, bite and lick her at once. Connor had obviously been a breast man for quite some time.

She popped open the button on his pants and unzipped, pleased to find a pair of easy-access boxers. When she reached in to find his cock, he shuddered against her. Smooth satin and steel, nicely formed and all hers. She couldn't quite reach his balls so she satisfied herself by pleasuring the base of his staff and running her other hand up and down.

He broke the kiss and sucked in a loud breath. "What are we doing?"

"Scratching an itch. Now, shut up and strip." She hopped off the desk and made quick work of her trousers and panties.

When she glanced at him, the sheer size and girth of his cock made her mouth water. Very soon she'd have to taste that wonderful looking organ, but not now. Right about then she wanted only to feel it inside her.

Oh God, he was fantastically hung. She took her time stroking him and getting to know his balls before she stood up. His pupils were dilated to the point that his eyes looked almost black.

She put her trousers on the desk, then slid up until she was sitting on them, and opened her legs wide. "Ride me, cowboy."

After a quick snap of a rubber on his staff, he was on her in seconds, his deliciously hard cock nudging her entrance. Alex grabbed his head and yanked him down to her breasts.

"Bite me."

Nothing excited her more than a little pain with her pleasure. As his teeth closed around her nipple, he plunged inside her hard and fast. She managed to suck in enough oxygen to avoid passing out, but just barely. He was perfect, so damn hard and big, he filled her until there wasn't an iota of space between them.

He mumbled something against her breast, then began to move within her, and he had a fantastic rhythm. She pushed against him as he slammed into her. The wet sounds of their joining mixed with the shallow gusts of breaths they managed to take.

Alex grabbed the edge of the desk and inched closer. Now he hit her clit with each thrust, heightening her pleasure. She wished he wore a cock ring, but perhaps another time. This was fast and furious fucking, exactly what she needed.

He switched breasts and bit the other, making her entire body clench. She was close to coming after only five minutes of being with him. Connor groaned and stopped moving.

"I'm going to come if you do that again."

Alex squeezed harder. "Then let's do it. I want to come *now*."

She slammed against him each time he pounded into her. Faster, harder, wetter. Alex's eyes rolled back in her head as the orgasm overtook her. She dug her fingernails into the desk as his teeth dug into her nipple. A scream rose in her throat, but she kept it contained, letting loose only a grunt.

He let her nipple go and straightened up to bury his spurting cock deep inside her. Alex rode the waves of her own orgasm as she pulsed around him, milking him, prolonging her own ecstasy until she saw stars behind her eyes.

Alex sucked in a lungful of air and realized she was shaking. Thank God she was sitting down or she might fall down. That was when she realized Connor was trembling too. He leaned into her and she felt his thunderous heartbeat against hers.

"Holy shit." Her voice was hoarse and a bit wobbly.

"Exactly what I was thinking." He pressed his forehead against hers. "This wasn't what I had in mind this afternoon."

Alex heard the regret in his voice, but she ignored it. Who cared if he didn't want to have a quickie in his office? It happened and she was glad of it. She'd needed it badly and obviously so had he.

He grabbed tissues from the box on the corner of the desk and handed her some. They spent the next few minutes cleaning up and locating their clothes. Alex tried to ignore him as he finished dressing.

The entire room smelled of sex and their musky odors. She breathed in deep, loving it. He, however, opened the window to allow a breeze in. When he turned around, he wouldn't meet her gaze.

So that was the way it would be.

"I'm sorry, Alex. I don't know what came over me."

She narrowed her gaze and stalked toward him, their positions now reversed between hunter and prey. He stood his ground, but didn't look at her until she grabbed his chin and forced him to.

"That, Connor, was a fantastic afternoon fuck. No need for apologies or regrets because I sure as hell don't have any." She cupped his balls. "I enjoyed myself and hope we can do this again when there's a bed nearby." Alex was still reeling from the encounter but meant every word she said. She and Connor seemed to be made for each other as far as sex was concerned. Her knees were still knocking together.

He opened his mouth to speak, but a knock at the door interrupted him before he could say a word. Alex kissed him hard, then picked up her laptop.

"Password?"

Connor looked flummoxed by the question.

"For the network. What's the password?"

"Oh, uh, zero, six, one, seven, eight, zero." He looked as if he wanted to punch something. Alex was pleased to note he'd been affected as much as she had from their encounter.

As she opened the door to leave, she realized the network password was her parents' anniversary. Her father surprised her with each little piece of information she learned at the ranch. If he'd loved his family so much, why had he abandoned them?

Confused and feeling completely unsettled, Alex wasn't sure if she was running from her own mistakes, her father's ghost or the man who turned her knees to jelly.

Connor got rid of the interruption quickly, unable and unwilling to talk to anyone right then. He needed time alone to think and recover from the afternoon's activities. As he closed and locked the door, he barely made it to his chair before he plopped down so hard the damn thing slid back two feet.

He stared at the desktop, realizing he'd just fucked Alex on yesterday's receipts. What the hell had happened to him that he would forget everything but her? He'd never felt that kind of primal need, the absolute heart-pounding need to join. It was as if he'd become an animal scenting his mate.

Truthfully, if Alex hadn't passed out at the hotel, it might have happened there, before he'd known who she was. The fact was, Alex and he were totally and completely sexually magnetized. He could almost feel the pull even when she wasn't in the building.

He would have put his head on the desk but he was afraid he'd catch a whiff of her scent. Connor was not the type of man to lose his head over a woman, especially one who threatened everything he'd built the last eight years. She was everything he didn't want in a woman. She was bossy and outspoken, and she cussed like a sailor.

Connor preferred a demure woman who didn't get dirty or argue constantly. Someone like Claire, although it would be extremely weird to be attracted to her since she was kind of like a quasi-sister-in-law. Yet did he really want a woman like her? The last dates he'd been on had been with women he'd met in bars, no surprise there, with big tits, big smiles and no brains. None of them liked horses and none of them had any idea he was more businessman than cowboy nowadays.

That blew the idea of liking demure women right out of the water. He picked them brassy and easy—Alex was the exact opposite, even if she had had sex with him less than a day after they'd met. He couldn't explain why, but it didn't make her slutty in his eyes. She didn't seem to be able to resist the pull between them any more than he could.

Although it was only two in the afternoon, he pulled out a

bottle of whiskey from the bottom drawer and poured himself a hefty double. Connor wasn't proud of his behavior or the fact he had lost control completely. Drinking didn't help any of that, but it did help his nerves a hell of a lot.

The whiskey burned as it went down his throat. He held his breath, waiting for the hooch to complete its path. When he finally let it out, he felt better, at least enough to be able to concentrate on business.

Connor put Alex out of his mind as much as he could and got back to reviewing the receipts.

CHAPTER FIVE

Alex went over the figures for the third time. Her eyes burned from squinting at the line items so intently the last few days. She closed them and pinched the bridge of her nose. It was no use going over them again—they were neat and balanced to the penny.

Not only was Connor using the best accounting software for small businesses, but the entries were flawless. Damn.

She looked up and realized the sun had almost set and she'd nearly missed it. Alex hopped up from the cozy sofa and ran for the door, ignoring the pins and needles in her legs from sitting with the laptop for too long.

As she limped outside, the purple, pink and orange colors in the sky made her breath catch. It was as if God had taken His paintbrush and swiped it across the horizon, leaving behind the most vibrant colors imaginable.

She sat down on the rocking chair and tried to remember that this was what was important in life. Enjoying herself, savoring the simplicity of a sunset and not focusing on the complexities of her past.

It was a hard thing to do. She'd spent so much time hiding from the past, from those feelings, that coming back to Wyoming was supposed to be cathartic, a way to close the door to that past. So far she'd done nothing but make things worse.

Alex hugged her knees to her chest and watched the sunset until nothing was left but the deep, dark blue of twilight. Her stomach rumbled noisily and she reluctantly got up from the rocking chair.

Perhaps it would be better to have a meal in the cabin rather than go to the mess hall. Feeling like she was hiding, Alex ordered room service and waited for her burger to arrive. Being in the VIP cabin must have given her certain privileges, because the food arrived in less than twenty minutes.

A knock at the door startled her. She realized she'd been staring out the window at the darkening sky since she'd placed the room service order. When she opened the door, Claire stood there with a tray of food.

Alex felt all the blood rush to her cheeks as she was confronted with the woman who had replaced her mother. At first, she wanted to slam the door, but she resisted the urge. Instead she gripped the wood so tightly a splinter lodged in her finger. "I don't think I'm ready to talk to you yet."

"I know, but Connor told me you were staying here, and I really wanted the chance to speak to you." She shuffled her feet. "May I come in, please?"

Alex wanted to shout no, truly slam the door and act like the hurt teenager she'd been ten years earlier. She could have, but decided her behavior so far in Wyoming had not been ideal. Perhaps acting like an adult might be in order.

"Okay, fine." Alex opened the door so Claire could come in. Her body was wound so tightly that if someone had poked her with a pin, she might have exploded. The idea that this woman, the person who had replaced her mother, was speaking to her was almost surreal.

"Alex, thank you for letting me in." Claire set the tray on the coffee table. "I know it can't be easy for you to be here, or find out about Grant and Daniel."

"An understatement." Alex flopped down on the couch and picked up the tin covering the food. She didn't even feel like eating anymore, but she picked up a French fry anyway.

"May I sit?"

Alex gestured to the couch. Her stomach was clenched so tight, she could hardly swallow. "Sure, why not."

Claire looked perfectly put together with her raven black hair in a bob, her white blouse and black slacks. Even her nails were manicured, unlike Alex's messy nails that had never seen a manicurist in her life.

"I waited a few days before I came over. I thought perhaps you needed some time to adjust. You see, I want us to come to an understanding, if we can. Grant wasn't proud of what he'd done. I hope you know that. He did try to find you but without much success. His one regret was never making peace with you." Claire offered her everything Alex wanted to hear, and nothing she wanted to accept.

"It's nice to hear that, but it would have been better coming from him." Alex managed to swallow the food in her mouth but didn't pick up anything else. "You were there at my mother's funeral. Do you remember that day?"

Claire blushed; at least she had some measure of guilt. "Yes, I do. I know the past isn't easy for either of us, but I thought if I made the first gesture, it would help us begin the healing process."

Alex shook her head. "The healing process is not the problem. I don't need any help with that. What I need help with is finding my place here, and to do that, I need time. I can't just forget everything and pretend we're a happy family."

Claire nodded tightly. "I can understand that, but I hope you change your mind. Daniel is excited to have a big sister and he's a wonderful boy. He takes after your fa—What I mean to say is, he's afraid to approach you. If you could find it in your heart to give him a chance, it would be wonderful."

Ah yes, she needed to be friendly with the boy who'd finally fulfilled her father's wish for a son. Alex, the girl who tried so hard to be a boy, went so far as to shave her head when she was ten so she looked like one. Claire had no idea what she was asking, and Alex couldn't even begin to explain it to her.

"Tell me something, Claire. At my mother's funeral, why were you there? Were you with my father as his girlfriend?" Alex didn't really want to know the answer, but she couldn't stop herself from asking.

Claire sighed. "I met your father in Denver. He was sitting on a park bench and crying. At first I didn't talk to him but I saw him every day for a week in the same place, looking sadder than any human being I'd ever seen. I've always tended to collect wounded souls, and Grant called to that side of me."

Alex was perversely glad he'd been sad in Denver.

"We had meals together and I found him to be a good man, a man who had lost his way. I, um, didn't know he was married." Claire looked decidedly uncomfortable. "Until one day he got a call and I found out his wife had passed away. I didn't want to go with him, but he begged me. We got on a plane and came to Wyoming. I almost had to hold him up to get him inside the house." Claire met her gaze. "When he saw you, I felt your pain, and I knew it had been a mistake to travel with Grant."

"You felt my pain?" Alex didn't know what to believe.

"I wanted to tell you I'm sorry for causing you pain. It wasn't my intention and to this day I remember the look on your face." Claire's eyes filled with tears. "I truly am sorry for being the cause of it."

Alex took a breath and swallowed the lump in her throat. "How did you end up marrying him?"

Claire shook her head. "I stayed on to help him with the ranch and eventually I fell in love with him. He was a good man for all his mistakes; he had a good soul. Grant did make mistakes; he was the first to admit that."

"Again, an understatement." Alex could write an opus about the mistakes her father had made, right after she wrote her own.

Claire stared down at her clenched hands. "All I'm asking is for you to give Daniel a chance. Give us a chance."

Alex wanted to say no. She wanted to tell Claire to go to hell, but something in the other woman's gaze told her she was telling the truth about all of it. No doubt Alex's father had used her as well. "I'm not making any promises. There are things you can't possibly know about me or my relationship with my father." Alex rose on shaky legs. "If you don't mind, I think we're done talking for now."

"Of course. Thank you for hearing me out." Claire made her way to the door with a significant amount of grace, a skill Alex woefully lacked.

As Alex closed the door behind her stepmother, she slid down the wall and covered her face with her hands. She tried to cry as quietly as she could.

The morning sun burned Connor's eyes as he stepped out of his cabin. He'd stayed up too late trying to avoid thinking about Alex and catch up on the work he'd ignored while trying to balance the receipts. One thing Connor hated about his job was the books. He would gladly shovel horse shit eight hours a day to avoid them. It also was the one thing he really had to force himself to do. Although schedules were the most complex task, balancing the guests coming in with the employees and their various specialties was almost an art form; accounting was still his nemesis.

His back ached right along with his neck, but another day of paperwork awaited him, including a visit from Michael Bailey, Grant's attorney. Connor really didn't look forward to it, or to Alex's reaction to the will. She was obviously brimming with passion, with fury at her father. Confronting what Grant had left behind would be exhausting for everyone.

After grabbing coffee and a muffin, and ignoring Bernice's glower, Connor headed for his office. He polished off the muffin on the way, barely tasting the sweet corn flavor. The coffee was strong and black, the way he liked it.

He nodded to a few people but didn't stop to talk. Normally he would have, but he was tied into knots. His new obsession with Alex was affecting his work, his sleep and his temper.

With determination, he dove into work, and before he knew it, Michael poked his head into the office. Connor looked up from the schedules, surprised to see it was ten o'clock already.

"I don't think I've seen you work so hard before." Michael grinned at him as he stepped into the office. The attorney was a few years older than Connor, with blond hair and blue eyes. A boy next door with an athletic physique and charm.

"Shut up, Mike." Connor sipped at the cold coffee, then made a face at the bitter dregs. He set it aside and sighed hard.

Michael sat in the chair and raised his brows. "I've brought Grant's will with me, as you asked. Now, tell me what the hell is going on."

"Alex Finley arrived four days ago. I almost fell out of my chair when she told me who she was. Jesus, Mike, I never expected her to show up." Connor ran his hands through his hair and leaned back in the chair. "She's got me chasing my own damn tail. I'm not sleeping and—well, it's been a rough week."

"How's Claire taking it? And Daniel?" Mike lost his teasing attitude, concern evident on his face.

"Claire is trying to make inroads with Alex, but it isn't going to be easy. Daniel has no idea what's going on; he's just thrilled to have a big sister, even if she ignores him." Connor picked up the coffee cup, then set it down before he swallowed the nasty crap again. "Thanks for coming by when you got back into town."

"No worries. I was glad to come after I got your call. Nancy hadn't scheduled anything for me this morning since I got in late last night." Mike hid a yawn behind his hand. "Tell me what she's like."

Connor thought about Alex, about all the moments he'd spent with her, and about the storm cloud that seemed to follow her.

"She's got his chin and his eyes. Other than that, I figure she looks like her mother. Kind of short, curvy." And oh, those curves kept him up at night, literally.

"Now, that's an interesting answer. You just described what she looks like and not a thing about what she's like." Mike's gaze was probing, like only a lawyer could do.

Connor frowned at his friend. "She's outspoken, bossy and demanding."

Mike chuckled. "Oh, so that's how it is."

"How what is?"

"You have had a total of three ladies in your life in eight years. Relationships with them all started the same, with you thinking they were outspoken, bossy or demanding." Mike pointed at him. "You are in trouble if she's got all three qualities."

Connor's cheeks heated. "That's a load of bullshit and you know it. I am not in trouble because of Alex Finley."

He glanced up to see her in the doorway. His stomach flipped, then twisted so tight he tasted the muffin.

She glanced at Mike; then her gaze swung back at him. "Should I ask why you were talking about me and trouble?"

Connor stood. "Sorry, Alex. I was just filling Mike in on the last four days."

"And that involved me and trouble." Color was high on her face.

"This is awkward." Mike stood and held out his hand. "Michael Bailey, attorney."

Alex shook his hand. "Alex Finley, prodigal daughter."

Mike smiled. "Witty and beautiful. Now I understand why there was trouble."

She crossed her arms under her breasts, pushing the amazing

mounds up, making Connor lose track of why he was trying to forget what it was about Alex that made him obsess.

"Did Connor tell you I wanted to see the will? I understand I own half the ranch, and I'd like to get the details of exactly what it all means." She walked into Connor's office and sat down, her spine stiffer than his wake-up woody that morning.

Mike sat down, his lawyer face firmly back in place. "Of course, Miss Finley. Please accept my condolences on the loss of your father. He was a good man, a good client."

Connor hadn't had a chance to tell Mike exactly how angry Alex seemed to be with her father.

"Funny, I remember him being an asshole. Now, let me see the will, please." She kept her voice even but the steel in it was sharp enough to cut through bone.

Mike nodded, but Connor could see he was holding his tongue. The lawyer was an even-tempered man, but Alex tested everyone's patience. Fury poured off her into the air, making it pulse in the office.

After opening his briefcase, Mike handed Alex a sheaf of papers. "The will is relatively simple. He made it after Daniel was born, so it's recent."

As she took the papers, Connor noticed her hands shook. He didn't know if it was anger or fear, or perhaps another unnamed emotion coursing through her. She was a myriad of deep corners he had yet to explore.

The only sounds in the office were the muffled noises from outside and the scrape of paper as she read the will once, then twice. Her knuckles whitened with each pass. Connor saw the color drain from her face and he realized she was more than just angry. She was suffering.

"Do you have any questions?" Mike watched her without any expression on his face.

Alex didn't answer at first. She stared down at the will as a nearly silent, uneven sigh escaped her lips.

"His mother holds the ranch in trust for him, right?"

Connor didn't have to ask whom she was talking about. Daniel owned the other half of the ranch.

"Yes, until he reaches twenty-one, she holds the power of attorney for him," Mike answered matter-of-factly.

"So what if I want to sell my half? Do I need her permission?"

Connor's body tensed even further. This was what he wanted, to buy her half of the ranch, so why did he feel as though he wanted to tell her not to sell? It made no sense whatsoever. How could he reach his dream if he closed the door on it?

"Are you interested in selling?" Mike's voice had hardened a little. He didn't know Alex or anything about her relationship with Grant. Connor didn't know much but he knew it was complicated.

"Maybe. This ranch isn't my home anymore. I don't know what it is." Alex glanced at Connor and he saw the raw pain in her eyes. She looked back down at the will.

He wanted to pull her into his arms. Foolish man.

"If you decide you want to sell, you would need to review the state laws regarding this type of situation and procure an attorney. Since I was Grant's attorney, I'm Claire and Daniel's now. You'd want to protect your interests." What Mike didn't say was he wouldn't help her break up Finley's, but Connor heard it anyway.

Alex either didn't hear or chose to ignore it. "Then I'll look into getting my own attorney."

"There's one more thing." Mike pulled out an envelope and held it out for Alex. "He left this for you."

Connor would have sworn she couldn't get any paler, but as her gaze settled on the envelope, she looked like a glass of milk. He was afraid she'd run to the bathroom again to vomit. Connor readied himself to follow her, then realized what he was doing.

He was preparing to take care of her. Well, holy fucking shit.

"I don't want it."

"It's yours whether you want it or not, Miss Finley." Mike put the envelope on the desk in front of her. "I'm going to find Bernice and get some coffee. Connor, you can find me in the mess hall."

The attorney left the room, obviously unwilling to be there with Alex any longer. Grant had been loved by everyone, including Mike. As a young attorney, he'd been given a chance to make his career by the rancher. Loyalty to Grant Finley ran deep, even after his death.

Alex stared at the envelope, then stood so abruptly, it slid toward Connor. "I've got to get out of here."

He didn't get a word in before she ran out the door. It wasn't even eleven in the morning and he was already caught up in Alex's pain.

Connor finally finished his work after nine p.m. Bernice had disapprovingly brought him dinner at seven, for which he'd been absurdly grateful. He'd missed lunch, and the food was absolutely delicious in his lonely office.

The main building was quiet, with only the soft murmur of a few guests near the fireplace. He nodded to Jeremiah, the night clerk, as he stepped out the door. The moon was a bright coin in the velvet black sky. He shivered as the cool air surrounded him, made him wish he'd actually brought a coat.

The hot coffee that morning had warmed him up so much he hadn't thought to bring one. Now he regretted the lack as he walked to his cabin, his breath coming in white puffs.

The horses were all in the barns, likely with their jackets on and ready for the cool fall night. The music of the night creatures filled his ears as he walked, his boots the only other sound.

Until he heard a woman's voice somewhere in the distance. He stopped and cocked his head to listen. The voice was far away, near the hill that led to the fishing hole, perhaps near the family cemetery. Somehow he knew it was Alex even before he turned to follow the sound. She hadn't reappeared since she'd left his office in the morning. He had tried not to think about where she was, unsuccessfully.

As he got closer, he realized it was definitely Alex and, if he wasn't mistaken, she'd been drinking. He shivered as he approached her location. She was in the cemetery, which meant she was either visiting her mother or yelling at her father. His money was on the latter, considering she'd had a gander at his will that morning.

The moon painted the hill in silver, outlining the sole human occupant aboveground. She was pacing back and forth, the glint of a bottle in her hand. He could almost smell the bourbon, apparently her drink of choice.

At first he was going to simply walk up and make her go back to the VIP cabin; then he thought twice and decided to see what she was doing out there first. For all he knew, she might simply need to visit her parents' graves. Fat chance, but it was still a possibility.

He stood just out of her sight, but close enough to hear her. At first it was just mumbling, but then her words grew sharper and louder.

"I mean, Jesus Christ, Daddy, how do you expect me to handle this? I don't want to like Claire and I sure as hell don't want to like Daniel. Although I'm sure he was everything you wanted and finally got." Her voice caught on a small sob. "You're going to force me to stay here a year before I can sell. What kind of shit is that? I don't want to stay here. I want to be somewhere else, anywhere else."

Connor immediately felt guilty for eavesdropping on her private moment. But if he stood up then, she would see him and it would make matters worse. Her circle widened and she came within ten feet of him. He was stuck right where he was until she was finished. That would teach him to meddle in her life.

"I came home to have it out with you and here I am shouting at your gravestone. How ironic is that? You predicted I'd take so many risks I'd put myself in an early grave, and guess what? It wasn't me. You beat me to it."

She took too many risks? Connor wondered exactly what that meant. Obviously Grant had disapproved.

Alex swung her arms wide. "Nope, I'm the lucky one who's a fucking orphan. Little Orphan Alex." A strangled chuckle sounded. "Well, let me tell you, the sun will not come out tomorrow. The sun might not ever come out."

She fell to her knees, the bottle forgotten on the grass beside her knees. "I just wanted to know why. Why did you leave us? Why did you think I was something to throw away?"

Her voice was so full of agony, Connor closed his eyes and tried to block it out. He'd definitely made a mistake and was paying for it now. Alex didn't need him intruding on her private thoughts, and he sure as hell didn't need to hear just how much pain she was in.

It reminded him too much of himself ten years ago.

Connor got to his feet, making enough noise that she heard him. It was enough to stop her tirade, thank God.

"Who's there?"

"It's Connor. C'mon, Alex, let me walk you back to the cabin."

She snorted. "Connor? Ah, the first son of the great Grant Finley. Did you know he always wanted a son? That's why he named me Alex—not Alexandra, just Alex." Her laugh sounded more like a sob.

Connor picked up the bottle and dumped it out into the grass, then held out his hand. "You're drunk again."

She sighed, long and hard. "I know. I wasn't intending on drinking but somebody left that primo hooch in the cabin, and after that lawyer left, whew! I needed a drink."

Connor wondered what Alex had been doing in the hours in between but didn't ask. If she wanted to tell him, she would. He managed to get her to her feet, but she was staggering.

"How much did you drink, anyway?" He struggled to keep her upright. This was too familiar, a complete déjà vu from four days ago.

"Too much. Not enough. I dunno." She grabbed hold of his shirt. "You are freakin' hot, Connor. You make my nipples pop whenever I catch a whiff of that cologne or see you in those tight jeans. Dayum, man, seriously nice package."

Unbelievably, Connor felt his cheeks heat. How the hell this tiny, buxom woman with a penchant for bourbon made a man like him blush was beyond explanation.

"Glad you like it. Now, let's get you in the cabin." He dropped the empty bottle on the side of the trail, making a mental note to retrieve it before the morning fishermen passed by.

Before they'd made it twenty feet, he was ready to strangle Alex. She was a sloppy drunk, one who had a big mouth and didn't know when to shut up. At thirty feet, he'd had enough and simply picked her up and threw her over his shoulder, fireman style.

She whooped and made a choking noise as her stomach pressed against his shoulder. He hoped she wouldn't yak all over his back. That would be a perfect end to a fucked-up day, though.

As he punched in the combination to open the gate to the VIP cabin, she seemed to come back to life.

"That's my birthday, you know."

"What's your birthday?" He set her on her feet so he could get the front door open.

"The combination." She pointed shakily at the gate. "He didn't forget me, Connor."

Connor didn't want to look at her, but he did anyway. In her blue eyes he saw ancient pain and grief so sharp, it cut into him. Grant had not done right by this girl—that was for certain—but it wasn't Connor's place to judge his friend. She had to work it out for herself, but she also had to stop drinking.

They made it inside and she pulled his head down for a kiss. She tasted of booze, desperation and longing—the wrong mixture. Connor broke the kiss and held her at arm's length.

"I'm not going to repeat what we did yesterday on my desk. You need to drink some water and then get some sleep." Ignoring her protests, he gave her a bottle of water from the minibar and pushed her toward the bedroom.

She sat down and struggled to unlace the silly boots she wore. "Help me, Connor."

With a thespian-worthy sigh, he removed her boots, again. Then, with as much objectivity as he could muster, he managed to get her down to her panties and T-shirt. Her breasts were simply glorious in the moonlight streaming through the window, but he knew it wasn't the time or the place. Alex had too many issues to work through for him to climb under the sheets with her.

She cupped his cheek. "You're too nice for me. I need to be punished. I need a bad boy." She kissed him hard.

"Yep, I am a nice guy—now, drink the water."

She made a face but dutifully finished the water, then climbed into bed. It was strange to be tucking her in, but that was just what Connor did. The day had started out on a strange note, and here it was ending on an even stranger one.

Alex looked up at him, her eyes luminous in the semidarkness of the room. "I like you, Galahad."

His heart did a complete somersault as the earth moved beneath his feet. "You're still drunk."

"I'm sober enough to know what I'm saying. I'll regret saying it, but it won't change the fact that it's true." She touched his cheek. "You're so perfect, it makes my heart hurt to look at you."

Connor shook his head. "I'm far from perfect, Alex. I wasn't always the upstanding businessman. Believe me, I was inches away from spending my life in prison when, uh, when I got the opportunity here at Finley's."

He'd almost told her Grant had saved his life, but it wasn't the right time for sharing that particular piece of information.

"Ah, but you have a good heart. A gentleman, a knight, a cowboy." She smiled, and he saw the woman behind the anger, and knew that he could fall for her if he wasn't careful. They were more alike than she realized.

"Good night, Alex." He started to rise but she pulled him down.

"You must kiss me good night, Galahad."

It was the third time she'd called him that. Obviously Maid Alex had a thing for Camelot. "Nope, just go to sleep."

"Not gonna sleep unless I get a kiss." She had morphed into coy and mischievous.

Connor, recognizing a losing battle, leaned down and brushed a kiss on her cheek. "Good night, Alex."

To his surprise she didn't protest the chaste kiss or push for a deeper one. She snuggled down into the covers and he sat there, oddly comforted by the fact he had made sure she was safe again.

Grant would be proud of him.

Alex woke suddenly, instantly awake in the plush, pillowed bed. She sat straight up and looked around, confused by her surroundings. The entire previous day rushed through her memory and she flopped back on the bed and groaned.

Interestingly enough, she didn't have a hangover, although she distinctly remembered swilling bourbon straight from the bottle. There was the fucking lawyer, the cemetery, the moon and . . . Connor. Again.

Did the man have nothing better to do than rescue her from her own stupidity? Apparently not, judging by the fact that he'd brought her home and tucked her in again. She wished he'd done more than tuck her in, especially after getting a taste of just how passionate he was.

Alex knew they were very compatible sexually and wanted to explore that relationship further. She didn't need to have something long-term to enjoy herself. In fact, she'd done her best to avoid deep relationships, but she had developed trust with her partners over the years.

It was a beautiful morning judging by the sunshine streaming through the windows. She rolled out of bed and showered, the hot water reviving her nicely. There was a one-cup coffeemaker with little tiny cups of grounds for each. She happily made herself two cups and sipped them as she nibbled on the bread left on the tray from room service the night before.

Although she was hungry, the bread and coffee were all she wanted at the moment. She dressed in jeans and sneakers, determined to take her first ride in ten years. The thought of hopping on Rusty's back was more appealing than any gourmet breakfast.

The cool air felt nice against her shower-warmed skin. She actually felt good that morning, which was a surprise considering the fact that it was the second night in a week that she'd drank too much. Perhaps whatever Connor did helped prevent whatever hangover she might have gotten.

It was before eight and there were only employees up and about. The fishermen were likely already at their task, which left the pretend cowboys. She surmised they were at the mess hall chowing down on Bernice's eggs and bacon.

As she stepped into the enormous barn, the smells washed over her, catapulting her back to the past, to the very memories she'd avoided. Alex had loved horses, loved riding, loved everything about life on a ranch. She'd started on the back of a horse before she'd even gotten comfortable on her own two feet.

Alex had lived and breathed ranching. Her throat tightened at the realization that she'd hidden not only from her father but also from herself for the ten years she'd been gone. She'd truly missed all of it. She resented that, whoever was to blame for it.

The barn was quiet except for the sounds of the horses, the wuffles, an occasional neigh, the scrape of the horseshoes in the hay and a low murmur from somewhere in the back. She glanced down at her sneakers and made a promise to find a store that sold real boots as soon as possible.

She walked in, pleased to see how clean and organized the barn was. If Connor did anything halfway, she'd probably have to search twenty years to find it. He ran a tight ship, that was obvious, and in this case the horses were well cared for.

Alex strolled past the stalls, studying each horse's name tag and breed before taking the time to look at them, say hello and blow into their nostrils so they learned her scent. She couldn't remember the last time she'd had so much fun or relaxed so easily.

Horses always had that effect on her, and she was so glad it was still true. They were friendly for the most part, although some were standoffish. They had personalities just like people, but most people didn't know that. She found Rusty halfway down and was thrilled when he immediately came to her. She scratched him behind the ear and he gave her all kinds of horsey love.

After she finished meeting the horses, she made her way back to the front of the barn to the tack room. There were rows of neatly laid-out saddles, bits, bridles and headstalls. A pile of blankets lay in the corner, ready for use.

It was just as neat as the barn, and Alex started wondering if Connor had a form of OCD. No one's tack room and barn were that damn neat. She checked everything and found it well-oiled and in great shape, of course. Alex begrudgingly admitted that it was in as great a shape as the books. She made a face at a fancy saddle with silver conchos decorating it. Could something be just a bit out of place and make her feel as if she were at a ranch?

"Can I help you?"

Alex turned to find a man in his forties, bowlegged as all men who spend too much time in the saddle are. He had some silver mixed in with his jet-black hair, and the standard cowboy garb of jeans and a button-down blue shirt. He pushed back his cream-colored hat and put his hands on his hips as he looked her over.

"I wanted to ride Rusty this morning. I didn't want to disturb the exceedingly neat tack but I need a saddle I can sit on." She touched the chinks hanging from the walls. "One of these days I'll wear these again too."

"You Alex Finley?"

Obviously Connor had put the word out about her. "Yep, sure am." She held out her hand. "Pleasure to meet you."

"I'm Julio, head groomsman here at Finley's." His hand was big, warm and callused, barely squeezing hers before letting go.

"Can you help me get Rusty ready?"

"Sure thing, Ms. Finley. I think I've got the perfect saddle for you that'll fit that big bay."

They spent the next ten minutes getting everything ready and saddling Rusty. Excitement bubbled in Alex's stomach as they finally tightened the cinch and led the horse out of the barn. The sun made her eyes sting after being in the shady barn for so long, but she didn't care. She was about to take a ride for the first time in ten years.

"There's a mounting block over yonder." Julio pointed to a long block on the ground, obviously there for all the cowgirls who rode during their vacations.

Alex knew her limitations and her lack of height. Accepting the inevitable, she led Rusty over to the mounting block and climbed up on his back with more ease than she expected. From up on top of the big horse, she felt as if she were a giant, that she could conquer the world if only she could ride him forever.

It was a freeing, amazing sensation and it made a smile break out across her face. Julio smiled up at her as he adjusted the stirrups.

"Keep to the trails until you get to know the terrain again. A lot can happen in ten years to change things." He wasn't bossy, but rather doling out advice he'd give to any guest at the ranch. Alex didn't take offense and planned to take that advice to heart. She didn't fancy getting lost on her first week back.

"Will do. Thanks, Julio."

Alex used her knees to guide Rusty as she turned toward the signs for the trails, for the first time absurdly glad there were signs around. At first she thought they were tacky and a symptom of what was wrong on the dude ranch, but without them, she might not have even found the trail.

As much as she hated to admit it, Connor had done a good job of managing, running and laying out the ranch. She still didn't take to the fact that her childhood home was inhabited by strangers, though. Her mother would have hated it. In fact, if they closed the dude ranch the next day and everyone left, Alex would be pleased as punch.

Of course, that would mean all the people there, including Bernice, would be out of a job. Alex had no money to pay anyone to work at the ranch, and there was the small matter of her little brother.

The thought of having a brother made her break out in a cold sweat. She'd spent so long competing against someone that wasn't there—namely a brother—that to find out that person existed was devastating. He looked healthy, obviously hearty and, although he favored his mother, he had the Finley chin.

Alex wanted to hate him, so much that she could taste it. If she thought about it, though, it was more resentment than hate. She resented the fact he'd had her father, that Grant had been a father to him, acting with love and guidance, whereas she'd had nothing. As though Daniel had stolen him.

She sucked in a breath as the truth hit her square between the eyes. She was green-eyed jealous of the boy. He was a kid, for God's sake, and Alex wanted to keep him out of her sight because she was jealous of whatever relationship he'd had with their father.

It wasn't Daniel's fault that their father had been a selfish asshole. Yet it was the sins of the father being visited on the sons, or daughter and son in this case. Alex couldn't imagine seeing the kid every day, a constant reminder of what she wasn't, and could never be. It would be a year from hell.

She made it to the trailhead and examined the signs, selecting the easy trail for her first ride, per Julio's instructions. As much as she wanted to simply let the horse have its head and ride hell-bent for leather, she listened to her common sense this time.

The sun peeked its way through the trees as she picked her way along the trail. The burbling of a brook, the birds, a chattering squirrel and Rusty's hooves were the only sounds. It was almost as if she'd landed in another planet after living in L.A. for ten years. Life actually existed outside of fast food, movies and trendy nightclubs. The sky could be blue, the air clean and the world much simpler.

It was interesting that she'd blocked out a good deal of her memories of Wyoming. She'd let the bad stuff overwhelm the good in her head. This, however, was definitely the good stuff. A morning ride used to be her ritual, what she did no matter what the weather. Although there were times her mother forced her to stay indoors during a blizzard so as not to risk the horse's life along with her own.

Alex took a deep breath, pushing aside the bad stuff so she could focus on the good. For the most part, she succeeded. The land began to seep into her bones again, the love of the wide-open sky, the majestic mountains. She was born and bred in Wyoming; it was a part of her, a part she had denied for so long, too long.

After a glorious hour of riding, she returned to the barn refreshed and feeling much better than when she'd woken that morning. There were a lot more people around, many of the guests were milling around the barn at various stages of getting ready to ride.

She wasn't concerned with Rusty's next rider since Connor told her he was reserved for VIPs, and since she was the one staying in the VIP cabin, there wasn't anyone else. As she hopped off his back, her legs and behind groaned. She forgot just how many muscles she used when riding.

They, however, reminded her with a vengeance. She hobbled a bit as she led Rusty back into the barn to rub him down. It had been a leisurely ride so he didn't need too much attention, but she was responsible for it. One of the ranch hands unsaddled him and she managed a tight grin, although her ass felt like someone had punched her.

Alex realized she'd been dumb enough not to stretch before riding and now was paying the price. After she rubbed Rusty down and finished replacing the tack she'd used, Alex headed for the door, eager to return to the cabin and use the jet tub she'd spotted in the bathroom.

"No, Buttons, you can't have any more peppermint sticks. Mama says they're making you fat." A child's voice came from the second stall, where the pony was located, if she wasn't mistaken. "Ginger doesn't eat too many and she's not fat like you. The little kids can't ride you if your belly is too wide."

Alex wanted to leave, but curiosity compelled her and her steps slowed. She peeked over the stall door and saw the black-haired Daniel using a curry brush on the shaggy pony. He looked so serious with his brow furrowed and his tongue sticking out the corner of his mouth.

She was immediately awash in memories of her childhood, of her father teaching her how to take care of a horse. Alex wasn't ready for the wall of sadness and poignancy that hit her. She stepped away before the boy saw her and hightailed it out of the barn.

Alex didn't want to think about her father, or her brother, and particularly not in the same thought. She tried to remind herself the kid had no blame for her issues, that he was as innocent in the situation as she was, but regardless of logic, her heart controlled her actions. Ignoring the pain in her muscles, Alex ran to the cabin. Ran from her memories and the pain.

CHAPTER SIX

After hiding from everyone for the next two days, Alex ventured into the world of humans again Sunday morning. The sky was steel gray and she had a feeling there would be no riding, judging by the pregnant clouds that filled the sky.

It might be a good thing since her behind and legs were still on fire from her ride the other day. She'd taken a long bath, but she felt every second of the time she'd spent on Rusty. Her gait was slow as she walked gingerly toward the mess hall.

The last day had given her the opportunity to center herself and think about everything that had happened since she'd arrived in Wyoming. The heart of her issues related to her parents, and since they were both dead, she had to accept that there would be no catharsis, no way to resolve anything.

It sucked big-time, and left her completely frustrated. She realized she couldn't take it out on everyone around her, but that didn't mean she was about to lie down and let everything happen around her. She'd spent ten years burying her head in the sand and that time had passed.

Connor was about to have an accountant join the running of the ranch, like it or not. There was one skill she had, and that was her talent for numbers. David had paid to have her trained and she'd served as his personal accountant for nearly eight years.

She ate a quick breakfast, retrieved her laptop and went straight to the main building. It still felt odd to walk into her childhood home and realize it was a hotel. If asked, she didn't think she could explain how she felt about it—almost as if she'd stepped into another dimension.

Connor's office door was closed but that didn't mean he was busy or gone. Besides, she was half owner in the ranch, so a closed door meant nothing. But just in case, she knocked.

"What?" came a sharp word from within.

"It's Alex."

A few beats passed before the door opened. Connor stood in the doorway, his eyes bloodshot, his hair sticking every which way and his clothes looking as if he'd spent the last two days in them.

"You look like shit."

He grimaced. "Thanks. Did you come all the way down here to tell me that?"

Alex shook her head. She hadn't actually meant to blurt that out. "No, sorry. I came here to talk to you about the books and the accounting."

"I suppose they look like shit too." He appeared to be in a rotten mood. She bit her tongue at the impulse to ask why.

"No, actually, they don't." She gestured to the office behind him. "Can we sit and talk in there?"

She didn't want to call it his office—kind of peevish, she knew, but just the same that was how she felt.

"Fine, but I only have a few minutes. I've got things to do." He opened the door so she could walk in.

Alex felt the heat from his body, along with the odor of frustration and a day without a shower. It should have put her off, but for some reason it didn't. She'd already had sex with the man, after all, so his emanations shouldn't bother her.

His mood, however, did.

He flopped down in his chair and she noted the receipts scattered around the desktop. She vaguely remembered sitting on those during their episode a few days ago.

"So what about the books?" He picked up a pen and started tapping it, much to her annoyance.

Alex looked for the right way to tell him what she wanted. "The books are in good shape, nearly spotless, and that's saying something. However, the accounting entries are vague; there doesn't seem to be enough detail in them. If you want to make more money, you've got to keep a better eye on what you're spending."

One brown brow went up. "You have experience as an accountant?"

"As a matter of fact I do, for eight years now." She gestured to the desktop mess. "I'd say you have a need for one."

"I've been handling it just fine." He scowled. "I don't need help."

She gave him a dubious look. "Your accounting entries tell me differently. I think you're not being truthful with me, Connor."

"I expect you have a lot of experience with that."

Stung, Alex managed to keep her composure even if she wanted to smack him upside the head. "There's no need to be defensive.

I have every right to be a part of this ranch legally. No matter how obnoxious you want to be."

He ran his hands through his hair. "I don't have a lot of patience right now, especially for you."

"Especially for me? What does that mean?" Alex managed to keep her voice steady. The longer Connor talked, the more she grew annoyed with him. Again.

"You come in here and throw everything off center, including me. I can't balance these damn receipts and for some reason, I fucked you on this desk a few days ago." He looked as shocked as she felt. "I didn't mean to say that."

"Yes, you did." Alex knew the truth when she heard it even if it packed a punch. "I can balance the receipts and take over the books. I know some excellent accounting techniques and ways to cut costs."

"I don't want you to." He almost pooched out his lip, appearing suddenly like a little boy who didn't want to share his marbles.

"Too bad. I can take this to the legal dogs if you want. I don't think you do, and truthfully neither do I." She leaned forward and focused on the desk rather than on his green eyes. "I need to find my place here, Connor. It's important. I have to stay here an entire year or I lose my share of the ranch."

Alex wanted to tell him that she felt out of place, out of sorts and floundering like a fish. Numbers, accounting, balancing it all would be like a piece of normalcy in a storm rivaling a hurricane. She desperately needed to anchor herself, and accounting had been that anchor for eight years.

Aside from that, she was already falling in love with the land and the ranch again. Perhaps she could find her place if she used her skills as an accountant. It was so hard to be in limbo, without a real direction.

When she looked up, he was staring at her hard, his eyes bloodshot with dark circles beneath them. "I don't trust you."

She snorted. "That makes two of us."

"I would want to check everything you do until I feel otherwise."

Alex could hardly believe he'd given in to her request already. "I would expect no less. I've seen how tight you run this ship."

His brows went up. "Have you been checking up on me?"

"No, but I've got eyes." She recalled how cleanly, smoothly and exactly things were done at the ranch. Although she wouldn't admit it to him, it impressed her. All except his accounting techniques.

"I know. I heard you rode Rusty on Friday." He started putting the receipts into a neat stack. Her gaze went to his fingers and she couldn't help but remember just how skilled they were.

A blast of heat brushed through her, making the small hairs on her body stand up. He must've sensed it because his pupils dilated and his nostrils flared. It was like sensing when another animal was in heat.

Alex surely felt like an animal.

"He's still got a smooth gait." She noted a small tremor in her voice, reflected in the rest of her. "Are those all the receipts from this week?"

He handed her the stack. "Yep, and the entries are already in the system, but something's not right. I hope you can figure out what's wrong because I sure as hell can't."

She took the stack of papers from him; the feel of the weight in her hands was comfortable and comforting. "Thanks, I think."

He barked out a rusty chuckle. "You're welcome, I think." Connor pinched the bridge of his nose.

"I'd say you need to go to sleep." Oh, the images of his bed flew through her brain and made her nipples pop. Jesus, did she have no control when it came to this man?

"Can't. I'll knock off early but I need to check on things first." He let loose a jaw-cracking yawn.

"It's going to rain."

"No, it's not."

"Yeah, it is. If you'd actually left this building, you'd notice the sky is full of clouds and it even smells like rain." Alex rose with the laptop and the receipts in her arms, unwilling to allow herself to lose control over Connor again. At least not so soon.

"Really? It's going to rain? Damn, that's going to mess up the schedule." Connor rose, swaying a bit on his feet.

"Let someone else do it. Go to bed and get some rest." She backed toward the door. "I'll let you know what I find later."

Before he could protest again, she slipped out of the room and headed away from Connor, away from the distraction. The papers felt warm in her arms, real. She couldn't wait to balance them.

Connor sat at the desk, staring at the closed door for a few minutes. He resisted the urge to chase her down and snatch back the receipts. The very idea that he'd given away control of the ranch books to her made him itch all over.

He prided himself on the control he exerted over the running of the ranch and himself. Alex had made him lose that control within three days of being there.

He wanted to send her away.

He wanted to keep her in his bed.

With a growl, he rose from his chair and went in search of breakfast. As he passed the front desk, Jennifer straightened up from reading a magazine and smiled.

"I'm going to eat, then go to bed. Tell Jed to keep everything on schedule and to wake me if he needs me." The words felt like gravel in his mouth, uncomfortable and rough. Yet he got them out just the same.

Apparently he surprised the hell out of Jennifer, who gaped at him as he passed. Was Alex right? Did he never allow his people to relax and do their jobs without looking over their shoulder?

It was an uncomfortable realization. Grant had taken him in, a pain-in-the-ass twenty-year-old with a chip on his shoulder bigger than Alex's. He'd been inches away from being convicted of a felony and destroying the rest of his life. Grant Finley had offered him a chance to build a real life and a real job. Although Connor had wanted to say no, the judge urged him to accept the offer.

Connor had never been more grateful for someone else's intervention. It had been a hard eight years, working his ass off to build Finley's. His blood, sweat and tears littered the beautiful land under his feet. However hard it had been, he wouldn't change a thing.

An aimless kid with nothing but time and an inclination to do the wrong thing was trouble with a capital T. Connor wasn't about to make excuses for himself. Lots of kids came from abusive homes, from poor parents, from last-chance neighborhoods. Not all of them made choices like he'd done to get himself into a hole so deep he couldn't get himself out.

Of course, not all of them had a man like Grant Finley to reach down and yank them out by the hair. With a wry grin he remembered walking into the ranch house and thinking it looked like shit. Then, of course, he'd said that to Grant.

The older man had narrowed his gaze and snapped, "Good thing you're here, then, Matthews. Better get used to working your ass off."

Connor shook off the memories, and the melancholy they brought, and went toward the mess hall. He glanced up and realized Alex was right—it was going to rain and hard if he wasn't mistaken. That always put the guests in an antsy mood.

He started to turn around and head back to the main house to find Jed, his second-in-command. Then he stopped himself and remembered he trusted Jed implicitly. The man had a degree in hotel management and had been one of the first employees Grant hired. He was smart enough to recognize they needed to activate Plan B—the entertainment.

Connor's steps were slow but steady as he walked into the mess hall and headed straight for the eggs. His stomach yowled noisily as the delicious smells tickled his nose. Bernice stood behind the counter, her expression unreadable.

"You know, if you keep going without sleep, you're not doing yourself or this ranch any favors."

"How do you know I haven't slept?" He reached for a plate and started heaping eggs onto it.

"If I hadn't been able to smell you, which I can by the way, I can tell by the state of your clothes, which I saw you wearing yesterday." She folded her arms across her more-than-ample bosom. "What kept you up this time?"

Connor always felt like a little kid being chastised by his teacher around Bernice. She was tough and no-nonsense, didn't take shit from anyone, but that didn't mean she didn't reduce him to two feet tall.

"Receipts," he blurted as he put half a dozen pieces of bacon on top of the eggs.

She handed him two biscuits. "You should ask Alex to do the books. She's an accountant, you know."

Connor didn't want to admit he hadn't known that fact until she'd told him that very morning. "As of twenty minutes ago, she's got the receipts and the books."

Bernice's brows went up. "Well, I'll be damned."

He didn't want to look at whatever expression she wore, so he took the biscuits and walked away. Quickly. He found an empty table and sat, then dug into the hot breakfast. It was as heavenly as it smelled and he ate like a madman.

A steaming mug of coffee appeared in front of him and he took a grateful gulp. He glanced up at Bernice with a mouthful of eggs, ensuring she wouldn't expect him to speak.

"I'm proud of you, Connor," was all she said before she walked away.

He swallowed the eggs and the lump that had formed in his throat. It had been more than two years since anyone had told him that. Bernice reminded him of how much he'd lost and how stupid he'd been since then.

It was time to attempt to get a life.

Monday morning came, and with it the sun, thank God. Connor balanced the muffin on top of the to-go cup and opened his office door. At first he could hardly believe what he was seeing; then he realized that Miss Alex Finley had set up her own workspace on his desk.

"What the hell are you doing?"

She glanced up from her laptop. "Working on the books. Just in case you forgot about giving me the job yesterday."

He gritted his teeth at her sarcasm. "It may come as a surprise to you, but this is my office. I work here, not you."

As he set the coffee and muffin down, she made a grab for it. Connor held firm to the cup, but she managed to snatch the muffin.

"Is this cinnamon chip? Oh, these were my favorites growing up. Bernice bakes the best muffins, doesn't she?"

As he watched her take a big bite of his breakfast, Connor had to hang on tight to his temper with both hands. It was like trying to control a team of eight with dental floss, but he managed.

"I let you do the accounting work, but I never intended for you to do it here. There isn't enough room." He sat down and booted up his own laptop.

She shrugged. "There's no other office free, so unless you want me working on the books in a public area where everyone can see exactly what I'm doing, then it's going to be here."

"What about your cabin?"

She picked up the next invoice and read it with her brow furrowed, concentrating on the trash collection fees. "The WiFi sucks that far away, so here I am. You'll just have to deal with it."

Connor gritted his teeth and counted to ten. The fact that she was right rankled him more than the fact that she stole his muffin. He should have made arrangements for her to have a private office, at least temporarily, until she decided Finley's wasn't the place for her.

"Couldn't you have asked me?"

One slender brow rose. "Ask permission to work in this office? I am half owner in this ranch, am I not? I don't think I need permission to contribute to the financial well-being of Finley's."

"I don't like sharing my office." Connor punched in his password with enough fervor to hurt his fingertips, which was saying a lot.

"I could tell." She smiled sweetly. "Is there a way to order more muffins and coffee? I'm starving."

Connor gestured to the door. "The mess hall is down on the south side of the ranch. You can't miss it. It's a big building with tables and chairs for people to eat."

Alex surprised him by laughing. "You make it hard to be a bitch sometimes, Matthews."

"Then don't be one."

"Ha, as if that's going to happen." She shook her head. "You're not getting off that easy. You will just have to deal with me playing in your sandbox." She popped a piece of muffin in her mouth.

"Then stop throwing sand in my face."

Alex smiled at him and went back to the invoices. At least it appeared she really was working, and he didn't know whether or not to be surprised. He tried to focus on the schedules but he kept glancing back at her while she worked.

She entered each invoice in the stack individually, then picked them up and reviewed them against what she entered. On the third pass, he had forgotten what he was doing and watched her reaction instead.

"What is it you're doing?"

"I'm categorizing the expenses properly. You put all the barn supplies into one lump instead of separating them by type. They should be split out that way to better track what you're spending."

She glanced over at him. "Did you know you've been paying about thirty percent more for feed than you did last year?"

He was startled by the figure. "What are you talking about? We haven't changed feed supplier or type of feed. I find it hard to believe—"

"Whether or not you believe me is irrelevant. I went back over these invoices for the last year and discovered what was happening." She gestured to the stack, which was when he realized they were all from Hanson's, the feed supply house.

What threw him off was that some were on blue paper, others on pink, and the top few were white. He didn't remember them changing the color of the invoice, but they obviously had. What else had he missed?

Connor realized she was waiting for him to ask the obvious question. "What was happening?"

Her face lit up as if she'd just discovered how to turn lead into gold. Alex obviously did enjoy accounting and all it entailed. "Hanson's supplies more than feed to the ranch. They also sell us saddle soap, some other leather conditioners and applicators, some stall cleaner, hay bags and winter stuff like bucket deicers. Each kind of supply was on a different invoice until about six months ago."

Despite his annoyance with Alex, he was interested in what she'd found. Hanson's did supply various types of supplies to them. They were reliable and their feed was good quality.

"Since you are being a stubborn ass, I'll tell you what I found. When they started billing everything together on the white invoices, someone got greedy and started charging more for the same amount of feed." She looked at him triumphantly.

Connor was impressed but skeptical. "What if the price of feed went up?"

"I checked with other suppliers online. Hanson's is by far the highest priced, well above what they should be charging. You're getting taken by a clever billing person at this place. I'll have a report ready in half an hour that details the discrepancies." She smiled and he saw just how attractive Alex was. He knew she was pretty but obviously when she was passionate about something, even accounting, her appeal went through the roof.

As long as it didn't go through his pants again. Jesus, this was the desk they'd had their afternoon quickie on. Now they were talking about feed invoices and pretending nothing happened.

"So, Sherlock, I suppose you want to confront them about this?"

"Hell yes! Let me get everything together and we can drive there and show them we know what they're up to. We can show them not to mess with Finley's." She ate the last of the muffin; then before he could stop her, she took his coffee and helped herself.

Alex made a face and handed the cup back to him. "Ugh, sugar in your coffee? What kind of cowboy are you?"

"The kind who can't jump in the car and shake some papers at our feed supplier." He threw the cup in the trash, unwilling to put his mouth where hers had been. It had a sexual overtone to it and he needed to keep thinking with his big head.

"Why not? Don't you do anything fun around here?" She sat back and stretched, pushing her breasts out like she was intentionally taunting him.

Perhaps she was and, damn it to hell, it was working. His dick stirred at the sight of her pillowy tits, at the nipples he could see just slightly hard beneath the T-shirt.

"See something you like, cowboy?" She'd caught him staring, of course.

Connor decided to play it cool, just as she'd been. "Yup, sure did. That's a mighty fine rack you got there, Alex. You must be proud."

Shock rippled across her face, but she quickly tucked it safely away. "Why, thank you, Connor. I am proud. My tits are my best feature, don't you think?" She leaned over the desk, affording him a view of the cleavage peeping up through the V-neck of the shirt.

His dick slapped against his zipper.

"Oh yeah, definitely." His voice cracked so he sounded like a little kid finding a dirty magazine for the first time.

She sat back down, bouncing on the seat as she did. No doubt designed to keep his attention on those incredible breasts of hers. The woman was evil incarnate.

"So are you coming with me to Hanson's or not?" Alex threw it out as a challenge. "According to the map website, it's only about twenty minutes from here."

Connor didn't want to go, to admit he'd been taken by a feed supplier simply because he had been a piss-poor accountant. He was supposed to manage every aspect of the ranch. "You're not going to let it go, are you?"

"Absolutely not. You want me to prove my salt as an accountant, and this is a perfect example of how I will do just that." She raised both brows and waited.

He felt his conviction to resist slipping away with every second she stared at him. "If we don't go, you're going to nag me, aren't you?"

"Oh, most assuredly." She rose with the invoices in hand. "Coming with?"

"Fine, but don't think this means I will do what you want me to do every day."

"Wouldn't dream of it."

They walked out of the office in single file, and he could almost feel her grinning behind him. Connor was annoyed, and yet also strangely aroused by their banter. She was smart, sassy and didn't give an inch.

He didn't know whether to kiss her or kick her out.

Connor drove to Hanson's in his pickup truck, saying he would run some errands while they were out. He wanted to make the trip "worthwhile," although Alex thought saving a great deal of money on feed was worth the trip alone.

She'd felt triumphant when he accepted her evaluation of the invoices and what had happened with the price of feed. It was something any accountant would have caught and she wondered how many other invoices she'd find with price discrepancies. It gave her a sense of purpose, like she was contributing something to the ranch besides her unwanted presence.

The scenery flew by as Alex stared out the window of the truck, country music playing softly on the radio. It was almost a comfortable silence, but she was well aware of the man in the cab with her.

Connor's scent, a combination of whatever soap he used and his own unique self, filled her nose. He was the first man to capture her attention simply by smelling good. Even if she fought with him every moment they were together, Connor had a scent she recognized at a base level; her body knew him, accepted him, even though she'd known him only a short time.

Alex knew she was in unknown territory with Connor. She had no idea where their relationship was heading, if anywhere. Of course, the fact that she actually enjoyed riding in the truck with him was an indication it was definitely going somewhere.

She pushed aside her inner wrangling and realized they had arrived at their destination.

Hanson's was in the next town over in a huge warehouse made up to look like a barn. The chipper sign announced there was a special on feed. Alex snorted. She would just bet they had a special.

When they pulled into a parking space, he turned to her. "Now, let me do the talking, please. Don't antagonize Martin."

"I don't plan on antagonizing anyone."

"What you plan on and what happens are not the same thing." He hopped out of the truck before she could respond.

Alex reached for the handle when it was snatched from her hands and the door opened. To her surprise, Connor stood there, holding it open for her. It had been a very long time since a gentleman held the car door for her, and now it appeared that in the cowboy country she returned to, it was status quo.

"Thank you," she murmured as she accepted his hand in getting down from the ridiculously high pickup.

They walked together into the feed store and Alex had a niggling memory of doing it with her father. It had been a monthly routine for them, something she'd either deliberately or accidentally forgotten. She didn't feel like dealing with that particular memory at the moment, so she pushed it aside before it could take over.

Connor walked over to the counter to a young man with carrot red hair and freckles. "Hey, Angus."

"Connor, didn't expect to see you today." The kid slid a glance at Alex. "And you brought a friend."

"This is Alex Finley. Alex, this is Angus Macgregor."

The redhead's brows shot up toward his hairline. "Finley?"

Connor cut off any questions before the other man could ask them. "Is Martin here? I need to talk to him."

"Oh, yeah, he's in the back. In his office." Angus stared at Alex.

She, on the other hand, decided to ignore Connor's order. Alex winked at the young man. His freckles almost exploded off his face.

Connor headed for a door behind the counter, with Alex following closely behind. Unfortunately or not, Angus was on her heels. Perhaps she shouldn't have flirted with him.

An older blond man was on the other side of the door. He wore a pair of half-glasses and was seated at a high workbench, seemingly at work fixing a bridle. He glanced up as they entered.

Before anyone else could speak, Angus launched into an excited stream of words. "It's Alex Finley. Can you believe it? We didn't think—"

"Angus, shut your yap." The man called Martin cut off the young man before he could finish. "Get your ass back out there and take care of customers." He turned back to them after Angus scuttled back through the door. "Connor, what brings you by?"

"We were in town running errands and wanted to stop by," Connor began.

Liar.

Alex stepped forward with the invoices tucked into a manila folder. "Hi, Martin, I'm Alex Finley, the prodigal daughter returned." She held up the folder. "I'm also an accountant and I need to talk to you about the last year's invoices."

Connor growled under his breath, but she ignored him.

"Ah, invoices?" Martin looked at her blankly over the top of the glasses. "I don't do those myself, of course. My nephew, Brian, started doing the books for me oh, about two years ago."

"Brian does the invoicing? Well, that's great news. Where can we find him?" Alex smiled at the older man and leaned forward to give him a good view. On cue, his gaze dropped to her breasts. Men were so predictable.

"Oh, ah, his desk is over yonder." Martin gestured to the corner of the room, behind a half wall.

"I'll just go pay him a visit while you two have a good talk." Alex left Connor sputtering while she went in search of Brian.

As she looked around the corner, she found a young man in his midtwenties wearing a pair of headphones and playing an online war game. She didn't know whether Martin knew it or not, but her gut told her his nephew was dirty. Alex would bet everything she owned on it, which was all of seven hundred dollars plus change.

"What are you doing?" Connor's hiss in her ear made her jump a foot in the air.

"Finding out who's stealing from you." She pushed against his bulk. "Now, let me do what you're paying me for. Or rather what you will be paying me for."

"I didn't say I'd pay you."

"Shut up, Connor." She made her way to the desk and plucked at the headphones tucked into a pair of somewhat dirty ears.

Brian glanced up at her and his eyes widened; then a grin spread across his broad face. "Hey, there, beautiful." Right on cue, his gaze dropped to her boobs.

"Hi, Brian. My name is Alex."

He glanced behind her. "You here with Connor?"

"Yes, sort of. You see, I am the new accountant at Finley's." She smiled and held up the folder. "I have been putting all the books in order and have a few questions for you."

Brian's playful flirting stopped and he wouldn't even look at the folder. "What are you talking about?"

"Brian, Brian, Brian. I'm from L.A., so don't try any bullshit with me. My guess is you decided to save money on the paper used for the colored invoices. Then you realized you could mix supplies on the white invoices and make a dirty set of books, tacking on thirty percent, which I can say for certain went directly into your pocket." She paused and cocked her head. "How am I doing so far?"

His face had turned a nice shade of white. Oh, she had the right guy, all right. "I—I don't know what you're—"

"Save it, Brian. With this paperwork in my hand, and likely a visit to another half dozen ranches, I can have you arrested and thrown in jail for embezzlement." She glanced at the computer screen. "And they don't have online gaming in prison."

Brian's face now flushed at the threat. "Wh-what do you want?"

"I want you to stop stealing from your uncle's clients, and refund every bit of that money. If you want to continue sending one invoice, then it had better be accurate. I'll be watching every line item on every one." She smiled and leaned forward until she was inches away from his frightened mud brown eyes. "I'll be watching," she repeated.

Brian swallowed and nodded.

"Thanks, Brian."

She stood up and faced Connor, who looked like he was ready to throttle her. "Ready to go?" Alex brushed past him, waiting for him to grab her.

He didn't. She didn't know whether to be disappointed or pleased.

They walked past Martin and said a polite good-bye to the confused older man. By the time they made it out to the truck, she could literally feel his annoyance. It was like an electric charge between them, a living, pulsing creature.

Connor yanked open the door and helped her in. His hand was like a block of wood, it was so tense beneath her fingers. Alex didn't care if he was angry or not. Finley's was being robbed and she'd just saved them quite a bit of money.

He slammed into the truck and let out a long breath. When he turned to her, she expected him to start yelling, but instead she literally saw him swallow down the anger. Connor obviously kept all his fury inside, which wasn't good for him, but in this case, it was good for her.

"Next time, listen to me and let me do the talking. That was embarrassing, to say the least." His gaze stayed on the windshield, never once looking at her. "I don't like your tactics."

"Tough shit. I got the job done and stopped a thief from skimming from his uncle and robbing you blind." She wanted to fight with him, but he wasn't living up to his end of the argument. It pissed her off.

Connor didn't remember the last time he'd been so angry. It wasn't all directed at Alex, but she was a big damn part of it. She'd sashayed into Hanson's as if she owned the place, confused Martin, then blackmailed his scumbag nephew into refunding Finley's money.

Therein lay the reason Connor was seething. He'd missed the fact that he had been ripped off for at least six months by a weasel like Brian.

He drove back to the ranch with a silent Alex in the cab, grateful at least for a short reprieve in the arguing. She'd been right about the invoices, but her methods were enough to make him see red.

Connor had spent too long in the bog of emotion and destructive behavior. He wouldn't let his hard-won self-control be tested by another wild child like Alex. No matter that he'd already lost control, more than once if he was honest with himself. He had to keep the reins tight in his hands from now on, no matter what shit she tried.

When they got back to the ranch, she hopped out of the truck without waiting for help. He heard her curse as she hit the pavement and stomped into the main building. No doubt she was going back to her perch in his office.

Connor took his time getting out of the pickup and went in search of a solution to his problem. He found it fifteen minutes later in a small storage closet in the back corner of the building. No doubt it had likely been a linen closet or something similar when the family lived there.

It was about to become Alex's new office.

He had to get her out of his space, to find some peace in the one place he used to feel safe. She'd infiltrated every nook and cranny on the ranch—he refused to let her stay in his office any longer. He'd never get anything done if she was there.

It didn't matter if he was putting her in a six-by-eight room with no windows. Connor refused to feel guilty about relocating her. She'd brought nothing but chaos and he couldn't handle that much more of it. He'd get a line run so she could have a phone in there. Other than office supplies, which they had plenty of in the étagère in his office, she would want for nothing.

With a grin worthy of any cartoon villain, Connor enlisted a few people to help him empty the storage unit of the various boxes of records. They carried them up to the attic where he found an antique desk gathering dust in the corner. It was perfect for what she needed so they cleaned it up and brought it back to the closet—or rather, Alex's office.

There was one electrical outlet, fortunately, so he swiped a corner table lamp from the lobby and stuck it on the desk. Cozy as a bug in a rug, even if it did look like a solitary confinement cell.

He asked one of the housekeeping staff to wipe everything down so it smelled piney fresh. Then, filled with something like glee, he went in search of Finley's newest accountant.

Alex couldn't make sense of Connor's filing system. The man had the folders labeled with vague titles such as "Supplies" or "Food." A man like him, with his perfectionist tendencies, should be better at the details. It surprised her as well as annoyed her. He was infuriating even when he wasn't in the room. She gave up trying to figure out what he'd been attempting to do with the files and yanked them all out of the drawer.

As she spread the files on the desk and started looking through them, she knew he'd be pissed. Alex, however, didn't care a whit. Perhaps it gave her a mild satisfaction to tweak his nose, but she wasn't doing this to annoy him. She was doing it to be a part of something larger, to make a difference in the world even if it involved a shady feed salesman.

She set to work looking through the files, labeling them more accurately, adding additional folders and placing them all in the filing cabinet in a logical order. It was a tedious task, but one she didn't mind in the least. Alex was so focused on what she was doing, she didn't realize so much time had passed until her stomach rumbled, reminding her it was lunchtime.

There were still at least three dozen folders to be reviewed and they were stacked on Connor's desk. She really shouldn't leave them there, but there was nowhere else to put them. Besides, it would annoy him, and she didn't mind that at all.

She stood up and stretched, then turned to leave the office. Claire stood in the doorway. Alex's heart did a flip-flop as she remembered their last conversation. Her emotions were still running high when it came to the woman who'd married her father.

"Connor's not here." Alex kept her gaze on the folders.

"I wasn't looking for him."

Alex's gaze snapped to hers. She tried to figure out what Claire was thinking but it was no use. She didn't know her well enough to read her face. "I was just going for lunch."

"May I join you?"

"Um . . ." Alex wasn't sure she was ready to face Claire across a table yet. She had to understand she represented everything wrong with Alex's past.

"I just wanted to talk to you about Daniel again." Claire's dark eyes pleaded with her to listen.

Alex sighed and leaned against the desk. He seemed like a good kid from what she'd seen of him, but that didn't necessarily mean she wanted to hang out with the kid. "I'm listening."

Claire stepped into the office. "It's been over a week since you got here. He's so excited to have a sister, someone he can look up to and emulate. Unfortunately you haven't been—or rather, you've been busy since you arrived, and he hasn't had a chance to get to know you."

Alex knew what was coming and dreaded it. She didn't want to be around kids, least of all the one who reminded her of her own failings as a child and as a woman.

"I'm working on the accounts now, so I don't have a lot of spare time."

"Just a ride or two a week is all I'm asking for. He's a really wonderful boy. Please." Claire obviously loved her son very much. Alex could hear it in her voice and it resonated within her. She remembered hearing the same tone in her own mother's voice.

Alex wasn't a cruel person, or one who enjoyed making others feel bad. She had no experience with children and didn't know whether Daniel would even like her when he got to know her. But the crux of the problem was that Alex had never been the boy Daniel now was and she damn well knew it. He reminded her of all she wasn't.

She knew it wasn't his fault, but it was so hard to simply dismiss those deep feelings.

"I'm not trying to aggravate you, Alex." Claire looked down at her shoes. "I know Grant left a mess behind and I just want you to understand that my son and I are not the enemy. He left us behind in that mess too."

With that, Claire left Alex alone in the office with a churning gut instead of a rumbling stomach. She sat back down, her appetite gone. The conversation with Claire hit Alex in an elemental way.

She wanted to continue thinking about how much she'd been hurt and how she was suffering. It was a bitter pill to swallow to think of someone else in the same boat she was—especially if that someone else was on the "to blame" list.

Alex wasn't a kid; she was a grown woman who could see right from wrong, yet she hugged her wounds to her. They were hers to wear, and the scars would last a lifetime. It didn't seem quite fair to allow anyone else to have the same privilege. It would likely sound petty to someone like the perfect Connor Matthews, but it was reality to Alex Finley.

"You're still here, I see." Thinking of the devil, Connor stood in the doorway, a smug expression on his handsome face.

"Where else would I be? The guy who runs this place is a disorganized slave driver."

That wiped the smugness off his face. "I'm not disorganized."

"Okay, then, an amateur accountant with haphazard tendencies and nearly nonexistent auditing abilities." She folded her arms and sighed. "What do you want anyway?"

"Way harsh there on my accounting. I did the best I could. It wasn't like I went to college or anything."

Now, that was extremely interesting. He didn't go to college, yet he ran this entire operation? What or who gave him the power to do that? Well, she knew who it was, but wondered what set Connor apart that he would be left in charge.

"That's what I'm here for. It'll take time to untangle the last two years, but as you can see I'm working on it." She gestured to the pile of files on the desk.

"What are you doing?"

"Organizing your receipts, invoices and tax records so you actually have your paperwork in order."

"Oh. I guess you'll need a filing cabinet in your office, then." He peered at the only one in his office, a four-drawer putty-colored behemoth. "That won't fit. I'll have to see if we can get one of those smaller two-drawer ones."

Alex stared at him. "Connor, have you been drinking?"

"What? No, of course not. I've been finding a place for you to work." The smugness crept back on his face.

That did not bode well for Alex.

"Where, pray tell, is this place?"

"Down the hall past the sitting room. It's been cleaned up and furnished already. But I forgot about the filing cabinet. I'll need to see if I can find one of those." He frowned at the folders as if they were to blame for him losing his mind.

"Why don't you show me this new office, then?" She rose and forced a smile to her face. "My day can't possibly get any worse."

Only minutes later, Alex chewed on those words and they tasted like old socks.

The "office" had been a linen closet when she lived there. Somehow Connor had decided the closet would be a great place for her to work. It was gloomy enough in there that she could hardly see.

"Is there a light or am I to work in the shadows like a scribe of old?" She peered in, unable to see clearly.

"There's a lamp. Wait; I'll turn it on." Connor stepped in and a snick sounded, the soft glow bathing the closet, or rather her office, in a warm glow.

He moved out of the way and Alex's breath caught in her throat when she saw the furniture. It was her mother's writing desk, a treasured antique that had belonged to her great-grandmother. As the story went, the desk had been a wedding gift from her husband, a carpenter and craftsman who had made it with his own hands.

Tears sprang to her eyes as she touched the newly polished top. The inlaid roses were in perfect condition, the quality of the furniture still evident even after a hundred years. Her fingers trembled as she traced the wooden flowers.

"Alex?"

She shook her head. "Where did you find this?"

"Um, up in the attic. It was covered in dust but in great shape. I thought it looked sorta feminine, and it was free." Connor sounded guilty, damn him. If only he was a complete ass and treated her like shit, she could ignore him. He had to go and be a gentleman again.

"It was my mother's." Her voice was very soft.

There were a few moments of silence and then a breath gushed out behind her. "Shit, I'm sorry. I had no idea. I really was trying to, um, find you a place to work."

"I know you were. You don't want me camped out in your office and you saw a way to solve the problem. It's kind of small." She managed a strangled chuckle. "I might have to step outside the room just to change my mind."

"So will you use it?"

He sounded hopeful, annoyingly so. She should refuse it, considering he was putting her in a closet. Yet the desk, well, that was a lovely surprise. It was a piece of her mother she could use every day. Of course, she could still annoy him as needed by simply walking down the hallway to his office.

"Yes, I'll use it, provided I can still come to you when I need to ask a question." She hoped she sounded innocent enough.

"Fine, and I'll see to putting a phone and a filing cabinet in there."

Alex turned to him and smiled. "I guess this is our first official agreement, then."

He looked startled. "I guess it is."

Her stomach picked that moment to yowl again. Connor didn't laugh but he did raise his brows. "Lunchtime?"

"Yeah, since I can't squeeze in a soda *and* a sandwich in my new closet, er, office, I'm going to the mess hall." She stepped out into the hallway where Connor stood. Alex didn't know whether or not to invite him to go, but he took the decision out of her hands.

"Me too. All that cleaning made me hungry."

Alex stifled the chuckle that threatened. No need to let Connor know she actually thought he was amusing. That was dangerous territory.

CHAPTER SEVEN

After two weeks at the ranch, Alex developed a routine that included rising early and going for a ride. She felt confident enough to take harder trails with each passing day and always returned with a grin on her face and a bit less pain in her behind.

Alex was now comfortable with taking care of the saddle and tack herself. The staff knew her on sight and she got to know everyone's names. Although she didn't want to like anyone, they made it hard not to. The one person she was still off center about was Connor. Until she was ready to deal with her feelings about the dude ranch and her father, she couldn't seem to pinpoint why the man occupied her thoughts so much.

And her dreams.

She'd had nothing but erotic, heart-pounding dreams that made her wake up with a wet pussy and aching nipples. Each morning she'd pushed aside the thoughts and gone riding instead. However, she knew it was a temporary solution, and the fact she'd already had sex with Connor made her a coward.

After she took a shower to clean up, Alex went for breakfast, determined to find Connor and talk about her future at the ranch. She had fit in comfortably doing the books, yet she needed to have an official title, rather than just the prodigal daughter. Her relationship with Connor, or whatever it was, complicated things a bit. Yet she still needed to talk to him as the guy who ran the ranch, oddly enough, about her "job" there. Eventually she would need a salary or stipend or whatever it was called.

Her other option was to sell her half of the ranch and move on. Of course, the will forced her to stay for a year, but she could simply do her time, then take off.

The one thing preventing her from Plan B was the fact that she was happy for the first time in a long time and it was because of being home again. After spending time at the ranch, riding the trails, feeling the power of the land around her, she felt the tug of staying there and making it her home again.

Alex walked into the mess hall to find it full of guests. It was only eight thirty, which meant they were all there stuffing themselves before heading out to play cowboy. She got herself a cup of delicious-smelling coffee and a bagel and found a spot at the end of one of the long tables far enough away so she wouldn't have to chat while she ate.

"Good morning."

She wanted to sigh in frustration, but instead she just gritted her teeth and looked up at the man who'd interrupted her solitary confinement.

He was simply gorgeous with salt-and-pepper hair, a hard, lean body in a light green button-down shirt and a pair of jeans that seemed to have been made for him. His cowboy hat was an expensive-looking chocolate brown color with a snakeskin band. His smile was bright and sexy as hell. He reminded her of David, only heterosexual.

Alex swallowed the bite of bagel she'd forgotten was in her mouth. "Good morning."

He pointed to the chair across from her. "Do you mind if I join you?"

"Please do." She smiled, enjoying the rush of a light arousal as his scent washed over her.

"You're Alex Finley?"

She nodded, disappointed he was only sitting there because he knew who she was. Perhaps she hoped he'd been hitting on her.

"James Howard, your neighbor." He held out his hand and shook hers with a squeeze.

"Nice to meet you." She didn't know what he was doing there and hoped like hell it wasn't to welcome her to the neighborhood. "Which ranch is yours?"

"Just west of here, on the other side of the creek." He sipped at the mug of coffee he'd brought to the table.

"Ah, the Latimers owned that when I was growing up." They had been grumpy but good folks. On more than one occasion they'd called Alex's parents and tattled on her for one transgression or another.

"Mr. Latimer passed on about eight years ago and his wife sold it to me, then moved to Colorado to be near her daughter." He smiled, a sexy, disarming grin. "I wondered if you would appear one day, give Connor a tweak in his, ah, business."

Alex's brows went up. So there was a rivalry, friendly or not, between Connor and their neighbor. How interesting.

"What brings you here today, Mr. Howard?" She ate her bagel, not caring what he thought of her cream-cheese laden breakfast. After all, she wasn't on a date or anything.

"I heard you were here."

She let that sit in the air for a minute while she chewed, then took a sip of coffee. "And I'm interesting to you?"

"Oh yes, definitely. Grant never spoke of you, so imagine our surprise when half the ranch went to you." James ran his finger along the rim of the mug and she noted he had beautifully manicured hands for a rancher. Obviously he didn't work his own property.

"If you don't mind me asking, what was your interest in me inheriting half of Finley's?" She already knew not to trust the man, and her instincts never let her down. Aside from that fact, she didn't trust anyone until they earned it.

"I've wanted to buy it for years, to expand my property out past the river and double my herd. Finley's is prime real estate, Ms. Finley." He smiled again. "You understand that I had to meet the woman I need to convince to sell to me."

"I only own half, Mr. Howard. It won't do you any good to convince me to sell if my step . . . Claire won't sell her son's portion." She felt uncomfortable discussing it even if her common sense told her to do all she could to sell the ranch, and obviously this man was interested. More than likely he'd pay her more than market share if he'd been trying to buy it for years.

"One step at a time, right?" He glanced at his watch, a nice Cartier with real diamonds, no doubt. "I wanted to invite you to dinner tonight. There's a lovely Italian restaurant in town and the food is actually quite good."

Alex still didn't quite trust the man, but he obviously had

money, and going out for food rather than eating in the mess hall had some appeal. Besides, she wanted to hear just how much he would offer for the ranch. If it was enough, she might be willing to do what she could to convince Claire to sell along with her. It was an easy solution to the emotional decision of whether to stay or not.

"Sure. Sounds nice." Very noncommittal but enough to make him look as if she'd said she would sell the ranch to him.

"Wonderful! I'll come by and pick you up around seven at the main building." He stood and took her hand, depositing a dry kiss on her knuckles.

She wanted to yank her hand away but figured it would be a bad start to a potential business relationship. Something about the man bugged her, but she couldn't say exactly what. "See you then."

James tipped his hat and headed for the door. Alex saw a man standing there blocking the exit and realized it was Connor. His hands were fisted at his sides and he looked at James as if he wanted to have a smackdown. When Connor's gaze met Alex's, she felt the power of it, and her entire body raced with goose bumps. She fought the urge to run.

Connor managed to keep his temper in check when he faced James, although he wanted to punch the smug son of a bitch in his perfect teeth. The man was a snake with legs whose only thought was how much could he get in his wallet and how fast could he get it.

James had done all he could to try to buy Finley's out from under Grant more than once. He had even tried to annex a full hundred acres of Finley property, and it happened to be the property with the river that fed the entire water system. The bastard had filed multiple lawsuits, complaints with the health department, agriculture department, even the revenue department. After unsuccessfully trying every legal angle imaginable, accidents around the ranch began to happen. Connor knew in his bones James was to blame for them.

He was a bastard who smiled as he stole the land out from under you.

And Alex had been eating breakfast with him. A surge of pure jealousy and something else surged through him, making him see red. It was unexpected and completely unwelcome.

"What are you doing here?" Connor gritted his teeth to keep the growl from escaping.

James's grin was almost feral. "Meeting the heiress, of course. Word has it she's not happy about the guest ranch business and wants out."

"Bullshit. I don't know where you're getting your information from but Alex isn't selling." He would make damn certain of that. "If I catch you on Finley property again, I'll have your ass hauled off to jail."

"Feeling threatened, Matthews? Tsk, tsk. I thought you were the tough, unmovable one." James's smile widened. "I'm glad to see I can shake your tree a bit."

Connor's nails dug into his palms as he resisted the urge to punch the asshole. "Get the fuck out of here, now." There was just so far he would control himself before he opened up that particular can of whoop-ass on the man.

James held up his hands. "I'm leaving, but just be aware I'm picking up Ms. Finley at seven tonight for dinner. Try not to have me arrested for trespassing on our first date."

With that, the man who'd spent too many years trying to steal Finley's property walked out of the mess hall, leaving Connor with unfulfilled rage coursing through him.

He walked toward Alex and reminded himself she had no idea what a dick James Howard truly was. She was, however, about to find out.

"What were you doing talking to James Howard?" It wasn't what he meant to say but that was what popped out when he opened his mouth.

"Excuse me?" Her brows went up and her lips tightened.

"You heard me. Having breakfast with a son of a bitch like that? What the hell were you thinking?" Connor couldn't seem to stop the flow of stupid from coming out of him.

"I was thinking I was hungry." She gestured to the half-eaten bagel.

He didn't give a shit about that. "You will not go out on a date with him tonight—is that clear? You're working for Finley's now, not to mention the fact that you own half. That man is not to be trusted."

Alex rose, her cheeks flushed and her eyes glittering. "Mr. Matthews, I believe this is a discussion to be had in private."

He glanced around, realizing that everyone in the mess hall had stopped what they were doing to watch his tirade. Shame crept through him, temporarily displacing the anger. "You're right. Let's go." Connor took her arm, but she shook it off.

"I will finish my breakfast, whether or not you approve. You can either sit down and behave like a civilized human being or leave until I'm done."

She sat back down and picked up the bagel. Connor wanted to

strangle her. The woman was pure cussed stubborn through and through. He sat down heavily across from her, not missing the fact that he was sitting in the same seat James Howard had just vacated.

She sipped her coffee, which he watched with avid interest since she pursed her lips each time she blew on it. It seemed that passion and anger were strange bedfellows, but they were there together wrestling inside him.

Connor wanted to sit there and wait for her to finish, but he couldn't. He rose abruptly, startling her in midbite.

"We'll talk later. I've got work to do."

She held up her finger and pointed to her mouth but he left before she finished chewing. Connor could not allow himself to lose control again and that meant keeping away from Alex for a while. He slammed out of the mess hall and headed for his office, aware her gaze followed him.

Alex stared at her meager collection of dresses and tried to find one that didn't look five years old. In truth she hadn't done much dating in the last ten years; it had been more of a casual relationship phase for her. As such, she'd gone to baseball games, parks, to the beach and to private homes.

It had been a dog's age since she'd actually gone on a date to a restaurant with a man. She and David would eat out weekly, but those weren't dates and the restaurants were never the kind she'd dress nicely for.

As a consequence, her wardrobe was woefully inadequate for the evening's event. Part of her wanted to find James's number and tell him she couldn't go. The other part wanted to thumb her nose at Connor's high-handedness and make as big a production out of the dinner as possible.

She chose to thumb her nose at him.

The standard black slacks and a royal blue blouse were presentable, along with a pair of black strappy heels. She put on makeup, a first since the funeral, and brushed her hair. Ready as she would ever be, Alex left the cabin and headed for the main building at ten minutes to seven.

She fully expected Connor to be waiting there like a guard dog, ready to light into her for consorting with the enemy. It was obvious there was bad blood between the men, but she simply refused to be the rope they played tug-of-war with. Alex fully intended on telling both of them that as soon as she had a chance.

She'd avoided Connor during the day and had a feeling he did the same. After the scene in the mess hall, he was likely embarrassed by the whole thing. She definitely was, considering he shook her like a recalcitrant puppy and tried to order her to stay home. Alex would not stand for it.

By the time she had made it to the main building, she'd built up a head of steam, ready to do battle with Connor, but he wasn't there. He also wasn't in his office; it was dark and empty. That left Alex vaguely disappointed; plus she hadn't been able to nail down her job with him either. Truthfully, he stirred her like no man had ever done, even when they were arguing. There was a lot of passion between them no matter how they interacted.

She went back out to the front of the building and found James standing beside a beautiful black Lexus sedan with a smile.

"Good evening, Ms. Finley. You look good enough to eat." His blatant come-on line nearly made her roll her eyes.

"I hope not, because I've heard silk gets stuck in your teeth."

He laughed softly, although there had not been an ounce of humor in her tone. "I'll remember that." James opened the car door and ushered her inside, shutting it behind her.

The car was plush, with leather seats—heated, which she discovered quickly—and every gadget imaginable on the dashboard. She recognized the man had money and obviously enjoyed the finer things in life. Nothing wrong with that, of course, but there weren't many ranchers who could afford that type of lifestyle.

"Hungry?"

"Actually, yes, I am." Alex put her seat belt on as he slid in and started the car.

With the wonderful low purr from the engine, they drove off into the twilight toward town. James made small talk about the weather and the changing leaves on the short drive into Lobos. It was pleasant if not boring and she wondered if he would do more than chatter aimlessly.

They pulled up to the restaurant and he again opened the car door for her, assisting her in getting out. She wondered if he did that all the time or if he was trying to impress her. Alex wasn't sure which she preferred.

They were brought directly to a secluded table by the window, covered with a pristine white tablecloth and with a bottle of Chianti waiting. The waiter held out her chair while she sat and Alex wondered if she'd stumbled into an alternate universe, because the high-class treatment did not happen in ranching country.

The smiling waiter, a swarthy, short man with blindingly white teeth, handed her a menu. "What would you like to drink, *signorina*?"

"Do you have Michelob Light?"

He looked as if she'd stepped on his foot. "Our beer selection is very limited, I'm afraid."

Oh, that wasn't good. Obviously this restaurant was completely displaced out here in God's country. "What do you have?"

"We have a complete wine selection." The waiter gestured to the small menu on the table.

"I don't drink wine. It gives me a headache and makes my nose run." She also didn't need to be drinking any more bourbon. That was a path she shouldn't go down for quite some time. "How about a diet soda, then?"

"But of course. And for you, sir?" He turned to James.

"A bottle of that Merlot I had the last time, if you have it. Full-bodied and naughty." James winked at her and she wanted to stab him with her fork.

"Of course, Signor Howard. I will be right back with it." The waiter picked up the bottle of Chianti and hurried off as if his ass were on fire but he could only walk from the flames.

"No wine?"

"Nope, never could drink it." She picked up a breadstick from the container on the table and started munching on it.

"Ah, that's too bad. I have developed a taste for it. I find that it cleanses my palate and makes food more enjoyable." He broke off a piece of her breadstick and popped it in his mouth. Alex felt completely off-kilter by the man.

"Did you want a breadstick?" she asked lamely.

He smiled. "No, I just wanted to taste yours."

Was he a sleazy seducer or simply a man who went after what he wanted? She couldn't get a bead on him and it bugged her.

"Why did you ask me to dinner, Mr. Howard?"

"Please call me James. We are neighbors and hopefully more; no need for formalities." He tapped his fingers on the tablecloth and she was again reminded of just how pristine those nails were.

"Alrighty, then please call me Alex." She sipped at the ice water that had been waiting for them on the table. It was a real crystal glass, another strange thing for Wyoming cattle country.

"I will. Alex." Another grin. "I have to admit, I didn't know what to expect. You have Grant's eyes and his chin, but the rest of you, the simply gorgeous rest of you, well, that's obviously not Grant." He laughed at his own funny.

"I've been told I favor my mother."

A sad face. "I understand she died ten years ago. My condolences."

She managed to nod at him. "It was a long time ago." A lie, or a small fib, but she didn't really want to share her private thoughts with the man. "Now, let's get back to my original question: Why did you ask me to dinner?"

He seemed to contemplate his fingernails for several moments before he met her gaze. "I want to buy Finley's ranch, which I told you before. When I met you this morning, well, I was intrigued."

That sure as hell wasn't an answer. "Let's cut the seductive bullshit, James, okay? I know you want the ranch, and right now a pile of money for it sounds right dandy. I seriously doubt you've asked Claire on a date and I don't think you swing the other way, which means Connor hasn't been sitting here either."

Alex waited for her words to sink in and she saw the expression on his face change from suave to surprised to respectful. "You are very different than I expected."

"Well, since I had no idea what to expect, it's all a surprise."

Alex was tired of playing word games. "Did you hope to seduce me into selling to you?"

In the dim light, she swore she saw him blush.

"The thought had crossed my mind, but you are a strong, independent and exceedingly intelligent woman. I don't think that would work."

"Nope."

He sighed and laced his hands together. "I'll be honest with you."

"Sounds peachy."

James managed a wry grin. "I've wanted to buy Finley's since before I bought my ranch. Grant wouldn't sell, wouldn't even consider it even when his business was new and floundering. I became more interested with each passing year, and now that he's gone, I find the brick wall named Connor Matthews in my way."

Alex silently agreed her nemesis was like an unmovable object. "And so you want me to ease the path so you can buy the ranch. Is that about it?"

"To be truthful, I do want to buy the ranch, but I find myself distracted by the new player on the field." He sounded hesitant, even embarrassed, to be admitting it to her. Gone was the suave seducer and in his place, a man intrigued by a younger woman.

She didn't know how she felt about that.

"I don't want to pressure you into anything, Alex. I just wanted you to know what I was thinking, how I felt."

Alex was saved by the timely arrival of the waiter with their drinks. As she sipped at the soda, she watched James as he checked the wine. She'd been witness to David testing many wines over the years, and James had the same kind of style. He swirled it in the bottom of the glass, then stuck his nose in and sniffed. When he took a sip and swished it around his mouth, Alex thought he looked like a chipmunk, but didn't think it prudent to mention that.

He swallowed the small bit of wine and made a strange noise with his tongue as he tasted the red vino. The man obviously really enjoyed it. She had the fleeting thought he might display the same patience and attention to detail in bed.

Alex firmly pushed that thought away. She didn't need to be thinking about the man's sexual tendencies when he was literally old enough to be her father. Aside from that, there was no chemistry between them, no spark, no fire, just a mild curiosity.

"What would you like to order for dinner, *signorina*?" The waiter stood poised by the table, no tablet in hand, just an expectant look on his face.

Alex glanced at the menu, realizing she hadn't decided yet. She loved white sauce more than red, something about the creamy quality that appealed to her.

"Do you have fettuccine Alfredo with chicken?"

"Yes, the chicken is blackened and tender. A delightful choice. And for you, Signor Howard?"

James didn't glance at the menu. "Mussels with clam sauce and angel-hair pasta. Fresh bread, olive oil dipping sauce."

"Of course." The waiter disappeared in a flash, leaving them alone again.

"Back to the ranch question," Alex began. "What exactly would you be willing to pay for it?"

James's brows went up. "A woman who knows what's important."

"I'm just being honest. I figured you'd appreciate honesty." She was torn between knowing that when her year was up, she could grab the money and run, leaving Wyoming behind, or find her place in God's country again.

"I'd have to determine market value and speak to my attorneys. It would be a fair price, I assure you." James took a sip of wine. "I wouldn't cheat my neighbors, after all."

Oh, Alex highly doubted that was the truth. No doubt James would get every possible angle he could to cheat anyone he could. She wasn't going to judge him for that; he was a businessman after all.

The rest of the meal passed with small talk about the economy, the latest gossip on Hollywood, and the pros and cons of muscle cars. Alex found herself relaxing with him, actually enjoying the dinner and the company. James was charming, no surprise, but he was also funny and had a great deal of intelligence.

Alex liked him and she wasn't sure how she felt about that. The man had obviously earned Connor's ire for a reason. She wasn't stupid enough not to realize James had one thought in mind, or perhaps two—to get the Finley ranch and get into her pants.

The first might be possible, the second unlikely.

The waiter brought deliciously decadent tiramisu for dessert and espresso strong enough to make her tingle as it went down her throat. She was full, relaxed and felt the best she had since arriving in Wyoming.

"Are you ready to go?" James rose and held out his hand.

"You might have to roll me to the car." She laughed as she rose, her too-full belly sloshing happily.

"I'm glad you enjoyed your dinner. It's my favorite restaurant." He tucked her hand in the crook of his arm and they walked out into the night air.

The cold hit her and she shivered, her body temperature low from all the digestion happening. The light jacket she'd brought wasn't even remotely adequate for the freezing cold. She shuddered, and when he put his arm around her, she was absurdly grateful for his body heat.

Until he leaned over to kiss her temple. "I'll warm you up, Alex." The tenor of his voice had changed, now a low, seductive pitch she didn't want to hear.

She stepped away even if she was shivering hard enough to make her teeth clack together. "I'm not in the market for that, James."

He reached for her, but she moved out of his reach. "Oh, c'mon, Alex, we're both adults with needs."

Alex shook her head. "Not even on a good day is that something I'd say yes to. Either you back off now or there won't be any further talk of selling."

The silence between them was thicker than the espresso. It was obvious James wasn't used to anyone telling him no, much less threatening him. But Alex wasn't just anyone, and she didn't take kindly to men trying to push her around, physically or verbally.

"You're quite a woman, Alex Finley." His voice had a resigned tone, which meant he was backing away. So there was a limit to how far he would go.

"Drive me home, James. I need to sleep off this dinner."

He unlocked the door and helped her inside; then they were on their way back to the ranch. Alex leaned her head on the window and asked herself what she was doing. There was no need to pussyfoot around with a man like James Howard. She'd either decide to sell her half of the ranch or she'd decide to stay.

A simple yet amazingly hard decision.

* * *

Connor looked at the clock for the umpteenth time and cursed under his breath. It was nearly eleven o'clock and Alex wasn't back yet. He'd heard from several people that she'd driven off in a black Lexus—James's car. And this was, of course, after Connor had told her not to go.

The woman had been there only a few weeks and she'd already tied him into knots. Now she was on a date with James Howard, consorting with the man who had done his best to snatch Finley's Ranch. She played with fire like a damn magician. Well, he didn't want to get burned. It was time he confronted her about all of this and let her know what he wanted.

Her half of Finley's.

He swallowed hard and realized his interactions so far with Alex had all been about sex or fighting. All passionate energy that left him drained, physically and emotionally. She lit a fire within him and he felt completely out of control.

Did he want to buy her out? Yes, he did. Did he want her to leave Finley's? No, he didn't. That left him in a conundrum of what to do. He couldn't have her dating James Howard, though.

His ire arose anew at the thought of her with that low-down bastard. Connor had never told anyone that he suspected Howard had something to do with accidents around the ranch. There were broken fences, tack that wore out long before it should, a few missing horses and even a fire at one of the cabins. Then Grant was killed and the accidents stopped.

It all seemed too coincidental to Connor, and he kept a close eye on all the happenings at the ranch. His tight management prevented anything else, but there was no way he'd relax his guard. Particularly since Howard seemed to have set his sights on the next generation of Finley's to get his hands on the property.

Connor had asked Grant once why James hadn't simply asked to pay for a tributary from the river if it was the water he wanted. Grant had told him, "That man doesn't want anything handed to him. If he doesn't take it, hunt it or steal it, then it ain't worth spit."

He remembered the conversation clearly because it was on the day Grant had died. Connor had never forgotten what his mentor told him. It had been a warning of sorts, one that Connor took very seriously.

He stood at the window of the cabin and looked out at the moonlit path. A solitary figure walked toward the fence. His body clenched at the realization it was Alex. She had a sweet swing to her hips and her hair bounced when she walked.

It was dark in the cabin but he wanted it that way. The moment she stepped up on the porch, he walked toward the door. She flicked on the porch light as his hand reached for the knob. Connor's temper returned in full force when he smelled perfume.

As she walked in the cabin, he yanked open the door. He didn't expect the foot to the stomach or the uppercut to the jaw. Connor landed hard on his ass and he did his best to suck in a breath. The light nearly blinded him, and he managed to hold up one hand in surrender.

"Alex," he gasped.

She stopped in midswing and her mouth dropped open. "Connor, what the hell are you doing?"

He managed to suck in some air. "I was waiting for you to get back."

"I can see that, but since this is my private residence while I'm here, there is no excuse for you waiting in here in the fucking dark." She slammed the door. "I repeat my question: What the hell are you doing?"

Connor's jaw throbbed from her punch. Damn, the woman had a hard set of knuckles. "Protecting you."

"I'm not your wife, your daughter or even your friend. There is no reason for you to protect me from anything." She threw her purse on the chair by the window. "You scared the absolute shit out of me."

"You beat the shit out of me, so I'd say we're even." He got to his feet and rubbed at his stomach. It still hurt like hell.

"No way are we even." She put her hands on her hips. "You need to get your ass out of here and never sneak in again whether I'm here or not."

Connor tried to tell himself to keep his temper in check but Alex pushed every button he had. "I have every right. You are putting this entire ranch in jeopardy by consorting with James Howard."

"Oh, here we go. Consorting with James? I don't even know what that means. A neighbor invited me for dinner, which by the way was delicious; I'm so full I could go for two days without eating again. Yet you turn it into some sort of spy mission?" She snorted. "How did you ever get to be in charge of this place anyway?"

He stepped toward her until he could feel her hot breath on his face. "I earned it. You didn't earn a thing."

A flash of hurt ran through her blue eyes. "I earned more than you can possibly imagine, so don't you ever throw that in my face again."

Connor ran his hands down his face. "You make me nuts, Alex. Absolutely loco."

"Ditto." She stepped back and opened the door. "Now, please leave."

"No. I'm not leaving until we get this sorted out." Connor knew he'd gone about this all wrong. "I'm sorry if I scared you. I was just . . . Hell, I don't know, worried, maybe jealous."

One brow went up. "That's interesting, but it's your problem, not mine."

"No, it's our problem. We've, ah, already had some interactions, and I think that's where this"—he gestured with his hands to the air between them—"whatever it is, began."

"Interactions? Are you talking about fucking on your desk?"

"Well, yeah, I guess."

She stared at him, her gaze steady and intense. Connor refused to squirm under the power of it, but he couldn't help but wonder what she was thinking.

Her brow furrowed. "You were jealous?"

Now he felt completely exposed, like an idiot who blurted out things without thinking. "Yeah, I guess." His breath gusted out at the confession.

She put her hands on her hips. "You know, I've never had anyone jealous before. Is this what it does to people? Makes them break into private houses?"

"It makes me fucking nuts." This time his words were low and gritty. She was driving him completely loco.

He watched her face, and to his surprise, Connor saw a change in her expression, from anger to arousal.

"That's actually a huge turn-on." She unbuttoned the top button of her blouse.

His body tightened fast and fierce.

The second button was history, then the third. "I'm angry, but damn if I don't want to throw you on that bed in there and fuck you."

The fourth button made sweat break out on his forehead. His dick roared to life when the fifth button revealed the black lace of her bra. Alex had a terrific rack, and the low-cut bra revealed cleavage fit for his hard-on.

She closed the door with a soft snick. He'd intended on telling her not to see James again, and here he was panting like a damn dog for her. What the hell was wrong with him?

"If you want to leave now, then go. If you stay, understand that I'm not drunk; I'm not out of control. I am open in the bedroom and like to experiment with whatever gives me pleasure."

Alex was throwing down the gauntlet, daring him to be scared of whatever it was she liked to do. Either that or she was hoping he'd accept her challenge and climb into bed with her. His heart thrummed with a hard beat as he listened to her breathing in the loud silence that surrounded them.

Before he even thought about what he was doing, he stepped toward her. Her expression was surprised for only a split second; then the sides of her mouth kicked up in a grin.

"Let's see what you've got, Matthews." She grabbed his shirt and pulled him down to her, slamming his lips onto hers.

Blood coursed through him as every nerve ending jangled. Her lips were demanding, their tongues rasping and dueling. Connor pulled her close, feeling her diamond-hard nipples against his chest. She was soft and curvy, yet felt like a bundle of hard arousal in his hands.

He backed her toward the bedroom, eager to see the entire bra and what lay beneath. Connor's arousal was sharp as a knife and he could not wait long to be inside her. The bedroom was dark, full of shadows from the moonlight streaming in through the window.

She scratched at his shirt. "Take it off, cowboy. I want to feel your skin on mine."

Connor nearly tore off his clothes as she did the same. He'd never felt the urgency he seemed to experience with Alex. In such a short amount of time, he'd been with her twice, inside her once. He was about to make it a second time.

"Later we'll take our time, but for now let's just fuck." She climbed onto the bed and he was beside her in seconds.

All he wanted to do was simply get inside her. Her cool, long fingers surrounded his hardened staff and he sucked in a breath.

"My, oh my, this is nice. I'll explore later." She ran her hand down him with expertise he was becoming familiar with. "Lie down."

The sheets were cool against his heated skin as he stretched out. He ached with a hardness he hadn't felt since he was a teenager, as if he'd blow his load in less than a minute.

She slid up his body, her hot lips leaving a trail up his legs that made him shake. He was completely at her mercy, under her control, and he didn't give a shit.

She straddled him and he felt the sweet heat from her pussy. God, she smelled so good, he wanted to taste her, but that would have to wait too. Her nearly shaven pussy touched his dick and he groaned low and deep in his throat.

Alex leaned down and bit his lip. "Come inside me."

With shaking hands—he'd be embarrassed about that later—he guided his staff into her wetness. The head slid in almost immediately and he held his breath. He wondered if he'd make it very long if he teased her, but she took the decision out of his hands when she slammed down, impaling herself on him.

He gasped at the same time she did. Jesus, she was perfect, so tight, so hot, so right. He closed his eyes and took control of his runaway arousal. It had to last at least a few minutes.

Connor took hold of her and she started to ride him. Her breasts bounced as she rolled her hips, pulling him deep inside her. She was tight, so fucking tight, enough to make him close his eyes to keep from coming.

"God, you feel good." He sounded completely unlike himself, husky and thick with arousal.

"You don't feel so bad yourself. In fact, your cock is like steel in there. So hard." She reached down and pinched his nipples.

The pain heightened his pleasure, jacking up the intensity of his response. He must have made a noise because she did it again.

"You like that, do you? Hmmm, so do I. You know, there's an amazing amount of pleasure to be had when you mix a little of the opposite with it. Kind of like salty and sweet." She leaned down and lapped at his lip, then bit it. "Delicious."

He reached up and pinched her nipples to return the favor.

"Harder."

Connor did it again, this time with a twist. Her pussy clenched around him and he sucked in a breath. She obviously had the right idea. He slammed into her as he pinched, and a moan burst from her throat.

"God, yes." She leaned back and reached behind her.

To his utter shock, her fingers grazed his balls. Very dexterous woman he had riding his dick. The combination of her nimble digits and her hot, tight cunt made his orgasm hit like a lightning bolt. It slammed into him and he raised up, grabbed her hips and buried himself deep inside her.

"Holy fuck."

Connor nearly went blind with the waves of pure pleasure washing over him. He heard her shout and she tightened around him so hard, it felt like his orgasm started again. It was the most powerful sensation he'd ever had. His breath stuttered as he held her tight against him, even as she bucked and her own orgasm ripped through her.

He started to see stars in front of his eyes when he was finally able to suck in a much-needed breath. The room was almost pulsing with the scents and sounds, the echoes of what they'd just done. Connor looked up at Alex and his heart tumbled even further.

She looked exquisite with her dark hair in a wild cloud, her eyes heavy-lidded with satiated lust, her skin glowing and flushed. Connor imagined what it would be like to wake up every morning to the sight.

"Now, that was what I'd call an after-dinner treat."

She bent down and lapped at his lip, then bit it until pain shot through him. He jerked and she kissed the spot, then with one last lick at the pulsing spot on his mouth, she rolled off him onto the bed.

Connor didn't know whether to be glad he'd discovered a side to him he didn't know about, or upset she'd brought it out. Only time would tell if the experience with her would change him.

Of course, he knew it already had.

Alex rolled over and realized there was a warm, naked man beside her. His scent told her it was Connor. She had fallen asleep, which was unbelievable since she'd never actually slept in a bed with a man, not even David. Yet she had with him. The question was why.

She sighed and snuggled into the fluffy pillow beneath her head. The sex had been explosive, the kind that made her knees shake and her heart tremble. That was the part that scared her—her heart had already gotten involved.

There had been nothing but pain for her at the ranch as a child, and now, thanks to Connor, there was much more. She'd found someone to respect, a lover, perhaps even a man to love. The very thought made her quake. Allowing him in would leave her open to so much pain and disappointment. She didn't know if she was ready for that.

The night air crept around them, making the room nearly cold outside the covers. She snuggled down and spooned up behind Connor. As soon as her breasts touched his back, she wanted more of him. More of the bone-melting sex she'd already had a taste of.

This time she wanted to show him a thing or two about how to prolong the pleasure. She scooted out of bed and headed for her suitcase, for her toy chest. The beautifully detailed wood-inlaid box had been a gift from David. He understood she had wanted to explore her sexuality, the salty she needed to have with the sweet.

She set the toy chest on the nightstand and crawled back into bed, shivering. Her cold feet landed on his warm calves and he shrieked like a girl. Alex laughed until her stomach hurt while he sat up and glared at her.

"Not funny, Alex."

"I was cold. I didn't mean to make you screech." She reached for him but he batted her hand away.

"Oh, you can't make it up to me now." He started to get out of the bed and she grabbed his thigh.

"Not so fast, big boy. We're not done yet." Her fingers crawled up his thigh, making lazy circles in the soft hairs.

She felt him shiver and slide back under the covers. Alex smiled and kissed his exposed shoulder, licking his skin until she reached his neck. She nibbled his earlobe, then sucked it into her mouth.

"What are you doing?"

"Seducing you. Is it working?" She laughed softly into his ear. "Two times we've fucked and two times it's been quick and hard. I'd like to take our time and enjoy it."

"Oh, I enjoyed it." His voice was low and hoarse.

"Believe me, cowboy, you'll enjoy this more." She reached down until she found his already hard cock. "Judging by this development, you're ready for me too."

She gripped him, loving the feel of satin-covered steel, the pulse beneath her hand, the life force emanating from him.

From the toy chest, she took out her favorite small vibrator, some lube and a cock ring, still in the package. A few years ago, she'd dated a guy who was into them, and had broken up with him before they had used it. It was a risky step to introduce it to Connor so early, but after the connections they'd made already, it seemed like a good idea to show him what she liked.

Alex threw back the covers and he howled. "Jesus, woman, what are you doing?"

"Having fun." She set the vibrator on the nightstand and straddled his thighs. His now-flagging cock was in the perfect condition for the cock ring.

His gaze followed her as she opened the package. When he didn't say a word, she put some lube on her fingers and slid her hand down his staff, followed by the cock ring. Immediately he pulsed in her hand, his erection growing firmer by the second.

It was the sexiest thing she'd done in a very long time. He hissed as she reached down and lightly scratched his balls.

"Feel good?"

"I've never used one."

"That didn't answer my question." She climbed off and lay beside him. "Does it feel good? Can you feel the blood pumping, making you harder?"

To her delight, he took his dick in his hand and squeezed. He closed his eyes and did it again.

"Oh yeah, cowboy, show me how you like it." She leaned forward and sucked at his nipple, watching him as he stroked himself. It was erotic and so fucking hot; she needed more so she spread her legs and started playing with herself, her other hand creeping up and pinching her own nipple hard.

The only noise in the room consisted of their breathing, the soft squelch of his hand covered in lube, and the moist sounds from her fingers fucking her own pussy.

Alex had a feeling Connor had never had an audience while he jacked off, but she found it to be incredibly erotic. She couldn't keep her eyes off the motion of his hand, up and down, squeezing as it went. It was like her own personal porn movie.

"Does it feel different when I'm inside you if I'm wearing this?"

"I don't have a cock so I can't tell you. Why don't we find out?" She got up on all fours and kissed him hard. "Let's put on your raincoat so you can fuck me from behind, cowboy."

Connor grinned, still holding his dick, and rose up on his knees. She resisted the urge to suck him as she slid on the condom. He came up behind her and spread her knees a bit wider. The cool air hit the heat of her pussy and she closed her eyes, tingling with anticipation.

Instead of his dick, though, his tongue swiped her from her clit to her ass. Pleasure zinged through her and she moaned. Obviously this man knew what he was doing and she pushed her head into the pillow to enjoy it.

When he picked up the vibrator and turned it on, she buzzed nearly as much as it did. He slid it inside her, fucking her with the small blue buddy.

"Feel good?" He mimicked her question.

Alex found herself unable to answer as he continued to bathe her with his tongue. Long, slow licks made her tremble with need. With the vibrator sliding in and out, he began to eat her in earnest, his tongue wide and rough on her sensitive skin. Connor nibbled at her clit, the sensation like small fireworks on the hot button.

One finger teased her ass and she clenched hard around the vibrator in her pussy. When his teeth closed around her clit, she bucked against him, holding back an orgasm by strength of will. She wasn't ready to come yet. He lapped at her, as her juices slid down her legs. His mouth left a trail of tingling pleasure with each lick.

"Come for me, baby."

She wanted to say no, wanted to tell him she didn't want to, but then he put his thumb inside her ass. Alex teetered on the edge of ecstasy, her eyes nearly rolling back in her head.

"I promise, you'll come again."

That was all she needed to hear, apparently. Her hands crept up to pinch her nipples hard. He increased the pace with the vibrator and sucked her clit hard, making it larger, making it tremble against his tongue. Then his teeth closed around her clit again and her body convulsed with the force of her orgasm. She screamed his name as wave after wave crashed over her. He continued to suck and nibble, prolonging her pleasure until she literally shook from it. The vibrator thumped as it hit the floor and she managed to pull in a breath.

Before she realized he'd stopped eating her, his cock was nudging her entrance and he plunged in. She moaned as her pussy welcomed him into its depths, clenching around him and holding on.

"You are so fucking tight." His voice was almost guttural, raw with need.

Alex couldn't have responded if she wanted to. Instead she pushed back against him and he understood her message. He pumped into her in short strokes, teasing her, teasing himself. She wanted him deeper, faster, harder, but he didn't oblige her. He must be experimenting with the different sensations caused by the cock ring.

He did feel harder, more engorged, within her, or perhaps it was because she was so damn snug around him after his fantastic cunnilingus. His strokes began to pick up and he went deeper. His cock left a trail of heat between her folds, bringing to life the pleasure she had already experienced with his mouth.

Deep, deeper, deepest. Connor used her hips like an anchor, pulling her onto his staff, impaling her, fucking her silly. She forgot her name, almost forgot to breathe, as the sensations built upon one another. Her body was so in tune with his, she knew the moment he felt his orgasm beginning. It was as if a switch went off within her and Alex joined him on the journey.

"I'm gonna come, Alex." He pulled out for a split second and nearly wept from the loss. She heard the cock ring hit the floor and then he was inside her again. "Now, baby, now," he chanted as he pumped into her faster and faster. *"Now."*

As if on command, her body was rocked with another earth-shattering orgasm, this one more powerful than the last. Stars danced behind her closed lids as she clenched around his pulsing cock, pulling him deeper yet inside her. Pure, unearthly pleasure echoed inside her again and again until she was shaking so hard, she became a boneless heap, sliding down onto the mattress and bringing Connor with her.

He kissed the nape of her neck and rolled off, then yanked the covers up. As the warmth of the down comforter surrounded her, Alex snuggled up against him and closed her eyes. Alex was certain, in her sleepy state, that she'd found her mate.

CHAPTER EIGHT

Confusion drove her from her bed as the sun was just waking up. Her body ached from the mind-blowing sex of the night before. She didn't even look at Connor as he lay snoring softly in the bed.

Alex hadn't meant to take things so far, so fast, with Connor. She washed quickly, then pulled on some clothes as her mind continued to whirl with thoughts. She'd put herself in a position where she'd need to decide whether or not to pursue a relationship with him.

Of course, her body cried out with the very idea of not being with Connor anymore. She'd become addicted to him already; like a junkie needing regular doses of a drug, she had to have some. He slept on as she crept outside and headed for the barn.

Perhaps a ride would help her clear her head, get it out from inside her ass. She damn well liked Connor, a lot, and that should be the easy part. The ranch, the legal tangles and her father were these shadowy figures that lurked between them.

Her stomach clenched as the reality of the last words in her father's will flitted through her memory. The ranch would be a guest ranch in perpetuity, and she had to stay for a year to get her share. Alex didn't know if she would survive. She couldn't bear to think of Finley's being a guest ranch, yet she could hardly remember what it was like before.

Alex shook her head, trying to dislodge all the whirling thoughts from her head. She yanked her hair into a ponytail and didn't worry about running into anyone. As she pulled down the cap on her head, she kept her eye on the damp path in front of her.

Thankfully the barn was empty and she saddled Rusty quickly. He was a bit sleepy-eyed but perked up when he saw her. After a few scratches behind the ear, she mounted him and took off for a midlevel trail. She needed a couple hours alone—her sanity depended on it.

She should have left a note for Connor but hadn't known what to write. The cold air made everything seem clearer, and she realized she should have just woken him up and told him she was going for a ride. Alex had a tendency to make everything more complicated than it was. It was an annoying habit she had trouble breaking.

The trail led her far from the woods, across the meadow and deep into the heart of the property. The terrain was vaguely familiar but she didn't know exactly where she was. Good thing the damn path was so well marked. If she wasn't careful, she might get lost.

The NO TRESPASSING sign was the first clue she was close to leaving Finley property. There was a fence with a rather nasty wire, which appeared to be electrified, and a sign every six feet. She knew for a fact they hadn't been there ten years ago.

Alex rode up closer and read the tiny letters at the bottom of the sign: HOWARD RANCH. Well, wasn't that a nice, neighborly thing to do. James obviously protected what was his—with force, if need be. It didn't surprise her, but it did disappoint her.

Although he'd tried to hit on her, and smooth-talk her into selling, she liked him. He was smart, funny and witty. But the fence and the signs told her there was much more beneath the surface of the handsome man. She'd suspected it, and here was evidence she'd been correct.

James Howard was a dangerous man.

"Good morning, beautiful."

As if she'd conjured him from her thoughts, James was there on a stunning quarter horse—show quality; if she wasn't mistaken. He smiled, but even at twenty feet away, Alex could feel the undercurrents of frustration and hunger.

"We both know I'm far from beautiful, but I'll take the good morning and give it right back to you." She couldn't quite manage a smile but she figured her expression was at least pleasant.

"Of course you're beautiful. Don't put yourself down, Alex. You are not only beautiful; you're sexy." This time his grin had just a smidge of sincerity to it, delivered of course with boyish charm.

"What are you doing out here and what the hell is up with this fence?" Alex wasn't one to be coy about asking a question. He had to know that from last night.

"I'm taking a ride, which is I assume what you are doing. As to the fence, well, the guests from Finley's seemed to think the entire world was their oyster. They used to cross over into my land, sometimes scare the cattle, lowering their value after they ran for an hour; a couple calves even got trampled. I am protecting what's mine from folks who have no business being out here." James's expression didn't change but his voice grew harder and sharper as he spoke.

She understood protecting property, and that included the livestock, but the fence went beyond that. The damn thing was electrified, which could cause the death of a calf too, perhaps even a human. That fence was pure rage, which she concluded was fueled by frustration. James wanted the land she was on and he couldn't get it.

"I meant to call you later and thank you for dinner."

That surprised her. "I should thank you; after all, you paid and drove."

He smiled. "That's what a gentleman is supposed to do. Your generation has forgotten what etiquette is."

"I won't argue that point." She agreed with him and even silently added that her generation had forgotten what manners were all about too. Alex had always found people her age tended to be annoying and vapid—James reminded her of the fact a man could be a gentleman. Perhaps that was why she liked him even though her instincts told her he was dangerous.

"I'm headed into Lobos later to pick up a few things and thought maybe you'd like to accompany me. Have lunch."

Two meals in two days? Oh, Connor would be pissed, or beyond pissed, really; heading into the realm of furious. Alex did need to go into town and buy a pair of boots, though. Since she had no schedule to follow, she had plenty of time to go do some shopping and have lunch.

And find out what else James was up to.

"I planned on going into town myself, so if you happen to run into me, then so be it." A white lie, since she hadn't actually made the plans until that second, but effective.

His open expression closed a bit. "Of course. I was just thinking about saving the expense of the gas. Those pickups get lousy mileage."

Alex figured she'd surprise the shit out of him when she drove up in the Camaro. It would be a gleeful, totally self-indulgent thing to do.

So, of course, she'd do it.

"Don't worry about that. I might see you later, then?"

"I look forward to it." James started to turn his horse. "Oh and by the way, Alex, don't touch the fence. It's electrified." His smile was pure mischief and not in a good way.

"I'll remember that. See you later, James." Before he could respond, she kneed Rusty into action and trotted away.

Her mind was still full of questions upon questions when she returned to the barn. While she was hoping it would be empty, there was no such luck.

When she dismounted, Daniel was standing in front of her, eyeballing her as if she were one of the horses.

"What do you want, kid?"

"Mama says you're my sister."

"So?" Alex led Rusty into the barn, brushing past the little pint-size version of Claire. She didn't need to deal with the nuisance right then. Her stress level was already too high.

"That means I'm your brother."

Alex rolled her eyes as she unsaddled Rusty and set the gear on the sawhorse near the tack room. "Brilliant deduction."

Daniel popped up in front of her, his blue eyes mirroring her own. She felt the world tilt a little as she confronted the male version of what she was "supposed" to be. Her father must've been over the moon when he was born.

"Well, your name is Finley and your eyes are blue. And you have the same butt chin as me." He pointed to her face with one grimy finger.

Alex barked a laugh, surprising both of them. "Butt chin? What does that mean?"

"It's got a crack in it, like a butt. Daddy had the butt chin too." Daniel was a damn precocious boy.

Alex didn't want to like him, and she sure as hell didn't want to spend time with him, but she didn't send him away. She walked Rusty to his stall and Daniel followed, chattering away.

"Are you gonna live here now? Mama says you are." He took the blanket off Rusty and folded it like a pro.

"I don't know yet." Alex handed him the headstall. "Put this away, brat."

"Connor calls me 'brat.' He says it means he loves me." Daniel's voice came from the tack room.

Alex shook her head. "I think Connor's yanking your chain."

A little black-haired head popped back into the stall door. "Yanking my chain? I don't get it."

"It means he's messing with you. Calling somebody 'brat' does not mean you love them." She rubbed Rusty down and checked his food and water.

When she turned to leave the stall, Daniel stood in the way, arms crossed over his chest and legs spread wide in a combat stance. His brows were drawn together in a fierce little scowl.

"You are wrong, big sister. Connor does love me even if you

tell me he doesn't. It's not a very nice thing to say, you know." He humphed loudly. "Mama says if you can't say nothing nice, don't say nothing at all."

Alex saw herself in everything about this kid. The attitude, the smart mouth, the fearless way he confronted her. Against her will, a grin played at the corner of her mouth.

"While I agree with your mama on principal, I can't always be nice. Nobody can." She walked up to him until she could lean down and be nose to nose with him. "Now, get along little doggie, before I make you."

He waved his hand in dismissal. "Connor says you're nice underneath all that sass and bluster. You wouldn't hurt a fly."

With that, the little scamp ran off, leaving her with an open mouth and more confused than she'd been before she had entered the barn.

Connor woke alone, with a pile of regrets and questions. Damn, he hadn't meant to be with Alex again, although "be with her" didn't even begin to describe all they'd done.

He glanced at the clock and could hardly believe it read 9:02. It was obviously a cloudy day because there was no sunshine streaming through the window. Instead it was a weak gray light filtered by the curtains, barely enough to see the wreckage of the bed.

The entire room smelled musky, like sex and sweat. He rolled out of bed and looked down at the sheets. The black cock ring lay there against the cream-colored sheets. He had never used one before, but damn if it hadn't made him fuck harder, come harder. Against his will, he picked it up.

Connor made his way to the bathroom, wondering for a moment

why she had a new cock ring, but not really wanting to know the answer. The memory of her putting it on him made a shiver race down his entire body. Alex was sex personified; beneath that tough exterior she was nothing but heat and passion.

She made him hard just thinking about her.

He clutched the ring in his hand, unwilling or unable to leave it for her to find. Somehow he wanted to take a piece of her with him when he left the cabin. Connor washed quickly, and cleaned the ring, tucking it deep in his pocket.

The clock read nine fourteen when he left, full of questions about where Alex was, where they were going and how he could possibly find a way to balance his budding relationship with her and the ranch.

Too many questions and no answers.

Alex walked toward the front of the ranch, hoping to see or perhaps hiding from Connor. He'd been missing from the cabin when she'd returned from her ride. She didn't know whether to be disappointed or glad. Their night had been intense enough to put her on the raggedy edge of bliss.

He obviously needed time away from her as much as she needed the same. Riding Rusty had been a good idea, but now she was almost regretting leaving the cabin. She knew the sexy, passionate man was already under her skin, and she needed to keep him from diving too deep into her heart.

Then there was James Howard, the sometimes scary, definitely pushy and charming neighbor who seemed to be intent on wooing her. For what end, she wasn't sure. She had already told him how she felt about selling the ranch, and to back off from any personal contact with her. Yet he'd invited her to lunch.

Alex didn't know if she would join him or not. As she rounded the corner and headed toward the Camaro to drive into town, she still hadn't made up her mind.

"Going somewhere?"

Connor's voice made her nearly jump out of her skin. She turned toward him with her heart pounding, and when she caught sight of him, it sped up even more.

God, he was so damn sexy a shiver snaked through her. Now that they'd been intimate again, their relationship had changed. While she still hated the fact that he had served as the son she could never be, she was most definitely involved with him. What their relationship was, well, she didn't know yet.

"Into town. I need some real boots and another pair of jeans." She shaded her eyes. "And maybe a hat."

Honestly she probably should have followed up on the salary from her accounting work. The seven hundred dollars or so she had left wouldn't last forever.

"I'll come with you."

She stared at him. "Excuse me?"

"I need some new boots too. If you're going into Lobos, we might as well go together." He stepped toward her, into the sunlight that caressed him like a lover's golden hand.

She swallowed hard, caught between the lover she'd invited into her bed and the man who wanted to be. "Don't you have work to do?"

"I'm the boss. I can take time off if I want to." He looked uncomfortable with the notion, but she already knew he was a workaholic.

"You don't mind shopping with a woman? You know I'll take ten times as long as you."

His gaze narrowed as he stepped into her personal space. "Why are you trying to prevent me from going?"

"No reason, just figured you had better things to do." She wondered if the lie was visible in her eyes.

"Not right now, I don't." He glanced behind her. "That's your car, isn't it?"

Alex turned to view the green Camaro, which had become a symbol of her independence. "Yes, it's mine."

And, damn, it felt so good to say that.

"Sweet ride. Can we take it?" He was already walking toward the car.

Before she could tell him he couldn't drive, he stopped in front of the passenger door and looked back at her expectantly. His green gaze was steady and she felt a bubble of excitement in her belly. It was her first nonbusiness outing with Connor.

"Okay, let's go."

Lobos looked different yet the same. There was a good-size strip mall just outside the main street. It had always been where the fall festival carnival had been held. Images of a Ferris wheel, tilt-a-whirl and stolen kisses behind the cotton candy booth ran through her head. This time they were good memories, not painful ones. She smiled as they got out of the car and headed for the Western store called Denny's Western Wear.

"Denny has the best boots, even if they might be a bit more expensive than the shoe store down yonder." Connor was being surprisingly helpful. Their relationship had been so tumultuous, she was wary to let down her guard completely with him. If ever.

He opened the door for her and a cowbell tinkled. As she passed him to step into the store, she caught a whiff of his scent. Her entire body clenched and she had to stop herself from falling on her face. Connor grabbed her elbow.

"Whoa, there, Alex."

She straightened up and gave him a pained smile. "Sorry. Now you know why I need boots."

He chuckled. "Then we'll make sure to get the ones with the no-tripping feature."

She tried to ignore her body's reaction, stuff it down deep in her pocket and forget it. It was damn hard.

The store seemed to be a collection of everything cowboy. From hats, to jeans, to boots, to outerwear, even some chaps and even the shorter style chinks. She liked it immediately.

"Boots are on the back wall there, women's on the left." Connor led her back, the smell of leather getting stronger as they walked.

There was a dizzying array of boots to choose from, more than she expected. "Um, where do I start?"

"Connor, I never expected to see you in the middle of a workday." A man approached them wearing a rather dramatic Western shirt with shiny buttons and serious piping. He was around fifty, with wide shoulders and chest, and red hair liberally sprinkled with gray topped by smiling blue eyes. "And with a lady. Wonders never cease. Next thing you know, you'll be holding doors for her."

Alex could not stop the bark of laughter from exploding.

"Shut up, Denny," Connor growled. "This is Alex Finley." He

turned to her. "Alex, this is Denny Wardman, an obnoxious fool who knows everything about boots."

"Hi, Denny. Nice to meet you." She held out her hand, which was immediately engulfed by Denny's enormous paw.

"Finley? Did you say Finley?" Denny's eyes widened. "Well, I'll be damned."

"Probably already are." Connor nudged him with an elbow. "Let go of her hand."

"Oh, shit. I mean, dammit, forget I said all that. My mama would tan my hide if she heard me cussing." Denny dropped her hand and she was tickled to see the man flustered. What was it about Western men that made them so embarrassed to curse around women?

"No worries. I've heard much worse, even said much worse." She grinned at him. "Now, according to Connor, you can help me figure out what boots I need." She glanced down at the stained sneakers. "These are obviously not going to last long in a horse barn."

Denny grimaced as he followed her gaze. "Would you be offended if I threw them away after we found you a pair of boots?"

Alex laughed. "Only if we can burn them and roast marshmallows."

Denny turned to Connor. "I like her. Don't you dare screw this one up."

Now it was Alex's turn to blush. "The boots?"

"Ah yes, first let's measure that foot of yours." Denny gestured to one of the captain's chairs lined up neatly in front of the wall of boots. "Have a seat and we'll get started."

The next forty-five minutes were spent experimenting with boots of all shapes and colors, not to mention sizes. There was ostrich, kangaroo, snake and bull hide, then pointy toed, round toed and somewhere in between.

It was a dizzying array of everything boots, making Alex glad Denny had such a wealth of knowledge. When he slid on a pair of chocolate brown Tony Lamas made of bull hide with a round toe, her feet nearly sighed with relief.

Denny sat back and looked up at her. "Well?"

"Wow. These are perfect." Alex stood and walked back and forth while Denny watched. "It's like they made them for me."

"I knew I'd find the right pair for you." He looked like a strutting peacock as he patted himself on the back with the success of the boot-finding mission. "They're waterproof too."

"They're great. Thank you, Denny. Really, thank you." She picked up the box and winced at the price. Two hundred dollars was a deep cut into her funds, but they really were perfect. They were sturdy, comfortable as hell, and even though they weren't pretty, there was a little bit of stitching that made them look, well, less boxy.

"And may I burn these now?" Denny held up the sneakers.

"With my blessing, yes." Alex picked up the empty box and headed toward the front of the store, realizing Connor was nowhere in sight.

"He's over by the hats." Denny was right beside her and she realized he knew exactly what, or rather whom, she was looking for. "He's a good man, had a hard life until he got here. Your daddy, well, he worked that man like a dog until he sweated out all the bad. Now he spends his time trying to prove to everyone he's just as competent as Grant was." Denny's gaze was serious for the first time that day. "Judging by the way you've been looking at each other, things are complicated already. Just don't hurt him; he's hard as steel on the outside, but beneath, he's more vulnerable than anyone I know."

Alex had no idea about Connor, didn't know about his relationship with her father, or that he had apparently been just as messed up as she'd been. Perhaps her father had straightened Grant out when he couldn't do the same with her. Another reason her father had loved him, and forgotten her.

She knew it wasn't Connor's fault, but it damn well made her heart clench in pain.

"Yeah, I know what you mean." She made her way over to the hats on the opposite side of the store, bypassing all the clothing. She'd look for jeans another day when she had more money to spend.

Connor was staring at a line of hats sitting on a bench. The hats were varying shades of brown in different styles. He was frowning at them when she walked up.

"What are you doing?"

"Looking for a hat."

"I can see that, but I'm fairly certain these wouldn't quite work for you." She picked up the caramel-colored one and popped it on her head. To her surprise, it fit perfectly.

"I was picking one out for you."

Her surprise turned to pleasure as she realized he'd been shopping for her. A man, shopping for *her.* What a strange and unusual world she'd returned to, where cowboys and honor still existed, not to mention chivalry.

"That one is just a bit too light for your hair." He picked up one near to the shade of the boots on her feet and plucked off the hat, plopping down the new one. "Try this one."

She stared at him, trying to read what was lurking in the depths of his green gaze. He adjusted the hat, then cupped her cheek, his thumb sliding gently across her chin.

"Perfect."

Alex leaned toward him and her lips grazed his. He sucked in a breath and leaned closer. Her arms started to rise of their own volition when someone cleared his throat behind them.

"The hat on the bill too?" Denny sounded utterly amused.

Alex wanted to smack him. She didn't know if it was because he interrupted them or because he thoroughly enjoyed doing it.

"Yep, put them all on the Finley Ranch bill. Our new accountant will be paying it at the end of the month." With a grin he took her hand, lacing his fingers with hers.

She stood there, unable to process what had just happened. Connor had simply paid for likely more than three hundred dollars' worth of boots and hat for her without any hesitation. It had been years since anyone had paid her way, particularly Finley Ranch money. She'd relied on herself for so long, even going so far as to pay David rent on the guesthouse, much to his consternation. Having someone take care of her was as foreign as the hat on her head, not necessarily uncomfortable, but unusual. She didn't know how to respond, particularly considering how freaking amazing his hand felt holding hers.

Alex felt young again. Her heart lightened and a smile crept across her face. Damned if she wasn't falling in love with him, this hard-as-nails cowboy with a passion that matched her own. Oh boy, she was definitely in trouble.

Connor leaned down and kissed her quick. "Anything else you need here?"

She turned to see herself in the mirror. The hat was perfect; the color highlighted the shades of her hair and the tone of her skin. She was surrounded by men who knew what she needed to wear, even if she didn't. The thought made her chuckle. If only David could see her now.

"No, nothing else." She glanced at Denny. "Thank you for your help."

Denny smiled and bowed in a courtly manner that made her think again of chivalrous gentlemen. "You are most welcome, my dear. Next time ditch the stiff and you and I can go have fun together."

"Shut up, Denny." Connor led her from the store, with Denny's laughter following them.

Alex couldn't remember a time she'd been so happy or content. That meant it likely wouldn't last.

Connor felt off center, as if he were watching everything happen instead of being there. The feel of Alex's small hand in his, however, was very real. She wore the boots and hat, looking much more like a Wyoming girl than the L.A. woman she'd been a week ago.

He hadn't intended on not working, or, for that matter, going with her into Lobos, but he had just the same. Connor hadn't taken a day off in eight years, not since his first day at Finley's. Even sick as a dog with the flu, he'd worked. Now, with barely a word to the staff, he'd driven off with Alex in her fierce Camaro.

The sun was warm on his face as they walked down the strip mall toward the car. He was content, almost happy. It was an unfamiliar sensation.

"Are you hungry for lunch? It's almost noon."

"Hungry enough to chew on my new hat. I missed breakfast." Alex glanced around. "Anyplace good to eat around here?"

"I forgot you haven't been here for ten years. There's a nice sandwich shop down at the end. They have a great club sandwich and make homemade chips." He hadn't been there in three years, but he'd seen the sign when they drove in.

"Sounds good to me. I'm starving." She leaned in a little closer and her breasts brushed his arm.

Connor almost forgot he was hungry at all.

"I didn't realize you were bringing a date for lunch."

Connor's contentment vanished suddenly as a dark cloud named James Howard intruded. He turned to find James standing at the entrance to the sandwich shop, a nasty grin on his face.

"What are you doing, Howard? Following us?" Connor snapped.

James looked at Alex. "I thought I was meeting Miss Finley for lunch."

Connor's stomach flipped. Twice. He turned to her and her mouth opened and closed, yet she didn't speak. Son of a bitch.

He backed away from her, letting her arm drop from his. "You thought it was a good idea to play us off each other, Alex?"

"No, I didn't. James asked me if I wanted to have lunch, but I never said yes." She didn't sound very convincing.

And Connor was definitely not convinced. "You were on your way to town when I saw you." He remembered that she had looked startled to see him. "In fact, you didn't even want me to come."

Alex's cheeks flushed. "I wasn't expecting you to come, but I'm glad you did."

"Hm, Alex, you shouldn't really have two dates for lunch." James tsked at her. "You knew I'd be here and yet you came with Connor. I think you are playing a dangerous game, Miss Finley."

She turned to James. "You are an asshole, you know that? I came into town to get boots. That's all."

"And a hat, apparently."

"It's none of your fucking business." She folded her arms, pushing her breasts up, making Connor wonder whether he was losing his mind if he could be distracted so easily.

"Alex, after the date we had the other night, I'm surprised." James moved closer to her, and Connor clenched his fists. "I thought we had a connection."

"The only connection we had was a business one. It was not a date. I told you I didn't want you in my pants and I meant it." Alex turned back to Connor. "I'm not so hungry anymore. If you want a lift back to the ranch, let's go."

"If she's in your bed, I think you'd do best to control that little filly before she—"

Connor didn't remember his fist actually moving from his side, but suddenly it connected with James's jaw and the older man went down like a sack of potatoes. Connor's fist hurt and he likely broke a finger, but damn, that felt good.

"What the hell are you doing? Did you want to pull it out and measure it too?" Alex shouted at him from ten feet down the sidewalk. "I haven't seen his yet, but I'm sure yours would be in the top two." She stalked back to him, shaking her finger like a scolding teacher.

He didn't expect James to reappear from behind him and punch him in the kidney. Pain exploded through him as he fell to his knees; then another punch landed on the side of his head.

Alex screeched and Connor saw her foot fly toward James just as his fist went toward Connor again. In a split second, she was flying over him, landing on her ass on the sidewalk with an audible thump; then her head smacked the concrete. Connor watched it as if it were a movie, not real, couldn't be real.

Alex looked up at them as blood leaked from her split lip and her eyes were unfocused. "Did you just punch me, James?" She sounded surprised and a bit loopy. When she touched her lip, she hissed, then stared at her hand, surprised to see blood.

Connor roared and stood up, ready to beat the absolute shit out of James Howard. Yet the older man was already by Alex's side, apologizing profusely, stuttering like the complete ass that he was.

"Get away from her."

"I don't think so, Matthews." James sounded different, almost concerned about Alex. Connor refused to believe the man would care about a thing other than himself.

"You probably just gave her a concussion, broke her jaw, if not knocked out a tooth. I'm only going to tell you one more time—get the fuck away from her." Connor didn't recognize his own voice, nor did he understand the red-hot fury currently coursing through him. It had been so long since he'd let the dark side loose, it shook him to the core.

"Both of you, shut up. Connor, help me up." Alex was her usual bossy self, but he simply complied since he agreed with her. Aside from that, if he said another word, he might really regret what came out of his mouth.

"Alex, I didn't mean to—"

"I said shut up and I meant you too, James. You're acting like a sixteen-year-old boy who can't control himself." She reached up to accept Connor's help and he was dismayed to realize how much she was shaking. He didn't know if it was because of the punch or the emotions that were running high.

James, the idiot, tried to push Connor out of the way and help her, but that backfired when Connor elbowed him. "Let me help, Matthews. You know I didn't mean to hurt her."

"She told you to shut up, so shut the fuck up." Connor resisted the urge to set Alex down and pound James into the concrete.

With the older man sputtering behind them, Connor simply scooped her into his arms and carried her to the Camaro. The sight of her blood made his grip tighten.

"Easy, cowboy, I think my ass is bruised enough for the day. God, and I had just gotten over being saddle sore." She let out a shaky breath.

Connor loosened his grip, feeling like an ass. "Sorry, baby. I didn't mean it. It's just that asshole pisses me off. And what the hell did he mean, you were meeting him for lunch?"

"Did you call me 'baby'?" Her words were slurred.

He had been beyond angry when he accused James of giving her a concussion, but judging by the way her pupils were dilated and her speech was slurred, it was likely true. Fear nudged aside fury.

"We're going to the emergency room."

"What? I'm fine, just need some ice and a Diet Coke. I'll be right as rain. Oh, what a pretty rainbow." Her head lolled against his shoulder. "You feel so good, Connor."

He managed to get her into the passenger seat and wrangle the keys from her pants pocket. Any other time, having his hands in her tight jeans would be a much more pleasurable experience. Now he felt like he was in a panic and was slower than a slug in molasses.

The emergency room was about fifteen miles away, not too far, and the road was pretty clear between Lobos and Chilroot, where the hospital was located.

It was the most hellish ride he'd taken in two years, not since the night he'd followed the ambulance there with Grant's broken body. The memory was not a good one to experience as he worried about Alex, particularly when she passed out two miles from the hospital.

Connor would kick James's ass from there to the state line the next time he saw him. The son of a bitch had no self-control, no inkling of how much destruction he left in his wake. Somebody needed to teach him a lesson, and man, Connor was ready to be the one to do it.

He screeched into the parking lot, glad Alex had such a fast car. Later on he'd ask her where she got it, but for now he simply parked and ran over to her side of the car.

He'd seen her asleep before, but he'd never seen her this vulnerable. Perhaps it was the blood, or perhaps it was his heart that was getting in the way. It didn't matter; all that mattered was getting her into the emergency room.

Connor picked her up and ran.

CHAPTER NINE

Alex woke to find Connor standing over her, his face a picture of pure worry. Her head hurt like hell along with her tailbone. She tried to swallow but she had no spit in her mouth.

"Alex." He took her hand in his clammy ones. "Thank God you're awake."

She croaked and pointed to her mouth. He fumbled with the pitcher beside the bed and poured her a glass. Alex was shocked to see his hand trembling.

"What happened?"

Connor slid her arm beneath her shoulders and helped her drink. The water was like the nectar of the gods, cool and sweet as it slid down her dry throat. Her lip stung and she realized her entire mouth hurt.

"James punched you." His voice was tight like a guitar string that had been wound too tight.

She had a vague memory of running into James in town, following clear memories of buying boots and a hat. Connor was there through all of it, a solid presence beside her. She was stupidly warmed by that fact—it had been a very long time since anyone had taken care of her.

"He punched me? Why did he punch me?"

Connor helped her lie back down before he answered. "We were, uh, fighting and you jumped in to stop it, I think, and, well, his punch went wild. You got it instead of me." His green gaze met hers. "I'm sorry."

She tried to remember what happened but it was fuzzy. "Why can't I remember?"

"You have a concussion."

"He punched me so hard I got a concussion?"

"No, that happened when you hit the sidewalk." Connor gently touched her head.

Now Alex was glad she didn't remember. The force of a concrete sidewalk meeting her noggin sounded bad enough to make her nauseated.

She glanced around and realized she was in a curtained-off area, still wearing her clothes. That meant she hadn't been admitted, which was a good thing.

"Can I leave?"

He frowned. "Don't you think you should spend the night? I mean, you have a head injury."

"I don't have insurance, Connor. As it is, I'll probably use up all my funds just paying for this visit." She sat up, then swayed when the room began to tilt.

"Whoa, there." Connor steadied her. "I'll pay for it. You're half owner in the ranch, so the money I spend will be yours anyway."

"That doesn't make me feel any better. I don't want you to pay for it simply because my father died and left me half of a dude ranch."

"It's a guest ranch."

"Shut up, Connor." She swung her legs around and tried to stand, but ended up in his arms. "Dammit."

"Don't push yourself, Alex. It's not worth it."

She was suddenly very tired of Connor and his care of her. "Back off. I can take care of myself. I've done it for ten years without you, so don't think you can just step in and be my sugar daddy." She pushed his hands away.

He looked shocked, even hurt, but his expression hardened and he held up his hands, stepping back. "Fine, then. You make your own decisions; pay the bill yourself. I would suggest you let me drive you back to the 'dude ranch,' though, or you might drive into a tree when you pass out again."

His sarcasm was as sharp as the pain in her head. "There's no need to shout, Matthews. I'm only a foot away from you, for Chrissakes." She made it to her own feet and waited until her stomach stopped flipping.

Slowly but surely Alex made her way to the nurses' station and argued her way into signing a waiver so she could leave the hospital. Her entire body hurt, but the worst was her head. When the nurse handed her post-concussion care instructions, the first thing she noticed was not to sleep for twenty-four hours.

She fought back tears as she limped outside, her perfect day ruined by a runaway punch.

Although she wanted to argue with him, Connor had been right about driving. It took every smidge of strength she had to make it to the Camaro; she wouldn't be able to drive it even if someone offered her everything she ever wanted in the world.

Instead she slumped down in the passenger seat and stared out at the passing scenery while he drove. Every two minutes, she'd feel him look at her.

"You're not sleeping, are you?"

"No. Now, shut up and leave me alone." She sounded petty, mean and childish, but she couldn't help it. Alex was no stranger to lousy days, but the loss of that incredibly wonderful feeling she'd had with Connor, well, that just really pissed her off. It shouldn't because she hadn't expected it to last, but just the same, she was mad beyond reason.

Connor pulled up to the handicapped parking spaces at the ranch and hopped out. She wanted to argue with him, but she felt horrible enough to selfishly covet the space long enough to get out of the car. The parking lot was fifty yards away, certainly too far to walk when she had a concussion, or perhaps she was just being a big baby. Likely both.

He helped her to one of the rocking chairs on the porch. "Sit tight and I'll park the car, then get one of the electric carts to take you to the cabin."

Connor had some speed; she'd give him that. He was in the car in seconds, the engine roaring to life. She never expected to see the green machine driving away from her battered body, though. If she didn't feel like shit, she might have laughed.

A couple walked past while she waited. No doubt she looked just as bad as she felt, like a prizefighter who'd lost the match. Somehow she managed to nod and look as if she was supposed to be sitting there battered and bruised. The woman looked at her in sympathy while the man shook his head as if Alex was a bad influence.

If only he knew.

"Alex? Holy shit, what happened to you? And where did you get those boots?"

She looked up to see Kent and Don in their L.A. finery standing on the porch. It was a hallucination—she knew it—but she burst into tears at the lovely, familiar sight. Then suddenly she was in Kent's arms and Don was rubbing her back. She didn't know how or why they were there, but she was so glad she wanted to cry. So she did.

"Oh, doll, don't cry," Kent crooned as he held her tight. This time there was no sexual content to their touch, as if that one night had expunged that entire need.

Alex refused to believe her relationship with Connor may have affected her sexual attraction to anyone else. That was too much to contemplate in her condition.

"Alex, what's going on?"

She peeked over Kent's shoulder to see Connor standing beside a golf cart, a scowl so deep she thought it might cause permanent damage to his forehead.

"Who are you?" Don challenged, his dark gaze checking out Connor's hard form.

"Who are you?" Connor gestured to both of them. "And what are you doing?"

"Comforting our friend." Kent turned to Connor, tucking Alex under his arm.

She had the unearthly urge to be tucked under Connor's arm instead.

"Well, I'm taking her to her cabin."

"Good, then we'll come with." Kent gestured to a small black suitcase. "Be a love, Donnie, and get my bag."

Without so much as an introduction, Kent swept past an

openmouthed Connor and climbed into the backseat of the cart. It was unreal, maybe a dream brought on by the concussion. Alex could hardly believe it when Don put two bags in the back bin, then sat in the passenger seat.

"You do work here, right? We're guests, so please ferry us to Alex's cabin." Kent sounded positively imperious.

"Alex?" Connor appeared next to her, his mouth set in a tight white line. "Do you know these men?" Behind the anger and stress in his face, she also saw concern. The urge to be comforted by him roared through her again.

"They're my friends from L.A., Kent and Don."

"Do you want me to drive you, all of you, to the cabin?"

Ever the chivalrous knight, the honorable cowboy. Connor wanted to be certain she knew what she was doing, that nothing untoward was happening between her and the other men. Her heart melted just a bit more.

"Yes, I do. There's a second bedroom they can have. I—I just need to sle—I mean relax." She managed to stop the tears, at least, even if she wanted to rewind the entire afternoon.

"Fine." Connor climbed into the driver's seat and glared at Don, who sat next to them. "The only reason I'm driving the two of you is because of her. If it were up to me, I'd make you walk to the bus station."

With that, he took off at a slow pace and she knew it was in deference to her. Connor really was a gentleman, for all his gruff ways and quirks; he was considerate, honorable and kind.

Damn, she really was falling in love with him.

The ride to the cabin took only five minutes, but by the time he stopped the cart, Alex was dizzy again. Without a word, Connor scooped her up, ignoring a protest from Kent, and carried her to the gate. He managed to punch in the code without dropping her and carry her up the steps and into the building.

The cool interior soothed her and she sighed with relief to be home, even if it wasn't really her home. It was where she belonged for now.

Connor brought her to the chaise lounge in the corner of the living room and set her down so gently, she thought it might take another five minutes. Then he set about turning on lights and covering her with a snuggly blanket. The violet on the table reminded her she was still alive and kicking, same as the plant.

Kent watched from the doorway in amusement. When he caught her gaze, he raised his brows and mouthed the word "hot." Alex shook her head at the incorrigible man.

Connor went into the kitchen and came back minutes later with a cup of coffee. She smelled the brew and realized it was exactly what she needed. Without her even knowing what she wanted, Connor did. What that meant, she had no idea.

The coffee was hot, with enough cream to make it a light tan color, exactly how she liked it. She felt pampered, maybe even loved a bit. Connor squatted beside her and looked her over, his soft touch never once causing her pain.

Alex wished Kent and Don weren't there. The thought surprised and shocked her. She wanted to be alone with Connor.

"You all set? I can stay if you want me to." He didn't look at the other men, but she knew what he was thinking just the same. Connor would enjoy throwing them out.

"No, you need to work. I'm fine. Kent and Don can help take care of me." She hid a huge yawn behind her hand.

He picked up the cordless phone and moved it beside her. "Call up to the main house if you need me." Connor kissed her forehead, nose and mouth, then pressed his forehead to hers and whispered, "I'm sorry this happened, baby."

He rose abruptly and thrust papers at Kent, anger vibrating from every muscle, bone and sinew in his body. "I don't want to leave her with you two yahoos, but obviously it's what she wants, so I will. These are the instructions for boneheaded women who check themselves out of the hospitals against medical advice. She's got a concussion, a bruised tailbone and plenty of other bruises and cuts. If she even once tells me she didn't get what she wanted, I'll throw your asses off this property. Am I clear?"

Without waiting for an answer, he slammed out of the cabin. Kent turned to Alex.

"Well, hell, girl, you didn't tell us you already found a man. And here we were worried about you."

This time instead of crying, Alex laughed, then winced as her head complained about the noise. She sipped her coffee and gazed at her friends. For the first time in a very long time, she felt safe and perhaps even loved.

Alex didn't sleep, as instructed, but dozed on and off as she watched the moon rise and set. The sweet sounds of the night creatures were her only company, aside from the sound of soft snores coming from the second bedroom. She suspected Kent had a sinus condition, but was too polite to tell him.

When dawn broke, her eyes were like sandpaper, her head still pounded hard enough to make her bones ache and, worst of all, she missed Connor. He'd left her alone with her friends, and seeing them was something she thought she desperately needed, but she found out she'd been wrong.

What she needed was a cowboy with a chip on his shoulder and a smart mouth, and the most beautiful green eyes.

She managed to get into the shower by herself. The hot spray soothed her aching body, but it did nothing for her headache. Alex slipped on her frumpiest, most comfy outfit and shuffled to the kitchen. Don sat at the table with a cup of coffee and a small smile.

"Good morning, Alex. How are you feeling?"

She sat down beside him. "Like shit, but better than the pounded shit I felt like yesterday."

He rose. "Coffee?"

"God, yes."

With brisk efficiency he made her a steaming mug and set the half-and-half beside it on the table. She smiled, realizing Don was the quiet one, but he missed nothing. As she sipped the nectar of the gods, he allowed her to enjoy the silence and the coffee.

"You love this cowboy of yours?"

Alex was surprised, to say the least. "Excuse me?"

"I saw the way he looked at you and the way you looked at him." Don shrugged. "It doesn't take a genius to see you've already got feelings for him."

She sipped at her coffee while she considered how to answer him. "I definitely have feelings for him, but I don't know if it's love, at least not yet."

Don nodded. "We came here to make sure you were okay. Kent nearly had heart failure when you showed up looking like you'd been in a brawl." He touched her chin gently. "I'm afraid you don't look much better, just more, ah, colorful."

Alex managed a small chuckle. "I can imagine. I avoided the mirror."

Another brief silence followed, a comfortable one in which friends simply enjoyed the morning brew.

"Will you stay here?"

She expected the question, but not the clench in her stomach at the thought. "I don't know." Her voice was soft and uncertain.

Don smiled at her. "Then we'll enjoy our cowboy weekend and try out the, ah, riding opportunities around the ranch. On Sunday, we'll say good-bye again."

Tears stung her eyes as the realization hit her. She did plan on staying; her heart was shouting what her choice would be. All she had to do was voice it aloud.

Connor didn't sleep much again. The combined lack of sleep over the last three weeks was totally kicking his ass. He dragged himself through everyday tasks, with barely a recollection of any of them.

He wanted to go see Alex, but he also respected her right to kick him out. It was partially his fault she'd been hurt, for one thing. And she had her two boyfriends from L.A. to take care of her, for another.

Their presence was a constant prick to his pride. He didn't know who the hell they were, but seeing her in the blond one's arms had nearly driven him to violence. Again. What she did and with whom she did it were not his concern or his business.

He made it through two days without picking a fight with anyone, a miracle in itself. By the time Sunday came, everyone started avoiding him instead of the other way around. When he left his office to have dinner, he saw Alex's two man friends waiting by the main house with their suitcases.

A sigh of relief escaped, much to his chagrin.

They spotted him as he walked toward them. The blond one cocked a brow and the dark one's expression was blank.

"It's Alex's cowboy."

"I can see that."

"You think he wants to pound us into the ground?"

"More than likely."

Connor didn't know what the hell they were talking about, but his heart thumped hard at the "Alex's cowboy" label. He wanted to ask them what they meant, but his pride kept him from doing so. "Are you leaving?" was what came out of his mouth.

"Anxious, honey? Don't worry; we're just waiting for a cab. We did call the only one in town." The blond had a smart mouth.

"Don't tease him, Kent. He's worried about her. Can't you see that?" The dark-haired man's stare was intense. "She's not going with us, but I'm going to warn you now we'll be back if she needs us."

Connor reminded himself they were leaving and Alex was staying. "She's lucky to have friends like you."

"Don't forget that, cowboy." The blond glanced behind him at the approaching cab, then met Connor's gaze. "I'm not going to repeat what Don said, but I will say don't hurt her. She's one amazing woman and deserves better than second place in anyone's life."

"I don't plan on hurting her. She's my, well, I don't know." Connor twisted in the wind with how to explain exactly what Alex was to him.

The blond man grinned. "It's okay. It's all part of the journey, right?"

As the two men walked away from him, he wanted to ask

them a thousand questions about Alex, but couldn't think of a single one.

The dark one glanced back at him. "Go to her. She's been lousy company and I think she misses you."

Connor felt a surge of cavemanlike satisfaction at the thought that she was miserable, particularly that she missed him. He didn't grin, even if he wanted to; he just nodded as they climbed in the cab and disappeared.

Anyone else watching might have said he ran to the VIP cabin. Connor would've told them it was just a fast walk.

Dusk was just settling like a blanket onto the daylight as he got to the gate. When he pressed the buttons to open it, he remembered the combination was Alex's birthday. She'd told him her father hadn't forgotten her. At the time he had dismissed it, but perhaps she was right. Grant never mentioned her, but perhaps he kept the pain private, maybe from shame or regret.

Connor promised himself he'd never have to code a lock with her birthday to remember her. If he had his way, she'd never leave Finley's Ranch.

He strode up to the door and threw it open. It banged against the wall, earning a startled yelp from inside. Connor could have knocked politely and asked to come in, but it wasn't the time for it. She looked up from the chaise lounge, a book in her hand and surprise on her face.

"Connor, what the hell are you doing?"

"Visiting you." He closed the door, then strode toward her and he saw her visibly shiver. With a predatory grin, he slid up the chaise toward her, the heat from her body almost sizzling as it came in contact with his.

"You're hot."

"I've been told that before."

"Stupid cowboy. You know what I meant." She didn't push him away or tell him to leave.

He braced himself over her and she sank lower into the chaise.

"No, I don't." He leaned down and began to rain kisses down her face, eyes, nose and mouth. She closed her eyes and let out a kittenish sigh. His dick roared to life.

"Your body is, um, really warm." Her voice was breathy and hitched on every other word.

Connor's inner caveman beat his chest in victory. She was missing him, and if he had his way, she wouldn't miss him anymore because he intended on seeing her every day. In bed or out.

"That's 'cause I'm near you." He shook with arousal, wondering how he'd made it three days without being with her.

He never felt so out of control, and rather than running from it, which he had been doing, he ran toward it.

She chuckled and then inhaled deeply. "You smell good. You always do."

Connor sniffed. "You smell like you need a shower."

She gasped and smacked his chest. "Connor!"

He captured her mouth, ceasing the reprimand he knew was coming. Her lips softened immediately beneath his, and her tongue lapped at the seam of his lips before he had a chance to reciprocate. Alex was passion and fire all inside one petite, buxom package.

God, how he loved her.

Connor's heart skipped a beat as his mind absorbed what his heart had just told him. *He loved her.* What the hell? That kind of shit happened only in movies, didn't it? Shaking off all thought completely until he had time to think about all of it, he allowed his body to take control. To feel, to taste, to enjoy.

His tongue danced with hers, the gentle rasp echoing through his body as he pressed his aching cock against her mound. He felt the heat of her pussy through his jeans and her sweats.

"Talk about hot, woman; you're about scorching me."

She reached down and cupped his dick, then squeezed. His eyes rolled back in his head. "I'm going to do more than that, I think."

Connor bit her nipples through the shirt and she arched up into him. He'd already discovered she liked a little pain with her pleasure, and apparently so did he.

"Let's take a shower together and I'll clean you up." He bit the other nipple and she moaned.

"Now, that sounds good to me." She returned the favor and pinched his nipples through his shirt.

His dick twitched at the sensation. Connor was no prude and had plenty of experience with women, but it had all been vanilla. Easy on the tongue but sweet.

Alex was more like an exotic flavor filled with hidden treasures to discover with each bite. He could hardly wait to taste her again.

After helping her up from the chaise, he led her to the bedroom and to the huge shower he'd had installed in the cabin. Grant had complained about the cost initially, but it fit the space perfectly, and there was room enough for two.

He turned on the water, and within moments, the room warmed up nicely, gentle puffs of steam filling the air. Alex was docile, unlike herself, but perhaps she needed to be. He wouldn't complain; he'd simply do what he needed to.

Connor pulled off her T-shirt and bra, followed by her sweatpants, tsking when he discovered she wasn't wearing panties. "Waiting for me?"

She grinned and shrugged. "You won't hear me confess that particular sin."

He shed his clothes quickly, then opened the shower door and bowed to her. "After you, m'lady."

Naked, Alex curtsied. "Why, thank you, kind sir."

The shower had two heads with alternating jets on three sides. Warm water doused them as they came together in an embrace. Heat rose from between their bodies and around them from the steam and water.

Connor's dick was already aching, hard as a damn stone against her soft belly. She obviously couldn't miss it, considering it was nearly fucking her belly button. He wanted her badly, but this wasn't the time to have a fierce mating. It was a time to make love.

He guided her back until her hair was under the spray. With a soft touch, he wet it thoroughly, then put shampoo in his hands.

"Turn around, baby."

She turned and sighed when his hands landed on her head. With a technique worthy of washing an infant, he shampooed her beautiful hair, paying careful attention to the injury at the back of her head. He pulled her back under the water and rinsed the locks until they squeaked beneath his touch.

Ignoring his own body's hunger, he soaped up a body sponge and began washing her. She finally met his gaze and he saw gratitude, affection and pleasure there.

He lathered in circles down her back, massaging her ass, dipping his fingers between her cheeks until she made a soft mewl. Then he meandered down her legs with the sponge, big circles, small circles, until he reached her feet.

"Now turn."

Alex complied, and he was pleased to see her nipples were like pink diamonds again, winking in the light with drops of water hanging from their tips. Against his will, he got to his knees and pulled one into his mouth and sucked.

She held his head in place and made sexy little moans deep in her throat. Connor kept his mouth on her nipple, licking, sucking and nibbling even as the sponge traveled up her legs, until he stopped at her pussy.

Alex spread her legs to give him access, and he pressed the sponge against her shaven lips. The rough sponge must have felt good because she clutched his head with her nails when he swiped her with it.

"Feel good, baby?"

"Mmmm, more."

He made circles on her pussy, then pulled it back and forth again. Then, when he could hardly wait another second, he dropped the sponge and replaced it with his hand. He rinsed the soap away, exposing a clean, pink cunt dripping wet.

"Back against the wall." He guided her until she was right in front of the side jets, then turned her until she faced them. "Now, don't move."

Connor reached up and pushed the button until the spray was an alternating sweep. It hit her sensitive nipples and she sucked in a breath.

"Holy shit."

As the water pleasured her upstairs, Connor pushed her legs apart and knelt between them. The pink flesh glistened, begging him to touch her, taste her. He wasn't about to resist. As his throbbing erection screamed to plunge into her beautiful pussy, he leaned forward and licked her instead.

This time she groaned. "Holy fuck."

"Make up your mind, baby. I prefer the fuck."

She chuckled. "Me too. Now, let me feel that tongue again, cowboy."

"Your wish is my command, m'lady."

Spreading her lips wider, he lapped at the hood protecting her clit until the plump nubbin grew larger. Her juices coated his tongue as he sucked at it. He could feel her tightening as the jets pleasured her nipples and his mouth pleasured her pussy.

He thrust two fingers inside her tight channel, groaning when he felt her clench around them. God, he needed to fuck her so badly.

As if she'd read his mind, she shook her head. "No, not fingers. I need your cock, now. Fuck."

Connor got to his feet as quickly as he could, then flipped her around until she faced him.

"C'mere, woman." He picked her up and she opened her legs to wrap them around his back. His dick brushed against her wet mound and he shivered at the touch.

Connor backed her into the shower wall until she was braced against it; then he eased into her hot, wet cunt. He closed his eyes as she closed around him like a hot fist. Damn, but it felt so good he almost came immediately.

"I won't last," he confessed against her neck as he plunged deep within her.

"Good, neither will I. Let's ride, cowboy." She kissed him, then thrust her tongue into his mouth, just as he was doing to her.

Sweet wet heat surrounded them, the steam and water making their bodies slick. Faster, harder, he pumped into her, pleasure catapulting him into a realm of ecstasy he'd never experienced.

He came so hard, so fast, he roared with it as he drove into her so deeply he touched her soul. She scratched at his back, her breath gusting past his ear as she shook in his arms. Connor's pleasure overwhelmed him, making his eyes sting with tears as he rode the waves crashing over him.

Then he started to remember where he was and the fact his legs were nearly crumpling. He let her down as slowly as he could. Her heart thumped as heavily as his, the heat in the shower making it hard to focus. He pushed the door open and cool air washed over them.

He washed them both again with only his hands, this time without arousal, without urgency or need. By the time he was done, she was nearly asleep in his arms. Connor wrapped her in a towel, then carried her to the bed to dry her off, then himself. They slid under the covers and spooned together.

Connor couldn't remember the last time he'd felt so at peace.

CHAPTER TEN

Another few days passed before Alex finally ventured out into the world. Connor walked her to the main building without fussing, for which she was grateful. After she settled in her office, she got to work on the receipts from the last week, and within a few hours she felt fantastic. Working with numbers had always calmed her, made her feel grounded in a world of chaos.

By midmorning, she realized that although she was content in her little niche, she missed Connor. That thought made her rock back in the chair. It was odd that she was apparently so infatuated with him, had gotten so used to his presence, that she missed him after only a few hours.

As if she'd conjured him, he poked his head in the door. "How are you doing?"

She almost blurted that she was missing him, but caught it just in time. "Good, just catching up on the mess you left for me."

He stepped into the doorway with a frown. "It's not a mess."

Connor wore a bright green shirt, making his eyes stand out like emeralds in his face. He was so damn sexy, her body stirred to life after a few days of slumber.

"Close the door."

His gaze widened as he realized her intentions. "We're going to get caught."

"No, we're not. Now, shut up and get undressed." Alex shut the door to her tiny office and leaned against it, unbuttoning her shirt as fast as she could.

"There's a new guest tour coming through in five minutes." Connor was undressing even as he admonished her.

"Too bad they won't get to have great sex too." Her body was already heating, her pussy wet with need. Every time she was around Connor, she was instantly aroused. At the moment, she didn't want to consider why. She just wanted him. "It makes it more exciting if there's a risk."

He stripped off his pants and stood there in a spectacular pair of tightie whities. Ye gods, the man was magnificent. That chest covered in whorls of chocolate brown hair, the muscles spanning from one side of his body to the other, six-pack abs earned the hard way through honest labor. Long, muscular legs covered in the same dark hair. Then of course there was the nice package between his legs currently pressing against the restrictive white cotton.

Alex yanked off the rest of her clothes until she was naked. His gaze immediately fell to her breasts, to the hardened pink nipples that were currently aching for attention.

"Tell me what you want." His voice was husky with need.

She hadn't considered where they'd fuck, just that she needed some right then and there. The office was convenient even if it was in a high-traffic area and it had a door.

"Sit in my chair, cowboy, and take off the damn underwear."

He turned and pulled them off with his back to her. She knew he was doing it on purpose, teasing her with the view of his dimpled ass, which was a spectacular sight, to be honest. When he sat in the chair, she got an eyeful of the delicious erection he was sporting.

Connor had a very nice cock, not too long, but thick, with a pulsing vein running its length. His balls hung heavy below it, like a pair of kiwifruit ripe for her hands, her tongue and teeth. She dropped to her knees and took him in her hands. Even if the desk was pushing into her hip, she needed to taste him before climbing aboard.

"Alex . . ."

"Shhh, be quiet. I hear the tour group in the lobby."

She gripped the base of his cock, squeezing as her other hand fondled his balls. His scent, man and the muskiness of his arousal, filled her nose as she bent down. One slow, long lick from base to tip made him jerk in the chair.

"Jeeeesus."

"If you don't shut up, I won't suck your cock."

He was quiet immediately, his hands gripping the edge of the chair. Alex smiled and bent down to continue. She lapped at the head of his staff, paying careful attention to the sensitive underside. His body tightened with each swipe of her tongue. He was clean with a slightly salty taste, simply scrumptious.

She licked him from top to bottom again and a tiny moan popped from his mouth. Alex stopped and looked up at him as voices were heard about ten feet from the door. The door that didn't lock.

The moment became so charged, the hairs on her arms stood up. She held his gaze as her mouth closed around him and slid down the entire length of him. His pupils dilated and his breath puffed out in tiny bursts. Alex sucked and licked as her mouth ascended only to lap at the head of his cock again. She could hear people discussing the various places within the main building.

Strangers were six feet away and she was sucking Connor off. It was enough to make her reach down and flick her own clit. She spread her legs for easier access, her hand finding just the right spot and rubbing in slow circles.

Connor realized what she was doing and another tiny moan popped out. Big man with no self-control. She was going to test him even further, to see just how far she could push him, how hot their sex could get.

Alex sucked him in earnest, bobbing her head down his length. She squeezed him as she bit at the soft skin and a squirt of pre-cum landed in the back of her mouth. Her thumb pressed the base of him as she returned to the head again to nibble.

"Alex." He whispered so softly she barely heard it. "Fuck me."

Her body clenched so hard, she almost came. She met his gaze, even as the voices grew closer. Yes, it was time. She wanted to come while the crowd was outside the door, when the danger of discovery was the greatest.

Alex stood and straddled him, guiding his pulsing cock to her pulsing pussy. She held the back of the chair and planted her feet on either side of it, then slid down onto him, inch by inch. He filled her completely, thick and hard, until he touched her womb. Alex's head dropped back as she jerked with the pure pleasure of having him inside her.

He held her hips and pushed her back up, then slammed her down. Alex let him do it a few times; clumsy as his movements were, it put her breasts level with his mouth. Then she took over, pushing her nipple between his lips. The voices were nearly at the door, and Alex knew she would come fast and hard.

His mouth closed around her nipple and he pulled her into his mouth, his tongue swirling around the aching tip. Alex wanted to cry out, to moan, but she swallowed it back down, her arousal that much stronger. She held on to the chair and rode him as if he were a stallion, her pillion perfect.

His grip on her hips tightened as she rode him, faster and faster, fucking him so hard he almost lost her breast, but he held on with his teeth. The pain sent waves through her, landing between her legs. The mix of pleasure and pain and the addition of the danger made her nearly mad with the need to fuck.

The voices were directly outside the door now, and anyone could open it. Licks of arousal flitted through her, leaving fire behind. His cock hit her womb again and she felt her orgasm building. She bent down and whispered, "Now."

His pace increased, as did hers. The wet sounds of her pussy seemed exceptionally loud in the small office. She reveled in it, loved it, embraced it, welcomed it. The pleasure started to overtake her and she tightened around him, her toes pushing against the floor as she rode the wave. His fingers dug into her hips and he bit her nipple again.

A powerful rush of ecstasy whooshed over her, leaving her blind and deaf to all but her blood pumping madly in her ears. He held on to her nipple, prolonging her own orgasm as he buried himself to the hilt inside her. His warm cum gushed deep within her pussy and she clenched around him, milking his cock for every drop.

Alex tried to suck in air, but her body was so tightly wound she could pull in only a short burst. He let her nipple loose and pressed his forehead against her chest. His body was shaking and she realized hers was as well. It had been powerful, mind-blowing sex. Outside the door was silent, the guests having moved on past.

She knew it was more than just a casual fuck in her office. It meant much more than that, but what, exactly, she wasn't ready to face. She pulled his hair until his head lolled back. His eyes were unfocused and hazy with pure pleasure. With a smile, she kissed him, running her tongue along his lower lip until he opened his mouth.

Their tongues slowly danced together as his dick pulsed in the throes of recovery. She cupped his face and stared into the depths of his beautiful green eyes.

"Again?" she challenged, not yet ready to leave the hot cocoon of her office.

His dick twitched again within her. "Give me five minutes."

Alex leaned back and pinched her own nipples, their tips sensitive from his attentions. "You've got two."

He laughed silently and hugged her to him. Alex knew at that moment she was already in love with him.

She walked with Connor by her side to the mess hall to eat lunch. Her body still hummed from the amazing sex in her office and she felt a certain languidness to her movements. Much of the staff smiled at them as they passed, as if they were part of a big secret. She realized he had been visiting her daily at the VIP cabin, and now she was going everywhere with him at her side. The staff must have noticed, which obviously led them to the conclusion that Connor and Alex were a couple.

It made Alex uncomfortable, if she was honest with herself. She hadn't yet committed to staying on at the ranch and she wasn't ready to be permanently attached to the man at her side either, even if her heart shouted with glee when he was around.

It made her stomach quiver to even contemplate handing over her heart and soul to him.

The coffee was heavenly enough to distract her from her odd mood. Connor didn't say much but he kept sneaking glances at her while he ate.

"Don't you want to have something besides coffee?" he said around a mouthful of potatoes.

She made a face. "Not what you have. Maybe a piece of toast."

He hopped up. "Be right back." His obvious chivalry secretly pleased her, which just added to her confusion.

"Where's Connor?" She looked up to see the desk clerk Jennifer standing with a bouquet of orange roses. Their scent was heavenly, not to mention the perfect buds.

"He'll be right back."

"Well, here's another bouquet, and he told me to bring them right to him. I heard he was here." Her curious gaze told Alex the girl wanted to ask her about the bruises, but didn't.

Alex realized what the girl had said and her stomach dropped at the dark thoughts that entered her mind. "Another bouquet?"

"Yeah, he's been giving them to guests since he knows you don't want them." Jennifer smiled. Her young, fresh face was so innocent it made Alex cringe inwardly.

"Why don't you leave them here and we'll take care of them." Alex managed to move her lips into what she thought was a smile.

Jennifer bobbed her head and set the vase down on the table. The roses Alex thought were so beautiful had just transformed into something very different.

"How many does this make?" Alex didn't want to know the answer but she had to ask.

"Well, three on Friday and Saturday, then only one yesterday because they had to come from Billings. Um, then just this one today." Jennifer must have seen something in Alex's expression because her happy smile disappeared. "Did I say something wrong?"

"No, you didn't. Thanks for bringing these." Alex could barely bring herself to appear unaffected. She felt her happiness shriveling into a desiccated corpse.

Jennifer walked away, frowning as she looked back at Alex. The girl didn't know what she had been brought into, a lie that now sat between Alex and Connor like an elephant. Or a vase of orange roses in September.

With a shaking hand, Alex reached out and took the envelope tucked in among the roses in the vase. As suspected, her name was on the outside. Her stomach jumped and the coffee burned as it nearly came back up at her.

She opened the envelope and pulled out the card.

Dearest Alex,

Please accept these roses as an apology, an offer of friendship and more.

Yours, James

Alex closed her eyes and squeezed the card in her hand. According to the girl, James had sent eight bouquets of roses and not one of them had ended up in her hands. Until this afternoon, that was—until Alex discovered Connor had decided to lie to her and control reality on her behalf.

Anger mixed with disappointment and sadness. She expected more from him, she truly did, or perhaps she just wanted more. A man who would let her be strong and make her own decisions. Connor was a cowboy, a man's man, who likely assumed he needed to stand between her and the interloper. Little did he know, everyone was an interloper in Alex's world.

She stood and took one rose from the vase, leaving the crumpled card and the mug on the table. If she confronted Connor right then, she might say something she'd regret later. For now, she needed to be alone and shake off the anger.

The cold afternoon air made her shiver as she walked down the path. Several people commented on the bright orange rose in her hand. One little old lady even told her the meaning of the color.

With a denture-straight smile, the woman touched the petals with one gnarled finger. "I used to be a florist before I retired and moved up here. Now I take care of the children in the program while their parents ride." She shook her head. "You are a lucky girl, you know. Orange roses represent desire, enthusiasm and passion. They're a mix of yellow and red; did you know that?"

Alex murmured, "No."

"Many times a man sends a woman orange roses when he's ready to make a change from friendship but not quite love, which is what red roses mean." She patted Alex's cheek in her grandmotherly way. "Whoever gave you these is telling you he has romantic feelings for you and he wants more than to just be a friend. Hang on to him, dearie."

After another few excruciating minutes with the older woman,

Alex escaped and found herself heading to the family cemetery. She hadn't missed her mother so much in ten years, but right about then her heart ached with the need to be in Katie Finley's arms.

The sun shined brightly on the cemetery, which was made up of about two dozen headstones, all Finleys. Her mother had a pink granite headstone, as pink was her favorite color and it also symbolized the fight against the breast cancer that had taken her life way too soon.

Alex laid the rose on the grass in front of the stone and sat down beside it, keeping her back to her father's grave. She didn't need him, or want to even remember he was there. He was the one who'd gotten her into the untenable situation she found herself in.

Alex spent the next half hour sitting with her mother and telling her about the weekend with Connor. Even if there was no one to answer, she felt better just getting it all out.

She felt a warm touch on her neck and didn't feel afraid; she simply felt loved. Her mother's spirit was telling her she wasn't alone and even if it was her imagination, it felt more real than much of the last ten years.

When she rose from the damp grass, she hadn't made any decisions about Connor, but she did know she had to speak to James, whether or not her lover liked it.

When he spotted the vase of roses and the empty table, Connor dropped the plate of toast with a loud crash.

"Shit."

He had kept the roses away from Alex the last several days, making all kinds of guests happy with fresh flowers. Connor knew he should have told her, but he assumed each bouquet was the last; then another one came, and another. Soon he found himself standing in a hole he'd dug himself, with no way to fill it in without admitting to Alex he'd been intercepting the flowers from James.

Now it was all in vain because someone had simply brought them to her in the mess hall. The crumpled card told him she knew exactly whom the roses were from.

"What did you do, Connor?" Bernice stood there with her hands on her hips glowering at him. "I told you to take care of her."

"I did, or at least I thought I was protecting her." He resisted the urge to throw the flowers on the floor and stomp on them.

Bernice shook her head. "Men are the most idiotic creatures on the planet. Looks like your protecting skills need a little bit more polishing."

"Thanks. I'll make a note of that." He squatted down to pick up the plate and scattered toast while Bernice stood over him tsking.

"You don't need to be sarcastic. That's a very old habit I thought you broke a long time ago."

He snorted. "I just hid it from you. Didn't want to hear you tell me how screwed up I was anymore. I already knew it."

There was a brief silence and then he heard the scrape of a chair. When he glanced up she was sitting in the seat Alex had vacated. Bernice looked as if he'd slapped her.

"Did I do that to you? Did I make you feel like you wasn't a good person?" Her brown gaze was confused and stricken.

Connor hadn't meant to hurt her feelings—actually he didn't know he could. Bernice was a tough old dame who didn't take shit from anyone, least of all a snot-nosed juvie with a record a mile long. After he cleaned up the toast, he sat down across from her and took her callused hands in his own.

"You were being honest with me, which I appreciated. You

never made me feel as if I wasn't good enough to be working at Finley's." He squeezed her hands. "I thought of you as a bossy aunt who happened to want to do what was best for me, even if I didn't like it."

Her expression softened a bit, but she still looked not quite right. "An aunt, eh? I thought I was more like a big sister."

She was at least thirty years older than him, but he wasn't about to point that out.

"Big sisters don't pull little brothers out of a jam at the sheriff's office after he steals their wallet." The memory of that particular night in jail made a chill crawl up his spine.

However, it seemed to cheer Bernice. "You were a little shit."

Connor smiled. "I was most definitely a little shit. Now I've got to go find Alex and try to make things right." God only knew how he was going to accomplish that without a burning bush or a parting of the sea.

Bernice's grip tightened. "I always tried to do my best with Alex, and then you. You both were like the kids I never had. Never mind aunt; I tried to act like a parent, but since I ain't got no kids, I was always afraid I did it wrong."

"You did it right."

"You work too hard and have no social life. She's been hiding for ten years. Tell me how I did it right." Bernice's scowl was back.

"Believe me, if you hadn't been there, I would have been in prison, not jail, and Alex wouldn't be the person she is." Connor stood and kissed her cheek. "So thank you for kicking my ass now and then, and for caring enough to do it. No matter what, I do love you, Bernice."

When she blushed, Connor thought perhaps a miracle was

possible. Maybe he could find another one to fix this particular fuckup with Alex. He left the mess hall and headed toward the VIP cabin.

Alex stood outside the main office and waited for James. He seemed surprised to get her call but eagerly offered to come by to pick her up. She knew she was playing a dangerous game between the two of them, but since she hadn't had an opportunity to speak to James since the fight in town, it was a necessary risk.

She was afraid Connor would appear and there would be another smackdown, or worse. Alex knew she had to get her head on straight before she talked to him, starting with settling the dust with James.

The Lexus pulled up and Alex jumped in without waiting for him to open the door. The surprise on his face was evident; then it was replaced by concern when he got a look at her colorful bruises.

"Jesus, Alex, I'm so sorry." He reached out to touch her but she pulled back.

"Don't think because I called you that I want to start any kind of relationship with you, least of all allow you to touch me because you feel guilty." She waited until he drew his hand back before she relaxed. "I figured we ought to talk and clear the air."

"I appreciate that. I really do." A blinding smile. "Where would you like to go?"

"Nowhere. Let's just sit here in the parking lot and talk."

A flash of anger in his gaze disappeared quickly to be replaced by a calm one. James was still playing games with her and it pissed her off.

He pulled the car into a corner spot, out of view of the main building, then shut off the engine. "I didn't mean to hurt you. I hope you realize I feel terrible about the whole thing. I wanted to apologize to you but I found out you had a concussion and I felt even worse."

"Eight bouquets definitely constitute an apology," she murmured.

James waved his hand. "There's a hothouse I use regularly. The roses were just a bit of brightness for you while you recovered."

"Orange roses mean you want to move from friendship to romance; did you know that?" She watched his face carefully enough that she saw the recognition in his gaze. Oh yeah, he knew exactly what orange roses meant.

"I thought of the sunset and how much you said you loved to watch it. The roses reminded me of it." He shook his head. "There was no other special meaning, I assure you."

Bullshit, of course.

"James, let me get straight to the point about why I called you. I am at a crossroads in my life and I'm still not sure which way I want to turn. I might stay at Finley's or I might move on." Her throat grew tight at the notion of leaving the land she'd come to love again. "Pressuring me to sell to you is not going to make my decision easier. While I appreciate the offer to buy the ranch, right now I just don't know what I want."

"But you're not saying no?"

"I am not saying no, but I'm not saying maybe either. I simply don't know yet." She wrapped her arms around herself as a chill crept up her spine. "I realize that sounds like a lot of bullshit but I'm asking for your patience to sort things out."

His gaze dropped to her breasts and she wanted to smack

him. Why did men always think it was a good thing to stare at a woman's tits? Jesus please us.

"James, my face is up here."

"What? Oh, of course, I just noticed you had a stain on your shirt." A lame excuse but she let it pass.

"As soon as I make a decision, I will call you and let you know. Until then, please just let me have time and space to think." She couldn't be clearer than that.

"Are you asking me to leave you alone?" This time the shock on his face was genuine. Obviously he'd never had a woman kick him out of her life before.

"Yes, I am. Give me some time and space—that's how you can make amends with me over the incident." She pointed to the side of her jaw where the yellow, purple, blue and black rainbow resided.

"Yes, of course. I will respect your wishes." He turned to her, and suddenly the suave seducer was back. "Just know that I will be at your beck and call if you need me."

"Sure thing." She put her hand on the door handle when he put a hand on her knee. "I'd remove that if I were you." What the hell was it with men in Wyoming who thought they could simply touch her whenever they wanted?

"Oh, I'm sorry." He sounded anything but as he took his hand back. "I just wanted to let you know I'm here if you need to talk."

Fat chance of that happening.

"Thanks for coming over." As she climbed out of the Lexus, she sucked in a lungful of fresh air.

Alex felt much better, with a clearer head than she'd had in the past couple of weeks. With a little wave to James, she closed the door and walked away. If she was lucky, it would be a while before he decided to woo her again. By then, she planned on having her decision made on where her future was.

Connor tried to swallow his anger, but it was really damn hard when he saw Alex climb out of the black Lexus. She had left him to be with James Howard again.

Son of a bitch.

He knew he just needed to go to work. It was already nearly ten o'clock and he hadn't even stepped foot in his office yet. He'd been looking for Alex all over the ranch, only to find her exiting James's car. Bernice warned him to behave himself, to treat Alex well and be patient.

He could hardly stomach the thought of being patient right about then. Maybe if she hadn't spent the last three nights in his arms, hadn't shown him exactly what she liked in bed and how she liked it. He'd become attached to her—hell, he had been arguing with himself on whether or not he was in love with her.

Now he knew he was and it hurt like a bitch.

Alex walked slowly through the parking lot, arms hugging her middle, with her gaze on the horizon. She never even looked toward him, never knew he was simmering in anger and hurt.

It seemed that every aspect of their relationship was full of so many ups and downs, he felt almost dizzy from the changes in altitude. If that was what love was, he wasn't sure he even wanted to follow her. What kind of idiot would open himself up to pain and misery, even if it meant experiencing intense pleasure and joy?

Connor started after her.

She wasn't walking fast so he caught up to her within a few

minutes. Judging by the direction she was going, Alex was headed toward the cabin. He didn't know whom he was angrier at, her or himself or James Howard.

"Alex."

She froze in place at the sound of his voice. "Connor."

He walked around until he was in front of her. She looked serious and wary, which she probably should be.

"I saw you with James Howard again."

"And?"

"The man punched you so hard, you got a concussion when you hit the ground. You're damn lucky you still have all your teeth."

Her gaze narrowed. "I don't need a history lesson."

"Obviously you do."

"Get out of my way, Connor. You're being an ass." She brushed past him without waiting for him to move.

That just pissed him off more. Alex had to see how destructive it was for her to be around James, for all their sakes.

When he grabbed her arm, she stopped again. "I should kick you for touching me."

That stung. "You had no objection to it last night or the night before or the night before that, as I recall."

"Let's not go there, Connor, okay? Right now I would like to be alone."

He didn't remove his hand and he literally felt her muscles tighten beneath his fingers.

"No, we're going to talk about this right now. You cannot imagine how much it makes me crazy to see you consorting with him." He sounded like a fool but the right words just wouldn't come.

"Consorting with him? Is this war and he's the enemy?" she snapped.

"Yes, actually, it is. I've told you that time and again but you won't listen. He is the enemy and he's tried to get his fucking hands on Finley's more than once. You're giving him the opportunity to succeed." Connor's entire body felt like it was on fire; fury simply made him see red. "I won't let you single-handedly destroy your father's legacy."

Connor didn't remember her moving, but in seconds he was on his back in the damp grass, the breath knocked from his body. Alex's knee was on his chest and she was literally vibrating with raw fury.

"Don't you *ever* throw that in my face again. *I* was my father's legacy and he did his best to destroy *me*." She was amazing, like a Valkyrie warrior queen. Connor was speechless at the sight. "I wanted to belong here. I have nowhere else to belong. Just so you know, I don't plan on destroying anything. Don't presume you can tell me what I can or can't do."

Alex lifted her knee up, then rose. That was when he saw the tears in her eyes, but it was only for a split second because she turned and walked away. He suspected she didn't allow herself the luxury of tears very often.

Connor knew Alex had issues with Grant, but he'd never probed her about what they were. Yet what he'd just seen made him realize Alex's problems began and ended with her late father. If Connor had any chance of a future with her, he had to find out exactly what those problems were and help her work through them.

Although he never considered himself to be a shining example of how to overcome a completely fucked-up life, he had done it. This time it was more important to help her, for him to step up, than he was willing to admit.

* * *

As she ran to the barn, Alex didn't care who saw her or what they thought of her. She needed to burn off her anger no matter how crazy she looked. Escaping from Finley's, from Connor and James, from her own inadequacies was more important than looking like an ass.

The sweet odor of horse, hay and manure greeted her when she burst through the door and sucked in a much-needed breath. Daniel was exiting the pony's stall and he jumped a foot in the air at her explosive entrance.

She gritted her teeth at his wary expression. Alex wanted to be alone until she calmed down. Judging by the kid's expression, he wasn't going to leave her alone, though. Truthfully he would remind her of exactly what she was trying to escape.

He clutched his chest dramatically. "What are you doing?"

"I needed to go for a ride."

"You scared me."

"Yeah, well, I thought everyone would be gone." She hoped Rusty was still in his stall, although the barn was empty of a lot of horses. No doubt the guests were out playing cowboy.

"I'm not gone."

"I can see that." She brushed past him and headed for the back of the barn. As suspected, Daniel was right on her heels.

"Can I go with you?"

"No, I'm not good company right now."

"Oh, c'mon. I can ride. I've been riding since I was two." He practically danced up and down beside her.

"I don't think so. It's not a good idea." She continued walking, trying her best to ignore the pleading.

"What if I say 'please'?"

"Sheesh, kid, did you want me to say it in Spanish? No."

"Crap." Daniel kicked at a beam, and a burst of hay floated toward the floor of the barn. "You know, it isn't easy to be a Finley, to never have any friends. I'm the only kid who lives here and nobody stays around long enough to be my friend. I thought maybe you would at least try, and, well, you're my sister."

That made Alex stop in her tracks. She heard a familiar tone in his voice, one she knew very well. It was loneliness, soul deep and painful. He was wrong about her not knowing what it felt like to be a Finley, to be so lonely she would beg someone who didn't like her for company. Oh, he was very wrong.

Alex had lived half her life dealing with it.

"Okay, you can come. But I'm not waiting long so you'd best get whatever you're riding saddled."

He let out a whoop and ran for the tack room. They spent the next five minutes saddling the horses without talking. The kid knew his stuff and was ready with a little pinto long before she finished.

She chalked it up to being rusty at taking care of horses. After all, she'd ridden many times in the last month, more than she had in ten years. The eager look on Daniel's face almost made her change her mind.

But she didn't. They led the horses out into the sunshine. Alex ignored the fact he mounted without assistance while she still used the mounting block. Once upon a time, she was as young and enthusiastic as this eight-year-old.

"Where are we going?"

"You live here, kid; why don't you pick a place?"

Daniel frowned as he adjusted the hat on his head. It was

strange how Alex had put hers on without even thinking about it. After only a week of owning a hat, she was already accustomed to not leaving the house without it.

"There's a secret trail on the north ridge. Only a few folks know about it and Dad showed it to me right before he . . . Well, I remember it 'cause I was on Buttons the pony and his legs were too short to go all the way up." Daniel turned his gaze on her and she saw the challenge in his blue eyes.

"It's hard, then?"

"Oh yeah, super hard." He smirked. "Unless you're chicken?"

"That particular insult went out of style thirty years ago. Now, let's ride to that trail so I can smush that cocky grin into the ground." She was pleased to see him grin, then spur his pinto into motion.

They rode single file toward the north side of the ranch, where there wasn't much but trees and rocks. It looked as if a horse couldn't even get through the line of huge boulders, but the kid simply rode toward them. Alex wanted to ask him what the hell he was doing, but she held her tongue, strangely trusting him.

When he made an abrupt left after a moss-covered giant, he disappeared from sight. There was a hidden path.

"Well, I'll be damned." Alex continued after him, wondering if the big bay would make it through the secret trail.

Daniel was waiting for her in the dappled sunshine of the woods. "Don't worry. Dad used to ride Rusty through here all the time. He can probably pick his way through without your help."

Alex felt the world shift beneath her as the boy compared her to her father. Her actions mirrored his as Daniel's mirrored hers. It was like she was looking into a room full of fun-house mirrors and didn't know which reflection was hers.

Her father had left a mess behind, and Alex was recognizing the fact that she'd blamed everyone else for the mistakes he'd made. Particularly this dark-haired boy who sported her eyes and her father's chin. He was lonely, just like her, and suffered, just like her. While Connor obviously spent time with the kid, he had a job to do, and an eight-year-old wasn't much help in running a ranch.

Alex's anger dissipated quickly, as if the trail held a magical quality that made her forget. Perhaps it did, or maybe she was finally coming to terms with the pain she'd carried with her for so long. Everyone made mistakes in their lives, some of them colossal enough to cause destruction or ruination.

Grant Finley had obviously tried to make up for his errors by putting everything into the ranch. She ignored most of the signs of his presence, but she couldn't ignore the boy whose blood ran through her veins.

The kid who was the closest thing to family she had. That thought was like a punch to her gut and her breath caught at the impact.

Family. Daniel was her *family.*

Alex blinked away the stinging in her eyes as she finally accepted what she'd found in Wyoming. She had lost all those she loved, had lived so long without having a family. Just recognizing what Daniel represented was enough to make her cry, apparently.

Alex took a drink of water from the bottle she'd grabbed from the barn refrigerator. The cool wetness helped her swallow the giant lump that had formed. She felt like a girl, a weak girl who had given in after fighting against a larger, stronger foe.

Only this time the foe was her own stubbornness and pride.

"What are you doing?" Daniel had ridden about twenty yards ahead of her. He twisted around and waved his arm at her. "You'll get lost if you don't keep up. You don't know this trail like me. I'm an expert."

Alex didn't laugh at him, although she did have to stifle a chuckle. "I needed a drink, oh, slave driver. I didn't know I needed your permission."

"Well, tell me next time. I ain't a mind reader, you know." He huffed like a grown man kept waiting at the door by a fussy female.

This time Alex did laugh. "You're obnoxious."

"So are you."

"At least we both agree on something." She spurred Rusty forward to join her brother.

Her brother. Her family.

Connor managed to focus on work for an hour, reviewing the reservations for the week, as well as the time sheets. It looked like several people had been putting in overtime to make up for his slacking off. Now he couldn't say whether or not it was worth it. After all, he'd now done more harm than good with Alex. She was angry at him, again, and this time he was afraid she wouldn't get over it.

A commotion out in the lobby reminded him the ranch was going on around him, without him. He rose, conscious of the stiffness in his muscles after zoning out at his desk for the last hour.

"Connor, you need to help me." Claire appeared in his doorway, panic evident on her pale face.

Connor's problems immediately forgotten, he went toward her. "What's wrong?"

"Daniel is missing."

Connor's stomach dropped. "Missing?"

"I haven't seen him in more than two hours and neither has anyone else." She looked behind him. "He's not here, is he?"

"No, he hasn't been here all day. We were supposed to go riding this weekend, but I was, uh, tied up." He didn't want to admit to Claire he was literally tied up. In Alex's bed. The very thought of what he'd been doing instead of going for a ride with Daniel made him ashamed.

The kid looked up to him as a big brother and he'd let him down. Now his worry was compounded by self-recrimination.

"When was the last time you saw him?"

Claire wrung her hands. "Breakfast, around eight o'clock. He was eating waffles when I left him to go talk to Eileen about the housekeeping assignments."

"Then let's start there and backtrack to find him." Connor took her elbow and they headed out to search.

"There's a stream up ahead. That's where we'd usually stop for lunch, then head back." Daniel sounded disappointed, as if he didn't want their ride to end.

"I didn't bring any food and it's got to be around ten thirty or eleven." She heard the sound of the stream, and its happy burble was soothing.

"I know." Daniel sighed. "But can we stay here and skip stones or hunt for treasure or something?"

Alex had no experience with kids, didn't even know how to entertain the kid. Hunting for treasure sounded so childish, and yet the thought of playing pretend for even a few hours was incredibly appealing.

"Hunt for treasure?"

Daniel stopped in a clearing by the stream and dismounted with incredibly agility. "Oh yeah, I used to do it all the time with my dad. You can find all kinds of stuff, like Indian arrowheads and fossils."

Alex should have known there would be some kind of rock a boy would consider a treasure. She stopped Rusty and looked around the clearing as she got down. The oaks spread their mighty arms wide above the grassy spot, making it into a paradise in the middle of the Wyoming woods.

The sun had warmed the air up enough to make it a perfect temperature, the rocks around the edge making natural seats. A fire pit with cold embers was in the middle of the grass, evidence there had been more than picnics taking place there. It was a romantic spot, truthfully, a nirvana for a couple to find peace and seclusion.

She shook her head at the whimsical thoughts that whirled around in her head. Who would have thought she'd be so inclined to such things? Certainly nothing in her life had been fairy tales and roses. Well, until she came back to Wyoming anyway. Then there'd been two men vying for her affections and obviously plenty of flowers and more.

"There are some caves on the other side of the ranch. Maybe we can go explore there another day." Daniel balanced on a round rock in the middle of the stream. He put his arms out and jumped to the next one. "C'mon, Alex, let's go hunting!"

Alex secured the reins to one of the enormous oak branches and followed her brother.

Connor was beginning to get a very bad feeling about Daniel's disappearance. It was going on lunchtime and Daniel seemed to have disappeared off the face of the planet. Claire was a sobbing mess in Bernice's arms when he left them in his office.

When he checked the VIP cabin, he realized Alex was not there. Maybe she'd gone off with James, but something told him she hadn't. He ran for the barn, his heart pounding as fear for Daniel whirled through him. The kid knew the ranch like the back of his hand. If he wanted to hide, he would have no problem avoiding detection for hours.

However, someone could have also snatched the boy without anyone noticing. That was his biggest fear, and he was sure it was Claire's as well. Daniel was an open, bighearted kid, too trusting. Connor tasted fear as he thought about all the terrible things that could happen to an eight-year-old.

The barn was busy with guests coming back after their morning rides. Connor caught Julio's attention and waited by the door for the older man to make his way through the milling people.

Julio must have seen something in Connor's gaze because he hurried. *"¿Qué pasa?"*

"Daniel is missing. Are there any horses gone that are unaccounted for?"

"Two of them. Rusty is gone, but Senorita Finley has been riding him. I thought perhaps she'd gone for a ride." Julio frowned. "But Raisinet is missing too. He's Daniel's favorite pinto."

"Shit."

Connor could hardly believe Alex would leave and go riding with Daniel, much less not tell anyone she'd done so. The woman had some measure of common sense. Then again, Daniel should have asked his mother's permission before going riding.

He punched the barn wall, eager for the pain that snaked up his arm from his fist. The first thing he'd do was yell at both of them; then he'd make sure they were all right.

"Can you tell what direction they rode?"

Julio shook his head. "No, too many tracks from the guests now."

"Damn. Can you saddle Thunder for me? I'll go look for them." Connor didn't wait for Julio to answer. He went straight for the phone on the wall to let Claire know the news.

Alex didn't remember the last time she'd had so much fun. Even when she slipped and her feet landed in the stream and Daniel told her, "They're cowboy boots so they're waterproof. Duh."

They knelt by the bend in the stream, the widest point that allowed them to get a drink. She cupped her hand and sucked up the delicious water. It dribbled down her chin and soon her blouse was as wet as her face.

She glanced at her brother. Daniel looked like he'd been swimming, he was so wet. Claire would likely not be pleased about that.

Her stomach rumbled and she glanced at her watch. It was two thirty, which meant they'd been gone for almost four hours. No wonder she was hungry, since she'd had only coffee for breakfast.

"Let's head back so we can get some lunch, kiddo. I'm starving."

Daniel wiped his face on an equally wet sleeve. "'Kay. I'm hungry too." He stood and dug into his pocket. "You didn't find a treasure so I'll share one with you." He handed her a pointy piece of stone. "This one is an arrowhead."

Alex stared at the stone, at the simple gift that meant so much.

David had given her presents over the years, and she appreciated each one. Yet he'd been a substitute family, a man who had given her shelter and friendship when she needed it most.

Yet this cold, wet stone in her hand meant more than every one of those gifts. Alex had been so confused, so hurt by the shit in her life, and with the simple gesture of a boy, the confusion was gone.

The arrowhead pointed the way for her; the path to take was right there in front of her. She closed her hand around the stone, the sharp edges digging into her fingers.

"Alex, you okay?"

She looked up at him and managed to nod. "Yeah, I think I finally am."

Connor got back to the barn at three, tired and annoyed. He'd gone down almost every trail and there'd been no sign of either horse or Daniel and Alex. The sun was sliding down the sky, which meant in three hours, dusk would make it hard to see and the cold would settle its blanket over the woods.

Where the hell were they?

Claire was pacing in the barn, her arms wrapped around her waist. When she spotted him, a small moan came out of her mouth.

"Let's call the police."

She nodded, her pale face enough to make him want to ride back out to find the missing siblings. Connor did the best he could to help and picked up the phone.

The sheriff arrived within fifteen minutes. Yancy Scanlon was a good lawman, one who had a young man's enthusiasm and strength. He was a lumbering six-and-a-half-foot dark-haired giant who had pushed more than one criminal toward a new direction in life simply by glowering.

He shook Connor's hand with his enormous paw. "How long has he been gone?"

"At least since nine. That's the last time he was spotted in the barn taking care of the ponies." Connor gestured toward Claire. "She's about beside herself with worry. It's not like Daniel to run off."

"So what changed?" Yancy hooked his thumbs in his belt.

"His sister arrived."

"Sister?"

"Yancy, you've got to start listening to gossip more. Don't you know Grant's daughter showed up a month ago?" Connor remembered what life had been like before she showed up, but it was distant.

"Grant's daughter is here? Where is she?" Yancy glanced around as if he expected her to come sashaying up.

"That's what you're here to find out. She's missing right along with Daniel. We think they're together, wherever the hell they are."

"Oh, that changes things a bit. How old is she?"

"Twenty-six."

Yancy rubbed his whiskered chin with one hand. "An adult woman who goes riding with her eight-year-old brother isn't usually a reason to call me."

Connor's jaw tightened. "It is when he didn't ask his mother for permission, hasn't been seen in over six hours and can't be found anywhere on the ranch or on the trails."

"Ah, gotcha." Yancy turned toward his men and started discussing the search patterns.

Connor heard the neigh of a horse and he cocked his head to listen. That was when he heard a laugh—*her* laugh. He took off running toward the north pasture and saw them riding toward the barn, side by side.

He let out a sigh of relief but didn't slow down until he reached them. Alex was smiling, her shirt obviously wet, and her expression more relaxed than he'd ever seen.

Connor wanted to strangle her.

As they approached, Daniel waved at him and they slowed to a stop. The boy must have seen something in Connor's face because his smile disappeared immediately.

"Where the hell have you been?"

Alex looked confused. "What's going on?"

Connor barely held his temper. "You disappeared with an eight-year-old boy for six hours. His mother is worried sick and the sheriff just got here to look for him."

She opened her mouth, then shut it.

"Don't you blame that child."

"I'm not planning on putting any blame on him." She met Daniel's gaze. "Let's get down there so your mom doesn't kill both of us."

"Oh, man, Alex, I'm in so much trouble." Daniel's face paled even further. "More than when I put the hot pepper in the pancake mix or when I hid all the saddle blankets."

"You did what?"

"Mom's gonna whoop me."

Connor would find out what happened later. "Get going. Now."

Daniel didn't even hesitate a second. He took off on the pinto, leaning low in the saddle. His hat even flew off but he kept going toward the barn.

Connor walked after him, picking up the boy's hat. It gave him the opportunity to accept the fact that the two of them were okay, unharmed and back at the ranch. Now, of course, he would have to relax before he talked to Alex. Connor had let his temper get the best of him too much since he'd met Alex.

He had to remember it never got him anywhere but in a shitload of trouble.

Alex rode up beside him, her face contemplative and, if he wasn't mistaken, contrite. Interesting change in his furious lover.

"I'm sorry if we worried you, Connor."

"We'll talk later." He damn sure wasn't ready to have this conversation with her yet.

"Fine. I can accept that."

"What you need to do is talk to Claire now." Connor gestured to the embracing mother and son down in the grass.

Alex rode toward them, leaving Connor by himself. Now, if he could stop shaking before he made it down there, it would be a miracle.

CHAPTER ELEVEN

Alex had never been in a situation like this. She'd been responsible for causing a significant amount of worry, and it had never occurred to her. The selfishness of taking Daniel with her, playing with him in the woods like a kid, well, it was almost embarrassing.

She gazed at Claire as she embraced Daniel. The expression on her face was one of love, in its purest form. That of a mother for her child.

Suddenly the resentment Alex had been holding tightly for Claire began to melt away. There was no rhyme or reason in how she held Claire accountable for her father's sins. The woman so obviously loved her son, it made Alex's heart hurt to watch them.

She missed her mother; the kind of hugs and affection that Alex had received were irreplaceable. She felt guilty for causing Claire so much worry. She dismounted and walked toward them, ready to face the music for the afternoon's activities.

"Claire, I—"

"Don't. Don't you dare tell me you're sorry. You are the adult here, the big sister he can't stop talking about. You can't possibly have an excuse for being so irresponsible." Claire's voice was like steel, her tone sharper than any knife.

Alex's guilt increased tenfold at the admonishment, which was well deserved, unfortunately. "I don't have an excuse. We spent the day together and it was, uh, fun. Time got away from us."

"You had fun?" Claire glanced at Daniel. "You had fun?"

"We went on a treasure hunt like I used to do with Daddy." Silent tears streamed down his face. "I'm sorry, Mama."

"And whether or not you accept my apology, I'm sorry too, Claire. You can't imagine how much." Alex hugged herself, since there was no one else around to do it.

Claire's shoulders dropped and she hugged her son again. "Ah, Daniel, there's never a dull day with you around."

"I guess you're Alex Finley."

Alex turned to find a giant beside her in the guise of a sheriff. The man blocked out the sun.

"Yes, good or bad, I'm Alex Finley."

He held out a big paw toward her. "Yancy Scanlon."

She took his hand and he barely squeezed it, although his hand practically swallowed hers. "Nice to meet you, Sheriff."

"Eh, call me Yancy. I'm glad I didn't have to search for you. Claire was about to tear me a new one, if you'll pardon the expression."

Alex's cheeks heated. "Sorry about that."

"No problem. We haven't had anything exciting happen around here in a while. It's good to keep us on our toes." Yancy looked behind her. "You need me to do anything else?"

She turned to find Connor, his face still set in granite.

"No. Thanks for coming out." Connor had never looked so fierce, and she found herself somewhat nervous to face him alone. That was a first for Alex.

He grabbed her arm. "We'll see you later, Yancy."

The big sheriff's brows went up but he just waved and walked away toward his deputies.

"Let's go, Finley." Connor marched her to Rusty. "You need to take care of your horse." He took the pinto's reins and, whether or not she liked it, they walked into the barn.

Everyone was outside, so the building was empty. Alex was glad of the chore; it brought her back to earth. The shock of realizing her mistake, her negative impact on not only Claire but everyone at the ranch, made her feel awful. Even if she felt closer to Daniel than she'd expected, her actions had caused a great deal of problems.

After unsaddling Rusty and rubbing him down, she went to the feed bin to get a scoop of oats for the bay. As she walked back with the food, she noticed the pinto's stall was closed, which meant Connor was finished. But he was nowhere in sight.

She poured the oats in Rusty's trough and he pushed her out of the way to get to it. Obviously grass hadn't been enough for the great horse. Alex closed the stall door and looked around, but still didn't see Connor.

Perhaps he was angry enough with her to go somewhere and cool off. The hairs on the back of her neck stood up and she knew that was the wrong assumption. He was close by, waiting for her.

Against her will, Alex felt a tingle race through her body, making her nipples pop and a pulse beat thick and heavy in her pussy. He was watching her.

There were two stalls at the back of the barn where the clean hay was kept. One of those doors was open and she walked toward it, confident she'd found out what he was up to.

When a hard body slammed into the back of her, she gasped in surprise. His arm snaked around her waist, pulling her flush against him and the already hard cock in his jeans. A moan escaped from her as his other hand traveled up and down her body, pausing to pinch her nipples hard.

He hadn't been the aggressor in their sex. Yet. Now that she'd shown him how she liked it, apparently Connor was ready to show her. Alex was more than ready for that.

Using his pelvis, he bumped her forward toward the stall. She tried to grab something, grip her boots into the floor, anything to halt his progress, to make things more challenging for him. Of course, he had her in the middle of the barn, and there was nothing to grab but him.

So she reached around and felt his hard-on. Her pussy clenched in anticipation of the fucking she'd get from him. It was life and death all over again, when people need to feel alive after an intense experience. Alex definitely felt alive now.

"You like this?"

She managed to make a sound of agreement although her body already told the truth for her.

"I can smell your cunt already. You want me, don't you?"

Alex squeezed him again. This time it was his turn to moan. He pressed his mouth against her ear and whispered harshly.

"I'm going to fuck you hard, up against the wall."

Alex almost creamed her jeans.

They entered the stall and he kicked it closed. Their harsh breathing echoed in the stall with bales of hay stacked every which way. Sounds from outside the barn were muted, but they told her there were people just a few feet from where they were. Anyone could hear them or see them.

Alex had never been an exhibitionist but the very idea they could be caught made her excitement notch up quite a bit. He turned her around and captured her mouth in a bruising kiss. This was no time for gentleness, and she didn't want any.

Their mouths opened and tongues dueled for control. He unbuttoned her blouse, then popped her bra clasp. His callused fingers tweaked and rolled her nipples until she nearly begged him to bite them. Her heart pounded so hard, her ribs ached—she'd never been so aroused in her life.

She yanked at his shirt and he pinned her arms against the wall. He took control and she wanted to fight it, wanted to grab it back from him, but this time Connor wouldn't let her.

"It's time you let me take the reins." He kept her pinned with his weight, sliding one leg between hers until her pussy rode his thigh.

As he pushed up against her clit, his mouth settled on one ripe nipple and bit hard. She swallowed the scream that threatened as she rode his leg.

"Take off your pants." He let her arms loose and she felt disoriented for a moment or two.

Then she heard his zipper and knew she had seconds before he'd be inside her. Her body shook with pure adrenaline as she fumbled with her clothes, standing stark naked within seconds.

He, on the other hand, had freed only his cock, which stood proudly in the shadows, jutting from his jeans.

"Suck it."

Alex didn't mind the order; in fact, she reveled in it as she dropped to her knees and took him. The hot maleness of him filled her mouth. God, he tasted so good. She grabbed the base of his shaft and massaged the sweet spot between his balls.

She lapped at the head, gently nipping the sensitive skin, smiling when he hissed. He groaned and grabbed her head, showing her what he wanted from her. Alex took his lead, eager to please him, eager to fuck him.

Her lips closed around the pulsing shaft. As she sucked him deep into her mouth, to the back of her throat, she pinched her nipple. She closed her teeth around him and bit lightly, making him jerk, pressing against the roof of her mouth.

Alex smiled inwardly and did it again. The saltiness of his precum coated her tongue. She fondled his balls and sucked harder. They tightened in her hands and she knew she had him close to coming, anticipating the gush of fluid for her to swallow.

He yanked her head away and pulled her to her feet. Connor turned her around, putting her hands on the wall and kicking her legs apart. His clothes rubbed against her as his cock slid between her wet folds.

He guided his staff into her welcoming entrance, then reached around to her breasts. Alex shook with need as he poised just barely inside her.

"Jesus, Connor, fuck me."

His fingers closed around her nipples and pinched just as he thrust inside her, embedding himself to the hilt. She bit her lip to keep the scream from exploding. Her body clenched around him so hard, she could barely tell where he ended and she began.

"So fucking tight," he whispered as he bit her earlobe and began moving inside her.

Deep, sharp thrusts, nearly impaling her on his dick. She had never known him to be so rough, and she loved it. This was a fierce fucking, a primal mating between animals. Their quickie in the cabin was nothing compared to this. It was intense; it was incredible. It wouldn't last for either of them.

Voices in the barn made her breath catch, and Connor paused. They could be caught at any moment, she naked with him fucking her. What a story that would make around the campfire.

"Come for me, baby," he commanded. "Now."

As if on cue, her body responded and she felt her pleasure building to its peak. She grunted as her hands dug into the walls, splinters lodging themselves in her skin. His grip tightened on her hips as he pounded into her, faster and faster.

The orgasm traveled north from her toes until it hit her pussy and the explosion made stars shine within her, around her, outside her.

Yes, yes, *yes*.

She shouted Connor's name in her mind as she came so hard, she stopped breathing, her heart stopped beating and her mind stopped thinking. It was the most amazing moment of her life.

He buried himself inside her as his own orgasm hit. The hot cum gushed inside her, filling her, making her own waves of pleasure continue off his. She pressed her forehead into the wood, trying to suck in a breath. Connor was shaking as much as she was.

The voices grew closer and he withdrew from inside her, leaving her a bit bereft. She wanted more, needed more, but now wasn't the time. They were about to be discovered. He shoved a bandanna at her.

"I know it's not ideal, but use it to clean up."

In the shadows he straightened his clothes while she pressed the cloth against her pulsing core. A little dizzy and trembling quite a bit, Alex managed to pull on her clothes. She picked up her boots as Connor came over and kissed her hard.

"I love you, Alex Finley."

With that, he left the stall, leaving her shaken and bewildered. The man had handed her his heart and walked away with hers.

Connor managed to keep his cool as he walked out of the barn. His entire body vibrated with enough energy to launch a damn space shuttle. He kept a grim expression on his face and sent everyone back to work, then walked Claire and Daniel back to their cabin.

What he wanted to do was run back to the barn and hold Alex until he stopped shaking.

He couldn't possibly explain what happened in that barn, but it was a turning point in their relationship. It was an elemental union that affected him right down to his bones. Then he'd actually told her he loved her.

Holy Mary and all the saints. He'd told her he *loved* her. Never mind if it was true or not; he had simply blurted what he was thinking, what he was feeling, without a thought to the consequences.

Claire was too distracted telling Daniel about how irresponsible he'd been, how worried she'd been, and how glad she was to have him safe. If she hadn't been so focused on the boy, she might have noticed Connor tripped four times, let the door slam in his face and walked through a pile of horse shit.

Oh yeah, he was in serious trouble, and her name was Alex Katherine Finley.

He felt like a heel leaving her alone in the hay stall. She'd looked as shocked as he felt. Alex also looked completely amazing, wonderful, and he had to stop himself from throwing her over his shoulder and carrying her off to his cabin.

It wasn't even four in the afternoon—he needed to do work that day other than worry and search. There was a stack of paperwork waiting for him, and he had to check all of Alex's accounting work from the previous week. Either that or he could simply let it go and trust she knew what she was doing.

Connor grabbed a soda on the way back to his office, fielding questions from curious employees. Everyone was glad to hear Daniel was safe, tutted about how little boys could cause such worry, and congratulated Connor on successfully finding him.

He didn't tell the truth—that the boy had been out for a ride with his big sister for the first time in his life. That the happiness on Daniel's face had been nearly blinding when they rode down the hill toward him. Connor had known the boy all his life, and he'd never seen such joy before. Something had happened between them out in the woods.

Connor wanted to yell at both of them for causing such strain, but he didn't. It was because of the joy, of the knowledge that whatever happened had changed their relationship. It was a stunning event, considering Connor expected Alex to fight her connection to Daniel for a very long time.

Yet apparently all they needed was a long ride in the woods and a treasure hunt. He would ask the two of them what exactly they were searching for later on. For now, Connor went back to his office and buried himself in getting the paperwork done.

He planned on locating Alex later and finishing what they'd started. Facing her after telling her of his love was nothing short of daunting. Yet he wouldn't dream of missing it for the world.

His future depended on it.

* * *

Alex filled the tub with bubbles and deliciously hot water. After her dunking in the stream, or at least partial dunking, the warmth of the tub was heavenly.

As she slid down into the water, her inner thighs stung a bit and she remembered exactly why. The sex in the barn with Connor had been intense, more so than anything else in her life. She closed her eyes and shivered at the memory even in the heat of the bath.

Connor was everything she didn't think she wanted in a man. He was bossy, opinionated and, worst of all, a cowboy. She'd run from all of that ten years ago; now she was back and found herself deeply involved with a man she barely knew.

Alex was exhausted from the ride, the emotion, the sex. She closed her eyes and lost herself in the pleasure of a bubble bath.

She didn't know if it was ten minutes or forty, but she woke suddenly, wrinkled and in lukewarm water. With aches and pains that were too much for a twenty-six-year-old body, she got herself up out of the water and wrapped herself in a warm, fluffy towel.

The sun was low on the horizon, which meant it was nearly the end of the day. She felt disoriented and tired, likely aftereffects of the injuries from the week before, the physical strain of the weekend, followed by the long ride and incredible sex.

Alex padded to the kitchen to make coffee and stopped in her tracks when she found Connor sitting at the table. Torn between anger and frustration at his behavior, she frowned at him.

"I told you not to come in here uninvited."

"I was born in Bakersfield, California. My mother was a waitress, my dad an auto-body guy. I had four older brothers and two dogs. We were a blue-collar family from a bad neighborhood." He sounded contemplative, even sad. "What the world didn't know was that my father was a thief, a man who ran a chop shop out of his garage."

Alex sat down at the table, her surprise and annoyance overshadowed by her own curiosity over Connor's story. "I didn't know you were from California."

A ghost of a smile flitted across his face. "There's a lot of things you don't know about me."

"Make me coffee and I'm ready to listen." She pushed aside any lingering tiredness as she watched him quickly make her a cup of steaming brew, then add just the right amount of cream.

That he knew exactly how she liked her coffee should have worried her. It didn't.

"Did your dad get caught?"

"My brothers had learned the business from him. They were a regular crime family, boosting cars and drinking, picking up women. Since I was the youngest, they held off on initiating me into the business until I was thirteen. To them, that was the golden age for learning the trade." His laugh was nowhere near humorous. "By fourteen, I could break into a car in thirteen seconds flat. I was quick and small, and that meant I could hide easily in tight spots. On my fifteenth birthday, my brothers crashed a society ball parking lot, manned by valets, to try to get me a Porsche."

She heard his voice tighten, winding up like a spring. Something terrible had marred that birthday, something that had changed the course of his life.

"What happened?"

He looked out the window, his gaze faraway and full of memories. "The valets were armed. Two of my brothers were killed point-blank, the other two wounded so badly that one of them died on the operating table. The other lost his sight in one eye and his right arm."

Alex gasped and took his cold hand in her own. "Did you see it happen?"

"Oh yeah, I had a front-row seat underneath the blue Porsche that was to be mine. My father came barreling in like a lunatic and they beat him until he lost consciousness. He was tried and convicted, sent to prison in Chino. My mother wept for weeks, barely leaving her bed to even eat." He swallowed hard enough that she actually heard it. "I was the only one left, the baby boy who had nothing that wasn't given to him by his brothers and father."

Alex took a sip of her coffee and tried to come up with the right words to express herself. She understood pain, all too well. He was obviously telling her a story he thought she needed to hear, perhaps to understand just who he was.

"My father was killed in prison during a gang fight, my oldest brother ended up in rehab depressed and suicidal, and my mother, well, she just kind of drifted away until her body caught up with her mind. Then I had no one left but myself."

"How old were you?"

"Sixteen."

She'd known there was a connection there, something that bonded them together even though they were so different. Both of them had lost their families at sixteen, had set off on their own in the cruel world to fend for themselves.

Her heart ached for the childhood Connor never had. At least the first fifteen years of her life had been idyllic compared to Connor's. It sounded like he loved his family, even if they were a bunch of criminals who'd paid the ultimate price for their crimes. Connor had to live with what they'd left behind, and fight against the awful memories.

"How did you end up in Wyoming?"

He shook his head. "I hitched my way out of Bakersfield, out of California, with twenty bucks and a huge chip on my shoulder for company. I spent two years hustling people out of money, trying not to sell myself unless I was desperate. Just surviving."

Alex felt tears spring to her eyes. "Oh, Connor."

"It's okay. You probably did the same thing. Maybe we even passed each other along the way." He shrugged one shoulder. "I had been put in foster homes, escaped, was arrested, over and over again. I stole your dad's wallet, you know. At the county fair, but by then I was eighteen and could have served real time for my crimes. He dragged me in front of a judge and asked to take responsibility for my sorry ass."

Connor kissed the back of her hand. "He might have been a shitty father to you, but he saved my life. I came to Finley's and spent years working off my rage, my self-pity and my piss-poor past. I wanted you to know just how much this ranch means to me."

Alex nodded. "I think I understand. I had help from someone who saved my life too."

"Then you do understand. I wouldn't be who I am if it weren't for Grant. The judge was going to put me in for hard time. It was only because Grant put his own ass on the line for me that I didn't go to prison." He finally met her gaze. "I still don't know why he did it, but I'll spend the rest of my life being grateful for it. I love this place, Alex, and everything about it."

"Thanks for telling me. I, uh, think I owe you an apology. A big one." She tried to clear the tightness in her throat with a gulp of coffee. "I didn't know about you and my father. I understand why you want to keep this ranch going and what it means to you. But you have to understand what it means to *me*. I've told you my father left my mother when she was dying. This place held the ghosts of my family. The pieces left behind when my mother died and my father ran."

Connor frowned. "Tell me."

Alex didn't intend on reliving the most excruciating moment in her life, but now that the door was open, the flood started. She needed to tell someone, to unburden herself of the enormous weight she'd carried for so long.

"My mother was dying of breast cancer. They didn't even catch it until it was at stage three, and within a month, it was already at stage four. It had metastasized throughout her organs, and all we could do was make her comfortable and watch her die." Alex's mouth went dry and her heart still beat, although it was so painful, her breath came in tiny gulps.

Connor seemed to sense she was struggling and he took her hands in his. The warmth of him helped a little but not much.

"You can tell me."

She let out a shaky sigh. "She wasted away to nothing, barely seventy-five pounds. Bernice could hardly be around her, my father had left a month before, and my mother was in agony. She cried for God to take her. I barely slept. It was like living in a hell I couldn't escape." The black, sick feeling crept through her, leaving bile in her mouth. She managed to take a sip of coffee.

"It's okay, baby; you don't have to go on."

"Yes, I do. Please. I need to get this out." She ignored the nausea and told herself she had to finish. She *had* to.

"Okay, then let's get comfortable."

Connor picked her up and carried her to the chaise lounge. He lay down and snuggled her into the crook of his arm. His warmth surrounded her, made her feel safe and secure. She breathed in his scent and felt stronger.

"I knew she wouldn't last more than a week or two, but every day felt like a hundred. I was only sixteen, still a kid, with a dying mother and an absent father." She closed her eyes, but the tears still slipped out from beneath her lids. "She begged me, Connor, *begged* me to give her the bottle of morphine and leave. I refused her every time she asked, but then one night when I'd had no sleep in three days and she'd been crying for the last twelve hours, I—I snapped."

"What do you mean, you snapped?" He sounded concerned, not judgmental, thank God.

"I gave her the bottle, knowing she was going to take all of them. I gave her the means to kill herself, Connor. *I killed my mother.*"

He held her while her body shook, her tears flowed and she grieved for the loss of her innocence, of her idyllic existence, of her family. Her guilt over her actions had festered within her, poisoning her soul bit by bit.

"You didn't kill her, Alex. She wanted to end it, not just for herself but for you. I'm sure she saw how you were suffering, how all of it was slowly sapping the life from you." He stroked her head. "I think she loved you enough to save you, to give you the peace of knowing she was no longer in pain."

It was what Alex needed to hear, to help lift the guilt that had nearly destroyed her. She held on to him, this man who had become a part of her life, the owner of her heart, the other half of her soul.

Alex slept in his arms, both of them relieved of their burdens, safe and loved. Together.

The snick of a light switch woke him. Connor squinted through the soft light to see Alex dressed in jeans and a T-shirt, her hair in a ponytail.

"Hey, there." She sipped at a bottle of water. "I'm thinking you haven't slept well lately."

"What makes you say that?" Perversely, he asked even though it was the absolute truth.

"Bags under your eyes, the fact that you snored loud enough to shake loose a couple of bats, and I've been making enough noise to wake the neighbors in Idaho but you didn't stir." She sat down and handed him a bottle of water.

Connor was surprised he'd slept, truthfully. He had meant to comfort Alex and in turn be comforted by her. They'd shared the darkest parts of themselves and cemented the bond between them. Then he'd fallen asleep so deeply she could hardly wake him.

"What time is it?" He sat up, his head muzzy and his eyes gritty.

"About eight. I was going to order supper in, but I didn't know how long you would sleep." She glanced at her feet, which were encased in red socks. "Actually, I didn't want to go alone, seeing as how everyone on this ranch is pissed at me."

Connor stifled a yawn. "Nah, no one is pissed at you. They were just worried about Daniel. The staff loves him and sometimes people forget he's only eight. This gave them a wake-up call to stop accepting whatever he does as status quo."

"So he won't be spiking the pancake mix again?"

"How did you find out about that?" Connor took a drink of water.

She shrugged "He told me."

Another time, another day, Connor would ask her what had happened during her afternoon with Daniel. For now, they'd had enough turmoil to last them at least a few days if not a week. Her stomach yowled into the silence, and sweetly enough, she blushed.

"Oops."

Connor grinned and kissed her quick. "Let's go see if Bernice has any food left for us."

"You might want to comb your hair first. It's, uh, looking like a rooster's head right about now." She played with his curls, a smile in her eyes.

Connor grabbed her and pulled her softness against him. Oh, but that was a mistake, yes indeedy. His body sprang to life even though it had been only hours since their intense encounter in the barn. Her eyes widened as she felt what he couldn't hide.

"Now?"

Regretfully, he shook his head. "No, not now. I don't think I would be able to walk if we did."

Connor held her close for a minute, reveling in the feeling of her heart beating against his, in the closeness they had developed. It was a new sensation to him, one he wasn't entirely sure of, or comfortable with. She brought out things in him he didn't know existed, and this cuddly, snuggly stuff was only the tip of it.

For pity's sake, he'd already told her he loved her. And she hadn't brought it up or returned the favor. He didn't want to believe that meant she didn't feel the same way. No, that couldn't be it. She was vulnerable and still recovering from a number of emotional blows. When she was ready, she would tell him she loved him.

Connor refused to accept any other scenario.

He leaned back and kissed her forehead, nose and lips. "Now, let's go get you fed before the wolves start howling in response to your belly."

Within a few minutes, they left the cabin and walked down the shadowy path to the mess hall. It was a quiet night, with a light breeze that just barely made the leaves whisper. Her hand was warm, tucked against his. Connor didn't remember the last time he felt so stress free, so relaxed, so content with life.

He didn't pretend to understand it. Connor usually analyzed everything to pieces before he accepted it, but not in this case. Something told him it was divine intervention that brought Alex back to the ranch, to meet him and become a part of who he was.

Maybe Grant was up there pulling a few strings, trying to make both his biological daughter and the son of his heart happy. In this case, happy together.

It was almost eight thirty by the time they made it to the mess hall and by then it was nearly empty. A few folks were cleaning up the tables and mopping the floors. Connor made a beeline for the kitchen. Knowing Bernice as he did, she would be waiting for him.

He pushed open the door to find her at the stove, her hands on her hips and a scowl on her face.

"It's about damn time. I was about to send out a search party for you. You know better than to—Alex, is that you?" Bernice craned her neck to see behind Connor.

Alex stepped forward, evidently reluctant to face the older woman's reaction. Obviously she'd been subject to more than her share of Bernice's lectures.

"Yep, it's me."

"Well, I have both of you problem children, then, don't I?

I can't believe the mess we had today with people running around like chickens with their heads cut off." Bernice shook her graying head. "I thought I'd have to smack a few upside the head with my frying pan. You should know better, young lady, than to keep that boy out so long without his mama knowing about it."

"I know, Bernice. I've already apologized to Claire."

"Claire? I ain't worried about her. She's stronger than she looks, even if she likes to cry like a baby herself. No, *I* need an apology. I about worried myself sick about both of you." Bernice waggled one finger. "In between this one not sleeping or eating and taking people's noses off with that sharp tongue of his, and you tearing around here like a twister, it's enough to drive a body to distraction."

Connor simply let her rant. He used to try to explain himself, but discovered the best method was to simply let her run out of steam. It was far less painful.

"Bernice, I didn't mean—"

"Oh, the world is full of good intentions. I know you didn't mean to cause no pain or suffering, or maybe you did. Ain't my place to judge, but I've watched you since you been here. Now, it's about time to let go of that yoke you're carrying on your neck and let the past go." Bernice was building up a good head of steam. Connor smelled the pot roast and gravy and his mouth watered, but he stood there and took his verbal lashing like a good boy.

"I did."

"And I don't just mean visiting your father's grave. I mean—Wait, what did you say?" Bernice stared at Alex and, for the first time since Connor knew her, she was speechless.

"I said I did." Alex walked toward her, arms outstretched. "I spent the day with Daniel and realized I wasn't alone in the world. I have family and it's here at Finley's. Then, well, then there's Connor."

He didn't know what that meant, but it sure as hell sounded good.

"You—you did?" Bernice's eyes were suspiciously moist. "Child, I am so proud of you." She pulled Alex into a bear hug so fierce, he heard a few joints pop. At least he hoped it was joints and not bones.

"Thank you, Bernice." Alex's voice was muffled by the bigger woman's embrace.

"Your mama would be proud too." Bernice held Alex at arm's length and met her gaze.

"You know, don't you? What I did." Alex was asking her mother's friend for forgiveness; he heard it in her voice.

"Oh, Alex, of course I knew. She begged me every time I saw her, but I was too much of a coward to help." Bernice hugged her again. "You are as brave as she was, the spitting image of that woman down to the steel in your spine."

This time when he gazed at Alex's face, the relief and joy he saw there made his throat tighten up. She had done what she could for her dying mother, had carried the burden of the guilt for so long, and was now able to set it aside. He hoped that meant she'd be staying at the ranch, staying in his life, for good.

"Can we eat now? I'm starving." His voice sounded husky and he wondered if they noticed.

"Typical man. There are only two parts of the body a man thinks with, and neither of them is on his shoulders." Bernice wiped her eyes with her apron and let out a huge sigh. "I made pot roast, so sit down at the corner table there and I'll serve up some for you. Connor, get you both a drink from the refrigerator."

He did as he was bade and came back with two cold beers. Alex took one with a grateful expression and took a long tug from the bottle. Connor sat down and did the same.

Bernice came over with two heaping plates of pot roast with gravy, potatoes, carrots and biscuits. Connor was hungrier than he'd been in months, maybe even years. They grinned at each other over the mountain of food.

"Well, whatcha waiting on? Dig in so I can get my old bones to bed tonight. Lord, what you children put me through." Bernice mumbled to herself as she went back to the stove and started clearing away the dishes she'd saved the food in for them.

As he dug into the delicious meal, he glanced up at Alex. She hadn't moved, or picked up her fork. He frowned, asking her without words what was wrong.

"Nothing's wrong. Don't worry. I'm just, well, I'm embarrassed to admit that I'm happy." She looked down at her plate. "I used to ignore the world around me, figuring nothing would ever touch me again. And I can't believe how different my life was a month ago. It sounds corny, but I'm glad to be sitting here in the mess hall kitchen eating with you."

"It's not corny at all. I'm pretty lucky too." He looked into her blue eyes and saw the future shining back at him. Before he said something stupid again, like tell her he loved her, he smiled. "I mean, Bernice never lets me eat back here."

Alex laughed and started eating. Connor ate with the knowledge they would have that conversation soon, but just not then. It had been too intense already and it was only Monday.

CHAPTER TWELVE

"I really do need to speak with you, Alex. It's quite urgent." James's normally smooth voice sounded off, as if he were in trouble. It wasn't Alex's business, of course, but he'd called her again.

Her tiny office was cozy and it had become her little hidey-hole. As soon as they hooked up the phone and somehow shoehorned in the filing cabinet, she was content with her little cave.

She leaned back in the chair and stared at the ceiling. "Can't we just talk on the phone? I'm working."

"Working? You're working at the ranch?" He sounded incredulous.

"I do have a brain, James, as well as accounting experience. I'm taking over the books."

The silence that followed her statement was uncomfortable to say the least. It was as if the air on the phone had gotten charged with a bolt of lightning.

"I hadn't realized you were doing anything at the ranch besides riding and living there." James's tone had changed but she couldn't put her finger on exactly what it had changed to.

"I can't just do nothing. I've worked for years and don't consider myself a woman of leisure, even if I own half a guest ranch." It sounded good to say that out loud. She didn't quite have the half ownership yet, but if she stayed there another eleven months, it would be hers.

"I can understand that. I respect hard work and a strong work ethic. You obviously have both." He was petting her with words again.

"Cut the shit, James. What do you want?" She was tired of being manipulated by the man.

"There's something that's come to my attention and I must speak to you in person about it. Please, Alex. I wouldn't ask if it wasn't important."

She believed he would but that was beside the point. It was four in the afternoon on a Friday and Connor hadn't said anything about evening plans. Alex could meet with James and then perhaps have dinner with Connor. In the VIP cabin.

"Fine, but I've only got an hour. Do you want to drive over here or meet in town?"

"Thank you, Alex, thank you. Why don't I drive over there again? We can meet in the parking lot as we did before." He truly did sound grateful, no matter what bullshit he was peddling.

Alex was going to tell him for certain there was no possibility she would sell her half of Finley's ranch. In the last month, it had become evident she belonged there; the land was in her blood, her heart and her soul. James would just have to recognize he wouldn't be able to annex the land.

"I'll be there in fifteen minutes. It looks like it's snowing so I won't stay long." With that he was gone.

Alex stood and shut down her laptop, eager to find Connor to discuss their plans. The idea they could have dinner together, perhaps in bed, was more than appealing. Food play was on her list of things to try one day. With a snowy, chilly night ahead, it was the perfect time.

She smiled as she walked down the hallway, amazed to find herself feeling happy. Who knew how much coming home would mean to her? She peeked in the door of Connor's office but it was dark and empty.

With only a small pout, she went back to her office to get her coat, hat and gloves. The air was beyond cold after the sun went down. The crispness of the morning air could make her nose hairs freeze; at night it made her lips blue. Strangely enough, she had missed that frigid taste in the air in California.

Fifteen minutes later, she peered out the window from the main office, waiting for James. In the pit of her stomach she was a little nervous and couldn't explain exactly why. He'd been a gentleman most of the time, except of course when he tried to grope her. And the time he punched her out.

An outsider might think she'd lost her mind by agreeing to meet with him. However to Alex this was the final time she was going to see him, a last farewell. They might run into each other in town—after all, Lobos was quite small—but she didn't intend on seeing him outside of casual contact again.

Connor would be happy about that, but she wasn't doing it for him. James almost represented the life she used to lead, the meaningless existence where she'd floated around like a cloud in the sky.

She'd been pushed by the wind to move this way and that, unable to get herself on the ground and steer her own destiny.

Wyoming had rescued her from that nebulous life, and James was the means for her to say good-bye to it, to David, to all she'd hidden behind for ten years. Put in perspective, this was a monumental parting of the ways.

Feeling stronger, Alex successfully squashed any nervousness she felt. She saw the black Lexus pull up and headed for the door. Claire was just walking in, her nose red from the cold air. She looked behind her and saw the car, then frowned at Alex.

"Where are you going, Alex?"

"I'm just talking to him, Claire." Alex buttoned her coat, waiting for her stepmother to read her the riot act, or at least disapprove. She did neither. "You're not going to tell me I'm nuts? Or that I shouldn't be consorting with the enemy?"

Claire unwrapped the scarf from around her head. "No, that's not my business, of course. You're a grown woman with a mind of your own. I wouldn't think you had any intention of listening to me anyway. You have that in common with your father."

Alex stopped in midmotion, surprised by the comparison. "Are you trying to say I'm stubborn like my father?"

Claire shrugged. "I'm saying nothing that I say will change your mind so I won't say anything. Simple as that."

"Then what were you going to tell me?"

"I was going to ask you to be careful. James has tried to paw me a time or two, and he's not a small man to fend off. I'm sure you know that, but I wanted to say it anyway." Claire hung her coat on the rack and peered out the window at the car. She frowned again.

Alex was shocked to realize Claire was concerned about her safety. This was a new development, one that made her feel, well, kind of warm inside. She smiled at her stepmother. "Don't worry. I've handled James's octopus-like tendencies before. I plan on having a ten-minute conversation with him, then having dinner with Connor."

Alex walked out the door with Claire's gaze following her, and to Alex's surprise, she was most definitely comforted by the concern. She and her stepmother were only about ten years apart in age, so she wasn't old enough to actually be her mother. However, it felt like an older sister was keeping an eye out for her, watching her back.

The cold air slapped Alex in the face as soon as she stepped outside. The air definitely smelled like snow; it would be a great night to be indoors beside a fire with a naked Connor beside her. The thought warmed her immediately and she could hardly wait to see him. If that was love, she'd have a second helping, and perhaps a third. Alex knew at that moment she'd tell him she loved him as soon as they were alone.

With a spring in her step, she went toward the waiting Lexus and knocked on the window. The exhaust puffed out clouds into the cold air.

Alex leaned toward the door and peered in. "James, if you're not going to talk to me, I'm going back inside."

She wasn't prepared for the clawlike grip on her neck. As she struggled, whoever it was reached out and opened the car door. Alex yelped as she was shoved inside.

Connor surveyed his handiwork in the VIP cabin and nearly patted himself on the back. He'd stocked up the logs for the fire, laid out a smorgasbord of fruit and other sweets on a platter and had a nice white wine chilling in a bucket.

He glanced at his watch and saw it was almost six already. Alex would likely be looking for him—he couldn't wait to surprise her. He had a feeling the fruit and sweets would be a part of their bed play, or maybe floor play, that night. His dick twitched at the thought of licking chocolate sauce from her nipples.

Oh yeah, time to find Alex.

Leaving a single lamp lit, he left the cabin and headed for the main office. He didn't tell her what he was doing because he wanted to surprise her. The hard truth was, they hadn't had a conversation about their relationship or their future. He wanted to have it, and soon, before any other disaster happened.

He nodded to everyone he saw, smiling like the lovesick fool he was. If Grant saw him now, he'd likely smack him upside the head and tell him to stop acting like a pussy and be a man. Grant was hard on the outside, and he expected everyone to march to that beat. Connor could see how it would be hard for a little girl, one who never felt as if she could please her father. Alex was tough for a reason, and it made Connor love her even more.

The lobby was deserted except for the night clerk, Dan Fielding, another college student, who waved as Connor passed by on his way to Alex's little office. He intended on giving her something bigger, but she'd settled in there as if it were a clubhouse. Perhaps in another month or so, they could find a more spacious spot for her.

The little room was empty and dark, as was his office and every other nook and cranny in the building. He walked back to the desk.

"Have you seen Alex?"

Dan shook his head. "No, but I've only been on shift ten minutes. Jennifer was working and I think I heard her say she was going to the mess hall for dinner."

"Thanks." Connor went back out into the cold, hoping he could catch Alex before she found his surprise. Outside, gently falling snowflakes began to dust the ground. It was getting colder faster than expected. He reached the mess hall in five minutes and found Jennifer chatting with Bernice. They both turned to look at him as he approached.

"You know, it's a good thing I'm not the jealous type or I'd pitch a fit over the way you've thrown me over for Alex." Bernice punched him in the arm.

Connor smiled. "You know I'll always love you, B." He kissed her cheek and to his utter surprise, she blushed. "Have you seen Alex?"

Jennifer frowned. "I saw her about five o'clock. She was talking with Claire and then went out the front door. I didn't see her come back in so I figured she was with you."

"No, she's not with me." Connor tried to ignore the niggling feeling of worry. "Thanks."

He took a moment to look around the mess hall, but Alex wasn't there. Claire and Daniel, however, were over in the corner at one of the private tables. Connor headed straight toward them, eager to find out what Claire knew about Alex's whereabouts.

Claire was smiling at her son when he walked up, and as soon as she saw him, the smile disappeared. "Connor, what are you doing here?"

That niggling feeling began to grow larger. "What do you mean?"

"I thought you were having dinner with Alex. She told me so herself when I saw her in the main building."

"At five o'clock."

"Yes, around five. She was, uh, taking care of some business and then said she was going to have dinner with you." Claire's expression became as worried as his. "Oh, Connor, I told her to be careful."

Thump, thump, thump. His heart beat madly as dread inched out worry.

"Why did you tell her to be careful? What was she doing?" He squatted beside the table since his legs began to shake.

Claire pinched her lips together and shook her head.

"Claire, dammit, tell me what she was doing that she needed to be careful."

"You shouldn't cuss, Connor. A gentleman never does it around a lady," Daniel piped in.

"She said she was only going to talk to him for ten minutes and then spend the evening with you. I didn't approve but I'm not her mother so I had no way to stop her."

Fear now joined dread and jumped up and down on his spine. "Who?" He didn't need to ask but did anyway.

"James Howard."

"Fuck."

"Connor, you cussed again." Daniel sounded as worried as Connor felt. The boy was smart enough to sense something was wrong.

"Tell me what you know, Claire. Now." Connor leaned in close to her. His mouth had gone cotton dry to accompany his racing heart and shaky legs.

"She told me she needed to talk to him, but it was only going to be ten minutes. Then she went out the door. It was too dark to see very far but I know it was James's Lexus." Claire's face had grown paler. "I'm sorry, Connor. I should have made sure she was okay."

"Alex is a grown woman and doesn't need a babysitter." Connor had trouble believing his own words, but at the moment he felt panic creeping over him. "She's been gone over an hour, nearly an hour and a half, and she intended on being gone ten minutes?"

"I thought she came back already. I'm sorry, Connor," Claire repeated. "I'll help look for her."

Grateful for the support, they left Daniel with Bernice and began their search of the grounds for Alex. As he suspected, she was nowhere to be found, not even in Rusty's stall. Connor's panic had given way to fury at James Howard. No doubt the son of a bitch was trying to find a way to force Alex to give in to him and sell her half of the ranch. He'd already tried that trick with Grant more than once.

Connor got back to his office with Claire on his heels and called the Howard ranch. Whoever answered the phone told him James was gone for the evening.

Connor's next call was to the sheriff's office.

Alex was furious. James was virtually keeping her prisoner in his car as they drove aimlessly around back roads in the pitch black, with snow coming down in buckets around them. It had started off as small flakes, but it was quickly turning into a full-on snowstorm.

"Take me back to Finley's and I won't press charges," she repeated for the umpteenth time.

"Not until you see reason." James flashed a smile at her. "I only want to relieve you of the burden of running a guest ranch. It's more headache than reward. You and I both know a California girl like you could never be happy in a backwoods place like this."

"Actually, I'm a Wyoming girl, born and bred, James, in case you'd forgotten. I'm happy at Finley's, plan on staying on, actually, and I am not selling. How clear do I have to make it?" She was tempted to get out of the car and walk, but she had no idea where she was, and the snow made it impossible to see more than three feet ahead of her. She was stuck in the damn Lexus until he decided to bring her back.

Rat bastard.

"Ah, but Alex, you don't understand. I won't take no for an answer. I must have the property or my ranch will wither and die." His coaxing tone had changed, becoming a bit darker and harder. "The water has dried up on my land and Finley's has an endless supply from the mountain stream. I need that water or my cattle will die."

"So we can put in a tributary and filter water to your property. We can cut a deal for the water, but you're not getting the land. I'm not selling and I'm not leaving. Ever." Alex firmly believed what she said, which meant she had made the decision to stay in Wyoming. A huge weight lifted off her shoulders and she knew she'd made the right choice.

James was quiet as the car silently rode along on the streets. The light snowflakes swirled on the pavement as they rode over them. It would have been a nice ride if she hadn't been with James. He made her tense and uncomfortable. Alex was the kind of woman who lived by her instincts about people and she'd been right to mistrust him from the start, no matter how charming he had been.

"I'm sorry to hear that, Alex. I had hoped you would be more open-minded about selling the ranch and about me." He sighed and fiddled with the zipper on his jacket. "Disappointing, to say the least."

"I suppose you'll just have to get over it. Now, take me back to Finley's, please." She'd had enough of the obtuse conversation. More than enough.

"I'm afraid I can't do that."

"Excuse me?" Her heart began to pound as she realized just how isolated they were out in the blackness of the night with only snow for company.

"Claire isn't as strong as you are. She'll give in to my demands if you're not around to influence her. The boy is of course no problem. Connor will need to be eliminated as well, though." James's voice had hardened, becoming as frigid as the air surrounding the car.

"'Eliminated as well'? James, what the hell are you talking about? This isn't an Old West movie where you can just off people you don't like." She managed not to sound afraid but it was very, very hard.

"Oh, but it is. You see, this is still the West, and men are still men if they own land. The more they own, the more powerful they are. I intend on being the most powerful man in the state of Wyoming." He turned to her, his face a mask of cold fury in the bluish light from the dashboard. "You will not be the bitch who ruins it for me."

Alex suffered a combination of shock, terror and rage. Before she could respond to his threat, she realized he wasn't just playing with his zipper; he had something in his coat.

The gleam of metal in the meager light was her only indication he had pulled out a gun and was pointing it at her.

Two thoughts flew through her mind. The first was that she hadn't told Connor she loved him and she'd regret that for the next ten seconds of her life. The second was that James intended to kill her.

Alex started fighting for her life.

* * *

Connor paced around the front of the main building and threw up his hands in disgust. "Yancy, what the fuck is going on? She's been gone for an hour and a half and no one has seen her. That bastard could have done anything to her by now."

He wanted to do something, anything, to help find her. He'd called around to everyone he knew, but no one had seen James or Alex. Frustration and fear were eating away at him.

The sheriff looked odd with his brown hat covered in snow, like a great big winter sculpture. "There's nothing I can do right now. It hasn't even been a day, much less two. That's the regulation for finding an adult who's missing."

Connor grabbed Yancy's coat. "I don't give a shit about the regulations. She's in trouble. I know it. I feel it in here." He thumped his chest.

"I can appreciate that, Connor, but your feeling ain't gonna count for much."

Red-hot rage poured through Connor. "It counts to me! I love her, Yancy. I won't let anything happen to her because of your bullshit rules. I'll find her myself."

"That doesn't sound like a smart idea."

Connor stalked toward his truck, determined to find Alex come hell or high water. He wouldn't let anyone or anything stop him, even a deputy the size of a Volkswagen. She was too important to him for that. Most of his life had been spent doing whatever he felt like, chasing a thrill, screwing around. It left no room for being afraid because he had to be fearless. Connor hadn't even been sure he could feel fear, but he knew the answer to that question now.

He was flat-out terrified something had happened to Alex.

"Connor, wait." Yancy was right on his heels. "I can't open an investigation yet, but I can help you look for her."

"Fine. You take your car and search in town and I'll start at Howard's place." Truthfully he wanted to tear over there and kick the shit out of the man, but he needed to find Alex first. Revenge could wait until after she was safe.

"Oh, no, you know I can't let you go on private property. He's had you arrested twice already for doing that. I'll go to Howard's ranch and you stay on the main roads and in town." Yancy leaned toward him, his bulk repeating the message a bit more forcefully.

Connor gritted his teeth. "Fine. I'll have the CB on channel three. You let me know the second you find anything."

"I can do that. Connor, listen, we'll find her. You know, maybe she just decided to skip town or go to a bar to relax."

Connor shook off Yancy's suggestion. "She didn't fucking leave and she didn't go to a bar. Alex is in trouble; do you understand that? Howard is a sneaky son of a bitch and he's up to something. Whatever it is it's bad, as bad as Grant."

Yancy frowned. "What do you mean as bad as Grant?"

He'd never told anyone of his suspicions about his friend's untimely death, but now he realized he should have. "I know you're the sheriff and you rely on evidence, but my gut and everything in my soul tells me Howard had something to do with Grant's accident."

Yancy's dark eyes widened. "What the hell would make you think that?"

"With Grant out of the way, James tried his best to hang around and convince Claire to sell the ranch. It was too convenient; he even had legal documents already drawn up at the fucking funeral. She told me he cornered her once, scared the hell out of her." Connor ground his teeth together. "The bastard was the first one at the scene when Grant was killed! He's the one that called you, remember? I could never prove anything, but he was acting odd and my gut told me James had something to do with Grant's death. He wanted the land, he wanted the water, he wanted everything that Finley's is, and now that includes Alex."

"Big accusations, Connor. Can you back them up?"

"Not yet, but I'll do my damnedest to find proof tomorrow. For now I'd like to haul ass out of here and look for Alex. Is that okay with you?" Connor was beyond having even a shred of patience. He was practically humming with a need to find her, keep her safe, tell her he loved her.

Before Yancy could answer, Connor jumped in his truck and shouted, "Channel three!" behind him as he slammed the door.

He didn't expect the passenger door to open. Claire climbed in without hesitation.

"She's my family too, even if she doesn't believe it yet. I should have kept watch, should have looked out for her. I'm her stepmother, for God's sake." Her chin trembled. "Grant would have wanted me to take care of her even if she's as stubborn as he was. I want to help find her."

Connor nodded, his already healthy respect for Claire going up a notch or two. They set off together into the inky darkness with only the headlights and the swirling snow for company.

The streets were nearly deserted, as they always got after six o'clock in a small town like Lobos. Having Claire in the passenger seat allowed him to look for Alex twice as fast. They both peered out the windows as they drove slowly down each street. No shadows revealed a Lexus, no parking lot a stray car, and no Alex.

By six forty-five, they had been through Lobos twice and

Connor was done taking the safe route. Yancy be damned, he had to look for them on the Howard property. It was huge, about forty thousand acres' worth.

Connor had been following the rules for so long, being a good ranch manager, a good friend, hell, even a good quasi-son to Bernice, brother to Claire and uncle to Daniel. It was time to shrug off the mantle of being what everyone expected him to be. This time Connor had to follow his heart.

He should get on the CB and tell the sheriff about where he was going, but he didn't. Claire didn't protest either as he drove out of town, heading straight for the Howard ranch. He was going to find Alex or die trying.

Life had kicked them both so many times, they couldn't lose each other now.

James held fast to the gun even as she scratched and yanked at his hand to try to take it from him. Alex's mouth was dry as dirt as they struggled for possession of the weapon. The car was still moving although the ride felt more like a bronc busting than a road.

They must have driven off-road, something a Lexus was not intended for. He pushed against her hold, the gun barrel turning with the sheer force of his strength. Alex should have jumped out of the car while they were still moving. Even if she was in the dark and snow, she would have found her way somehow.

Now, if she let go of his arm, he'd shoot her. If she even blinked, he would gain the upper hand. Alex was still trapped in the car, and this time she was fighting for her life.

He twisted her left wrist and she felt something pop, but Alex ignored the agony and held fast. She leaned forward and bit his hand. Warm blood coated her mouth as her teeth sunk into his skin.

"Fucking whore!" He let go of the wheel and grabbed a handful of her hair. As he yanked out clumps of her hair, Alex had never felt such pain before, but she didn't let go of his hand.

She was going to make him either let go of the gun or allow her to bite off his thumb. It was primal, brutal and bloody. Alex had wondered if she was ever put in a situation to fight or flee what she would do. Now she knew she would fight.

James leaned toward her and the car surged forward. His foot must've been too close to the gas pedal, but that didn't appear to faze him.

Tears burned her eyes as he tried to strangle her with his left hand. Suddenly there was a feeling of weightlessness; then a thunder slammed into them, as if the heavens opened up and smote both of them. Glass exploded around her and the roof of the car met her face. She heard a scream, which she vaguely realized was her own.

The last thing Alex heard was the gun going off.

Connor saw the headlights going around in crazy circles up ahead. He couldn't tell exactly what field the car was in because of the snow, but his gut told him it was Alex and James.

"There, do you see?" He pointed as they made their way down the hill toward the grazing fields.

Claire peered through the windshield. "I see something but I don't know what it is."

"It's that bastard; I know it is. If he's hurt her, I'm going to kill him." Connor didn't recognize his own voice, so deep was the hate and rage in his tone.

"I hope that's not true. You are too good of a person to commit murder." Claire could always be counted on to be the voice of reason.

In this case, Connor wasn't listening a bit. He fully intended on seeking revenge on James Howard for the death of Grant Finley and everything else he'd done to Alex. If she was hurt or—he swallowed hard at the thought—dead, there was no question in his mind he'd pull out the rifle from the rack behind him and blow James's head clean off his body.

As they neared the field, the CB radio crackled with Yancy's voice.

"Connor, where the hell are you?"

The headlights disappeared and Connor's stomach dropped to his knees. If he turned off the lights, or left the field completely, they would never find the car. He stomped on the gas and careened across the field toward where he'd last seen the headlights.

"Connor, come on back now. You hear me?"

Claire was wisely quiet as they bounced in the cab like a couple of pinballs. When they got close enough, he could see the tire tracks in the snow and followed them forward until he reached the edge of the ravine.

This time his stomach flipped sideways and his heart lodged in his throat. They'd driven off a cliff.

"No, no, no, no, hell no," he chanted as he slammed the truck into park and grabbed the flashlight from the seat beside him and jumped out. With more fear than he thought possible running through his veins, he ran across the slippery field toward the edge, where the tire tracks vanished into the blackness.

Connor heard Claire's voice as she picked up the radio. "Yancy, it's Claire. We're out in the north pasture area on James's ranch.

There's been some kind of accident. You'd better send the fire department and the ambulance. Hurry."

Connor leaned over the edge and shined the flashlight in a slow sweep. He couldn't see much but the light hit something metal. It was the rim of a tire still spinning as the car lay belly-up at the bottom of the ravine.

"Alex!" he shouted as he scrambled down the snowy bank. Branches and rocks cut up his hands but he barely noticed. All that mattered was getting to her. "Alex!"

"Can you see them?" Claire asked from the top of the cliff.

He didn't answer, couldn't have even if he wanted to. His throat had closed up so tight he could hardly get a breath in. Alex had to be okay, *had* to be.

The smell of oil and gas hit him as he made it to the car. He dropped to his knees and shined the flashlight through the ruined windshield. The sharp tang of blood filled his nose. It was everywhere.

Connor focused on what he had to do rather than on the fact the woman he loved might be dead. If she was injured, then getting her out was the top priority. Then he'd kill James if the man wasn't dead already.

"Alex, can you hear me?"

He heard a small moan and hoped it hadn't been the wind. Snow blew into his ears and eyes as he reached into the car and felt for something, anything. As the glass sliced up his hand, he felt an arm. He stuck his other arm in and felt around until he found another appendage.

Connor braced his feet on either side of the windshield and pulled. The moan grew louder and this time it sounded feminine.

"Alex, baby, is that you? Oh God, please let that be you."

He tugged again but she didn't move. Connor let loose a sob as he tried for a third time. Alex was stuck and he couldn't get her free.

"We need leverage to raise it up a bit and get her out."

Connor looked up to see both Yancy and Claire in the ravine with him. He sucked in a breath and managed to grunt an acknowledgment.

"Claire, you get down with Connor while I use this branch to lift up the front. Then both of you pull her out." Yancy managed to find an enormous branch of a tree and shoved it down as far as he could beneath the car. "Ready? Lift!"

Together they worked as one. The car rose up just about six inches and Connor pulled for all he was worth. The moan turned into a scream as Claire and Connor pulled Alex free of the car.

As soon as her legs were clear, Yancy let the car back down. Alex was bloody and unconscious, but alive. Connor hugged her to his chest, heedless of the tears rolling down his face. She was *alive.*

"Howard's dead." Yancy came back around from the driver's side of the car.

"Good, then I don't have to kill him." Connor's voice was raw with emotion.

As the sound of sirens filled the night air, Connor got to his feet and ascended the embankment with the precious cargo in his arms. He left a trail of blood in the white snow during the excruciating climb.

When he reached the top, he fell to his knees and held her against him again, this time sobbing openly. He'd never let her go again.

CHAPTER THIRTEEN

Everything was white, snowy white. Was she still out in the storm? Or was she dead and heaven was apparently as white as the scribes predicted?

Alex tried to move her arm and pain shot straight up into her shoulder. Nope, definitely not dead and not outside either. It was too warm to be outside. Beneath her hands she felt starchy sheets.

It was a hospital.

The entire nightmare ride came back at her in a rush. James with the gun, threatening to kill her, the accident, and blood. There had been so much blood. At least she'd survived and someone had found the car.

She managed to get her eyes at least half open and peered around her. There were her feet poking up beneath the white blanket. She wiggled them, which meant whatever injuries she'd suffered, it hadn't paralyzed her.

Turning her head proved difficult because she realized she was wearing a neck brace. That either meant they were concerned about spinal injuries, or worse and her neck was already damaged. She tried to swallow but her throat was beyond parched.

Holding up her right arm revealed a brace; no wonder it hurt. The left arm held an IV drip and a plethora of cuts and bruises. She reached up and felt her face and found some stitches near her hairline, more cuts and another array of stitches on her chin.

Various parts of her body woke up and loudly protested their treatment. There had definitely been a car accident; she remembered that now. What exactly happened after that was a mystery. She wondered if James survived, then hoped he did so she could send the bastard to jail for kidnapping and attempted murder.

"Alex?"

Connor's voice was like angels singing, and to her dismay, it also made her start crying. He appeared above her smiling like a lunatic and looking like he'd been in a brawl with a bear. His dark curls were sticking up every which way; he had huge dark circles under his eyes, at least two days' worth of whiskers on his face, and clothes wrinkled beyond repair.

He leaned down and embraced her as best he could. Although he didn't smell too fresh, he smelled like Connor, and that was ambrosia to her battered body and soul. She loved him with everything she had, everything she was.

It wasn't the near-death experience with James that led her to that conclusion. It was seeing him again, knowing she was a wreck and he was marginally better, knowing he loved her and accepted her with all her quirks and failings. She was also fairly certain that not all the tears on her cheeks were hers.

Alex needed to tell him she loved him. She'd promised herself she would as soon as she saw him again. However, when she tried to talk, she found the desertlike conditions in her mouth prevented it.

She tapped his shoulder until he looked at her, his green eyes as teary as hers. Alex cupped his cheek; the rasp of whiskers on her hand told her she was alive and her man was right there with her. If she didn't tell him soon, she'd simply explode. She opened her mouth and pantomimed drinking.

"Shit, I'm sorry. You need water." He fiddled with something beside the bed and then held up a rose-colored plastic cup with a straw. His hands trembled so bad, the straw bounced in the cup.

She took the cup in her left hand and managed to bring it close enough to her mouth to suck the cool water in. It was blissful, the sweetest water on the planet. She cleared her throat.

"I know I'm probably the world's worst cook. I have a temper, which you may not have noticed, but I'm admitting to it." She ignored his smirk. "I have a lot of unresolved issues with my past. I don't trust easily and am secretive too. But I am madly, hopelessly in love with you, Connor Matthews."

His mouth fell open and his face blanched. Her heart dropped to her knees at his reaction. Well, she hadn't expected to be rejected while in her hospital bed. Hurt roared through her and the fresh tears were nowhere near as joyful as the first batch. He turned away and started walking.

Alex shut her eyes to block out the sight of him. God, how could she have been so stupid? He didn't love her. It was heat of the moment—a great fuck and most men will tell a woman he loved her. It didn't mean *anything*.

A trembling touch on her left hand made her eyes pop open.

Connor was on his knees beside the bed, his eyes suspiciously wet again, but his entire face was smiling. He gently took her hand in his and, gentleman that he was, he avoided her injured right side.

"I am a good cook, although Bernice might debate me on that. I snore and I tend to leave dirty socks in balls on the floor. I also hog the covers and sing off-key in the shower." He leaned forward and touched her cheek with one finger. "I love you with every fiber of my being. Alex Katherine Finley, will you marry me?"

This time it was Alex's turn for her mouth to drop open. The last thing she ever expected in her life was a marriage proposal, or a man to love for that matter. It was so much, a gift worthy of someone with a better soul than she. It was selfish of her, but she grabbed hold of the gift and hung on tight. He was hers. She was his.

"I'll have to check my social calendar, but pencil me in as a yes." She managed a shaky smile. "Or better yet, use a pen."

Connor gently took her into his arms and she couldn't decide who was shaking more.

"Am I hurting you?"

She chuckled against his shoulder. "I don't think you could possibly hurt me right now. I must be hopped up on morphine or perhaps it's a combination of love and drugs."

He kissed the tender spot between her collarbone and neck. His warm breath fanned out across her skin. It felt wonderful, amazing and, surprisingly, arousing.

Connor set her back onto the bed just as slowly, then stepped back and surreptitiously wiped his eyes. "You up for visitors?"

Alex frowned. "What visitors?" She wasn't exactly looking her best, considering the stitches, bandages and the swanky hospital gown.

"They've been here since they brought you in last night and

refuse to go home." He kissed her forehead. "You inspire people to love you."

Alex was flummoxed. "I inspire people to love me? Who is waiting for me?"

"You don't know?" He tsked at her. "Your family."

She held her breath as he walked to the door and opened it. Connor disappeared for a few seconds; then he held the door open. In walked Claire, Bernice and then Daniel skidded in behind them. Yancy lurked by the door.

"These floors are so shiny. I could ski on my sneakers in here." Daniel whooped, earning severe frowns from his mother and Bernice. He glanced at Alex and his eyes widened. "Holy smokes, Alex. You look terrible."

"Daniel!" Claire admonished. "That's really not polite."

"She looks like she's been wrestling a cougar, but your mama's right. It ain't polite to say so." Bernice always had her own way of putting things. She was never going to change.

Claire came over and took Alex's hand. "I can't tell you how sorry I am this happened. I should have been looking out for you." Her brown eyes grew moist, and Alex's throat tightened up. "I am so glad you're all right."

At first Alex had trouble finding her voice. "You have nothing to be sorry for. I made the decision to speak to him. You had no responsibility for my welfare."

"Yes, I did. Whether or not you like it, we are your family and it's our job to protect you, to watch out for you, and to be there when you need us."

Alex was completely overwhelmed. Not only had she just had a marriage proposal, but her new family was accepting her with all her faults. It was nearly too much.

Daniel came up beside his mother. "Oh, wow, you put another dent in your butt chin. Too bad about that, but your butt was always bigger than mine."

Everyone laughed. Thank God for Daniel. He broke the tension as only a smart-ass kid could.

"Daniel, what am I going to do with you?" Claire grabbed him in a hug and laid a noogie on his head. "You crazy child."

Connor slid up on her right and put his arm above her on the pillow, as if he needed to be near her. Alex looked around her at her family, at the people who loved her and whom she loved. It was a moment she would remember for a lifetime. Truly a defining, shining second that she could tuck away into her heart and bring out to embrace now and again.

"Oh God, I look like a battering ram who lost." Alex peered at her face in the mirror and stuck out her tongue. "Geez, the last bruises haven't even completely faded yet. Now I really look like shit."

Connor came up behind her in the bathroom and wrapped his arms around her waist. "I think you look delicious. Good enough to eat." She smelled good, even tasted good as he lapped at her neck. Her breath caught and he felt her heart thudding beneath his arms.

"I'm going to hold you to that promise." Her voice was a bit husky and it skittered across his skin, raising goose bumps.

"Good, because I intend to keep it." He glanced around the hospital bathroom. "Are you ready to go?"

"After two days of lying on my ass in this skimpy cotton gown with my butt hanging out? What would make you think that?"

"Let's get going, then. Your reflection isn't going to change the longer you look at it." He ushered her out of the bathroom, then picked up the plastic bag marked BELONGINGS and they walked to the door.

Alex had been more than lucky. She had avoided any lasting injuries, walking away with a hairline fracture in her right wrist, three dozen stitches, more bruises than he could count, and a very sore head. There must have been an angel on her shoulder because James Howard had taken the brunt of the accident when the car rolled.

Although Connor hadn't seen his body, Yancy had been forthcoming in the extent of the man's fatal injuries. He'd even had a bullet in his knee, which he had yet to ask Alex about. She said James tried to kill her, but flat-out refused to talk about what happened inside the car before the accident. Alex asked him to be patient until she was ready.

He respected her request, but it concerned him that she wasn't being forthcoming about it, though perhaps in time she would be able to tell him. Now he'd never know if James had been responsible for Grant's death, but it didn't matter, or at least that was what he told himself. Both of them were dead so there was no one to blame. That didn't meant Connor didn't want to know, but because he couldn't know, he tried his best to not think about it.

After arguing for what seemed like an hour with the nurse about using a wheelchair, Alex walked slowly out of the hospital. Connor should have insisted on the wheelchair, but she was as stubborn as a mule. It had taken all his wheedling to get her to stay in the hospital an extra day so they could run a battery of tests to be sure there were no hidden injuries.

They made it to the front door of the hospital and she smiled up at him. He was afraid she would exhaust herself, but she looked as healthy as she could be given the circumstances.

"Wait here, please. I'm going to get the truck."

She started to protest, but he took off running before she could get a word out. He returned with the truck in only minutes, embarrassed to see his hands shaking. Connor had come so close to losing her, to spending the rest of his life missing her. The urge to protect her would be stronger than he would ever tell her.

He managed to calm his racing heart, barely, before he jumped out to help her into the truck. She made a face at him but praise be, she actually let him assist.

"You know, if you hadn't already done this for me, I'd think you were doing it because you think I'm too weak." She reached for the seat belt.

Connor breathed a sigh of relief. "You are a stubborn wench."

"Thank you. I pride myself on that." She grinned and he knew everything was going to be all right.

They drove away from the hospital in a comfortable silence. The sun shined brightly as they made their way back to the ranch. The snow had left nary a clue it had been there, although Connor was painfully aware of how much destruction it had caused them. He'd personally made sure Yancy destroyed the Lexus, making it into a cube of twisted metal in the junkyard.

Connor had been so very lucky in his life, despite the rough beginnings. If he hadn't found Grant, he would not have become a part of Finley's. If he hadn't been a part of Finley's, he would have never met Alex. If he hadn't met Alex, he wouldn't feel the way he did. It was unique to him to feel so close to another human being. He'd been protecting himself for a very long time. Alex blew those barriers to pieces.

He glanced at her and noticed her eyes were closed. Perhaps the walk to the truck was more than she anticipated. Connor slowed down to avoid jostling her too much.

"Now, that shit ain't gonna fly, Matthews." She didn't move an inch. "I'm simply keeping my eyes closed because I don't have sunglasses and the sun is too damn bright. Speed up and get me home."

Home. He smiled at the thought she had called Finley's "home" again. It was exactly what Grant would have wanted.

"Yes, ma'am. Anything else I can do for you?"

"Bring me to the cabin and make love to me."

Connor's entire body stood at attention, a heat only Alex could bring to him. He never expected her to want to be intimate so soon after being released from the hospital. On a deeper level, he understood her need. She could have died in that car in more ways than one. Alex was a fighter, a survivor who faced death and kicked its ass.

The specters of their pasts, the struggles and pain, needed to be washed away, cleansed from their lives for good. To move on with being together, being a part of a partnership, that was what they needed.

As they turned down the driveway to Finley's, a peace settled over Connor, spiced by a slow burn to be alone with her. He had a feeling if they parked in the employee lot, they would garner too much attention. Selfishly, he wanted to keep her to himself. So he passed the parking lot and drove across the grass and parked behind the barn.

"What are you doing?"

"Exactly what you wanted. Now, stay there until I come around to get you."

"Hm, bossy, aren't you?" She stayed put even if her tartness couldn't.

Connor hopped out and went into the shed to get a four-wheeler. It wasn't that far to the cabin but he didn't want her to walk, and besides, they could get there faster. When he came out of the shed, he saw her smile widen through the windshield of the truck.

He parked the four-wheeler and opened the passenger-side door of the truck. "Your chariot, m'lady."

"My redneck chariot."

Connor scooped her into his arms and bumped the door closed. He felt her warmth through his jacket, the sweet beating of her heart against his. They settled onto the four-wheeler and set off for the VIP cabin. The ride was silent, but their bodies were already preparing for what was to come.

She sat in front of him, cradled in the vee of his legs, her soft ass pressed up against his dick. Each bump on the trail was deliciously stimulating as they rubbed against each other. He heard her breathing change, becoming shorter and choppier, as was his. Connor didn't dare drive any faster because of the terrain and the fact she was recovering from a car accident.

It seemed like it took hours to reach the gate to the cabin, but he knew it was only ten minutes. As he punched the numbers in to open it, she slid off the four-wheeler and stood beside him, waiting.

He turned and met her gaze. "Ready?"

"More than you can imagine."

Connor scooped her up again and this time she didn't protest. He pushed the gate closed and walked up the steps, anxious and excited. When they got to the door, he didn't want to put her down to unlock it, but he couldn't reach the keys unless he did.

"Allow me."

She reached into his pocket, her slender fingers brushing his already half-erect dick. He sucked in a breath as she slid one digit up its length, almost as if she were making it longer by magic. Of course, it really was a certain kind of magic.

"God, you're so hard already."

"Get the keys and unlock the door," he said through clenched teeth. "Or I'll fuck you on this porch for all the world to see."

"Don't tempt me, Connor." She pulled out the keys and within seconds they were inside.

He carried her straight to the bedroom as her husky chuckle sent a zing through him. The bedroom was full of dappled sunlight as it danced through the leaves on the trees outside. The ivory comforter was still covered in red rose petals from his aborted seduction several nights ago. The scent of roses was in the air.

Connor set her on her feet, eager to feel her in his arms. She picked up one petal and brought it to her nose.

"You planned this?"

"Once upon a time."

"You're a romantic beneath that cowboy exterior. Red roses mean love, you know." Her gaze slid over him. "Although I really like the cowboy exterior."

His entire body pulsed with need for her, for Alex, the woman who held his heart in her small hands. She held out her arms, the blue splint a constant reminder of what she'd gone through. He didn't need to be told or asked what to do.

Connor took off her shirt, kissing each inch of skin as it was exposed. She sighed, a sound that went straight to his dick. When he slid off her sweatpants, she stepped out of them, standing there in a blue bra and panties. He ran his finger along the edge of the panties.

"I brought these to the hospital for you."

She shivered beneath his hand. "You went through my underwear drawer?"

"Absolutely. I even carried a pair around in my pocket." He grinned at her and she shook her head.

"And here I thought you were going to tell me you used one to masturbate." She tapped his chest. "I can't reach to unhook my bra, so you'll need to help."

"Did you have to ask?" He ran his hands along her belly, loving the feeling of the warm skin beneath his fingers. With a quick flick, he had her bra open and her magnificent breasts were free.

Connor pressed up against her, pushing his dick into her ass, reaching around to cup her tits.

"Mmm, that's nice." She leaned against him and put her hands on his. "Pinch them."

Connor knew every inch of her body, every nook and cranny. She didn't need to guide him, but the fact she did made him that much hotter. He complied with her order and rolled the pink nipples between his fingers, pinching lightly, then releasing and doing it again.

As her body heated, he could smell her arousal. It surrounded him, beckoned him to lose himself in her. Connor nuzzled her neck, inhaling her scent. He kissed her sweet skin, then lightly bit her. She sucked in a breath.

"Oh yeah, that's it. Now touch my pussy; make me feel good, Connor." She spread her legs to give him access.

His name on her lips as he pleasured her made his dick jump against her back. He slid his hand down her stomach and into her panties, then into the folds of her core. She was already slick with her own juices, which he used to spin lazy circles on her clit.

He pulled her earlobe into his mouth and sucked as his hand crept farther down into her wetness. Connor trembled with the need to be with her, feel her around him. Instead, he thrust two fingers into her channel while his thumb continued to pleasure her clit.

She moaned deep in her throat and leaned against him. "I think I want to get on the bed now, before I fall down."

Concerned he was pushing her too far, he removed his hands immediately. "Are you okay?"

She smiled. "More than okay. You were about to make me come, crazy man. Now, get naked and get in bed with me."

Connor picked her up and kissed her, then set her down on the bed. With a wicked grin, he hooked his thumbs on her panties and pulled them off. He leaned forward and kissed her pussy, the heat and taste from her core making his breath catch.

He looked at her, nude on the bed covered with petals, a picture come to life. A dream come true. As he undressed quickly, her gaze traveled all over him, making his dick jump when it was revealed. One brow rose and she crooked her finger at him.

"Let's use that thing before you hurt yourself."

Connor climbed onto the bed and lay beside her. He traced the stitches on her face with his finger, then kissed them.

"I can't believe I almost lost you."

She kissed his finger. "Not even close. Now, show me how much you love me."

"Your wish is my command, m'lady."

This was different from any other time they were together. It wasn't just sex for pleasure. It was making love, celebrating being together, showing how much they meant to each other.

Side by side, he raised her leg and slid into her slowly. Her body welcomed him, pulling him deeper within. She cupped his cheeks and kissed him. It was gentle; it was sweet; it was perfect.

His body had been ready for hers, eager to become one with her again. Within minutes he felt his orgasm building and he wanted to make sure she had her own pleasure. He reached between them and pinched her clit. Alex threw her head back and howled as she came, clenching around him fast and hard.

Connor captured her mouth as he came, spilling his seed into his mate, his woman, his love.

Alex knew what she had to do. It was midmorning a week after she'd returned to the ranch. Connor had basically moved into the VIP cabin with her until they could build a new one for themselves in the spring. They spent their nights curled beside each other, making love, exploring everything together.

Connor went to work every day, kissing her good-bye until he forgot where he needed to be and making love to her again before leaving. She was full of love, so much she could hardly take a breath in when she thought of what life had been like only a few months ago.

However, there was something she had yet to do. She dressed slowly, still sore in spots, pulling on her boots with great effort. The envelope from her father sat beneath the violet, as it had since she'd come home. She assumed Connor had put it there for her, for whenever she was ready to read it. After putting on a hat and down coat, she headed outside, the envelope clutched in her hand.

Alex realized life would not truly begin for her until she put the past behind her, forgave her father, forgave her mother and forgave herself.

She walked straight to the family cemetery, head down against the brisk wind that foretold another storm. It was past time for her to move on and she had finally gotten enough courage to do so.

Although she was shaking, Alex approached her parents' graves and knelt in the bed of fallen leaves. They crunched beneath her knees as she looked at one gravestone, then the other. Grant and Katherine had given her life, and now she was ready to live the life they wanted for her.

Alex opened the envelope with trembling hands and read the letter, the words her father had left for her.

My dearest Alex,

How can I find the words to say everything? So many things went wrong at once, so many mistakes were made. I looked for you but you had disappeared. I could have hired someone to find you, but so much time passed and I knew you didn't want to be found.

I hope you one day come back to the ranch, to me and your mother, to the land that is a part of who you are. Please know that I never meant to hurt you. I love you so very much, my daughter.

I made many mistakes as a father, but having you as a daughter was the one thing I did right. You showed me from the time you were two years old just how tough you were. I knew then you would be a formidable force, an amazing creature that would change the world.

When you left the ranch, you were so angry with me, furious at my betrayal, and you had every right to be.

My heart was broken in two first from Katie dying, then you leaving. I was lost until Claire reminded me I had a ranch to take care of, animals to watch over. Then I found myself falling in love with her. I met Connor and he seemed to need me as much as I needed him. When Daniel came along, I remembered what it felt like to hold you for the first time. We were an odd family, to be sure, but there was a hole in my life that never closed.

I am so sorry if we hurt you, dear Alex. You are my heart and I have always been so proud of you, love you so much. I never meant to do you harm. I hope you can find it in your heart to forgive me for everything. I want you to stay here on the ranch, to remember how much you loved it, to raise your children here and be happy.

If you're reading this, please know that I am up in heaven now with my sweet Katie girl by my side looking down at you. You are, and will always be, my beloved daughter.

Your loving father,
Grant Finley

Alex pressed the paper to her chest and wept. Deep, gulping sobs that echoed around her. Alex never knew her father loved her.

So many years of unhappiness, of time wasted, that she could have spent with her father. She wept until her tears were empty and her grief faded.

Shaking, Alex rose to her feet and stood between her parents' gravestones. Mistakes and regrets had nearly destroyed Alex. Now she had a second chance at everything.

Alex tucked the letter in her pocket and turned to leave the cemetery. There at the top of the hill stood Connor. Her heart leapt at the sight of him and she smiled up at the sky, at the clouds dancing above her.

"Thanks for finding Connor and bringing him here, Daddy. I think we're going to have a good life. Good-bye, Dad. Good-bye, Mom."

With her soul full of joy and her heart full of love, Alex ran toward her future husband and leapt into his arms.